No Such Thing as a

Lost Cause

A Brandy Alexander
Mystery

Shelly Fredman

Other books in the
Brandy Alexander Mystery Series

DEDICATION

In loving memory of
Caleb "Deuce" Fetzer

ACKNOWLEDGMENTS

I want to thank the following people, without whom I could not have written this book:

My "twin," Kris Zuercher, for spending countless hours reading rewrite after rewrite, and for helping me keep Brandy true to herself, my husband, Dudley Fetzer, for watching me go a little (okay, a lot) nuts and loving and supporting me anyway, my daughter, Corey Rose, for always knowing what a scene needs in order to make it better, Suzanne Dunham, for providing technical information, and for helping me with plot points, Audrey Matisa for offering up her wonderful talent to make the No Such Thing As…series visible on the Internet.

Special thanks to:
An'gel Ducote Molpus, for sharing so many hilarious "Brandy moments" on Facebook, Terri Dunn and Sassy Girls Book Club, for letting people know about my series, as well as to Joanna Banks-Morgan and Jill Dearden, for starting Facebook fan pages, and Anna Harp for maintaining our Yahoo group, Jerry Fest, for his help with the story line, Nick Carlson, for his technical advice, Carrie Gwaltney and Beth Dalebroux for being such strong Brandy supporters, and Marty Schatz, for our caffeine-induced brain storming sessions.

Kudos to:
Michael Canales for his brilliant cover art.

And huge shout outs to:
Judith Kristen, my "sister from another mother," author of A DATE WITH A BEATLE, ONCE UPON A TIME IN LIVERPOOL, MY NAME IS HENLEY, and THE MOOKIE SERIES, and to Pamela DuMond, author of the delightful Annie Graceland CUPCAKE mystery series.

Shelly Fredman

PROLOGUE

For a reasonably intelligent, passably cute, street-savvy, adult female, I have had my share of crappy luck in the romance department, but this just takes the cake. It all started a few weeks ago, when my heart got in the way of rational thinking and, well, I'm not sure, but I *may* have had unprotected sex. Okay, I did. I'm not making any excuses—but, really, you had to be there.

I tried not to dwell on the possible repercussions of my impulsive behavior, (or, as my friend Janine put it, "Brandy, how dumb can you be?") and concentrate on the happier aspects of my new relationship. But, two weeks and one missed period later, denial was no longer an option. And, as of thirty seconds ago, keeping it to myself didn't appear to be an option either.

"Is there something you want to tell me, Darlin'?"

"Um, no?"

"I think you meant yes." His tone was playful, but I knew he meant business.

Nicholas Santiago, beautiful, bad-ass mystery man, and my unofficial boyfriend of less than a week, stood at my bedroom door, holding a small box I'd mistakenly left on my bathroom counter. He turned it around so that I could see the words, written in pink, swirly script, surrounded by dancing daisies. Early Response Pregnancy Test.

"Oh, that," I laughed, acknowledging the box with a dismissive wave of my hand. "It's not what you think."

Eyebrows arched, Nick walked over to the bed. He was naked, except for the white, surgical bandage that cut across his otherwise perfect, caramel-colored chest. The bandage protected the site of a gunshot wound, and the incision that followed, to remove a bullet meant for me.

I reached out and took the box from him. "It's Fran's." Franny DiAngelo is Janine's twin sister and the first name that popped into my head.

"Fran, who just had a baby two weeks ago?"

"Yeah, well, she's not thinking clearly," I told him. "Birthin' a baby kills a lot of brain cells. You can't get them back, you know."

Nick studied me for a beat, and then he leaned down and kissed me softly on the mouth. My stomach got all skittery, and I made room for him to climb back into bed.

"It's tempting, Angel," he apologized, pulling on his jeans, "but I'm afraid I've got to get going. I have a business meeting in an hour."

"It's three a.m. Are we talking suit and tie business or Kevlar vest and semi-automatic?"

I don't know why I bothered asking. Nick won't discuss his work with me, which, however morally correct, I'm guessing falls on the far left side of legal. I would have pressed, but I had some business of my own to attend to.

Grabbing my tee shirt off the chair next to my bed, I yanked it over my head and followed him downstairs. He stopped when he reached the door.

"So, I'll see you later," I said, unconsciously shifting my weight from one foot to the other.

Nick took a step outside, and then in a flash he was back and pinning me up against the wall.

"Forget something?" I squeaked.

"Just this." He lifted my chin and kissed me, slow and

sultry. I closed my eyes and melted against him, forgetting for a moment that my world was on the verge of collapse.

"By the way," he said, catching me off-guard, "if you say you don't have anything to discuss, I believe you because I know you're always honest with me."

"What? Are you kidding me? I lie all the time!" *Unhh.* "What I meant was—"

He cut me a wry smile. "We'll talk later, Angel."

I watched as Nick disappeared into the middle of the night. Then I went back upstairs, and opened the box with the dancing daisies, peed on the stick, and waited two of the longest minutes of my life.

When the time was up I said a Hail Mary and looked down at the stick. A little plus sign appeared in the window. As my Bubie Heiki on my father's side of our Jewish-Italian family would say, "Oy vey."

CHAPTER ONE

"Are you throwing up?"

"No."

"Feeling dizzy?"

"No."

"Crying for no reason?"

"No...well, I did shed a few tears during a Huggies commercial, but who wouldn't? They're very moving."

"Uh oh."

"What?" I said, alarmed.

"Emotional response to baby-related items. This could mean something." Franny thought for a minute. "Do your boobs hurt?"

I felt around. "A little. Only I think it's my bra. I should stop buying underwear at Hal's Discount Mart."

I was talking to Fran from my cubicle at WINN, a local cable news station serving the Greater Philadelphia area. I am the community liaison to the many varied and exciting happenings around town. Want to know where to get the best frozen yogurt? I'm your go-to girl. Need hula dancers for your next party? I'll show you how to turn your living room into a tropical paradise! People tune in just to see what life-changing information I'll be dispensing next. This station would be nowhere without me.

I glanced around the room to see if anyone was listening in. Art Metropolis looked up from his desk and shot me a big, greasy smile. Art is WINN's political commentator and resident Nosy Nellie. I lowered my voice and continued.

"I've got a doctor's appointment this afternoon."

"Is Nick going with you?"

"No…um, I didn't exactly tell him yet."

Franny gave a very unladylike snort. "Oh, yeah. It's way better to wait until the baby's born. Guys really like to be surprised that way."

"Sarcasm isn't helping, DiAngelo."

The truth is I was scared. I've been in love with Nicholas Santiago since the day I first laid eyes on him, and after months of relentless pursuing on my part, and mega resistance on his, Nick finally admitted he loved me too. But, given the newness of our relationship, not to mention his lifestyle, dangerous by anyone's standards, and his family history, the last thing we needed to worry about was an unplanned pregnancy. I figured why bring it up until I was one-hundred percent sure.

A shadow crossed my desk and I looked up to see my boss, Eric, standing in front of me. At twenty-six, Eric is three years younger than I am. Eric's okay, except that he's something of a horn dog. He was leaning over trying to take a peek down my shirt, a loose-necked tee. Under normal circumstances, I would have threatened to smack him upside the head, but I needed a favor so I let it slide.

"Fran, I've gotta go." I hung up and tugged at the collar of my shirt. At least he had the decency to look sheepish.

"So, uh, when you're finished with the story on those freaks—I mean the *concerned citizens* who wanna fix the crack in the Liberty Bell, I need to talk to you about something," he said.

"How about now? I need to talk to you too."

I followed him down the hall to his office, a shrine to Philadelphia sports teams.

Eric sat down at his desk and began fiddling with a Charles Barkley Bobble Head. I settled into the chair across from him and jumped right in.

"Eric, I've been giving this a lot of thought, and I think it's time I moved onto hard news. I mean, how valuable is puff piece reporting anyway? When you think about it, it's really kind of a waste of air time. I want to sink my teeth into important issues, stuff that makes people think. And over the last several months, I believe I've proven I can take on hard hitting stories. I want—"

"We may have to let you go."

"*What?*"

Eric tugged on the Charles Barkley doll, absently twisting it around until the head snapped off. He looked at it, surprised, and laid it on his desk.

"I'm going to give it to you straight, Brandy. The station has been experiencing some economic downturn lately, and we're looking to cut back."

"But—but—Eric, you can't fire me! I bring a much-needed sense of whimsy, not to mention invaluable household tips into the dreary lives of our television-watching public. Our ratings went through the roof after my "behind the scenes" look at Clown College. And you should see the fan mail I got the day I worked the breakfast shift at Hooters!" (Okay, so it was one e-mail from an eighty-two year-old shut-in who asked me to be his new Meals on Wheels delivery gal, but *still…*)

"Brandy, I'm not arguing with you. Your report on waxing versus electronic hair removal was one of the biggest stories of the decade. Clearly, you're a front-runner for a Pulitzer."

"Fine, Eric, you've made your point, which is exactly why I wanted to talk to you in the first place. You know I can do more for the station. I'm working on an idea for a story right now. And they wouldn't have to pay me any extra—at least not right away. Eric, I need this job."

Eric picked up Charles Barkley's head and began tossing it back and forth in his hands, thinking. "Well, there is a paid position that just came available."

"Ooh, what is it? Do they need me to investigate that scandal at the docks? Oh, I know, there's been talk about corruption at the City Planners' Office. I could get on it right away."

"Uh, actually, I was thinking more along the lines of man's best friend."

"Oh no," I protested. "Not Godfrey the Traffic Dog. How am I ever going to be regarded as a serious reporter if I keep doing this kind of junk? Besides, it's a hundred and five degrees in that suit. Plus it makes me look fat."

"Now look, before you turn your nose up at this, just hear me out. If you take this on along with your current position, it's job stability. Godfrey is very popular with our audience, but after what happened with Kevin, they were thinking of retiring the character. You could restore Godfrey's good name."

I had my doubts. About two weeks ago, Kevin Sanders, the guy who played the safety-tip dispensing canine was driving home from work when he stopped off at a local bar for a nightcap, It wasn't the smartest move, seeing as he'd just come off a stint in rehab. Anyway, after downing his third rum and coke and being egged on by his drinking buddies, Kevin decided it would be *hilarious* to slip into his Godfrey costume and relieve himself next to a fire hydrant. *It was!* Only a passerby videotaped the whole thing and posted it on YouTube. The next thing he knew, he was paw cuffed and charged with indecent exposure.

I sighed. "Has the suit at least been cleaned?"

Eric grinned. "That's the spirit, Alexander. In the meantime," he added, "it wouldn't hurt to polish up your resume, just in case."

Twenty minutes later, (including a stop at Starbucks for a stress-relieving triple espresso on ice) I was on my way to

Dr. Claybourne's office for my appointment. I drove with the windows down in my parents' old Le Sabre, a car I inherited when they moved to Boca. The air conditioner had sacrificed its life in the battle against the summer heat, and I couldn't afford to resuscitate it. Nick offered to lend me his truck, but I've got a thing about taking favors, no matter how much fun it might be to repay them.

The summer air was hot and sticky and smelled like doughnuts. Philly has about three thousand doughnut shops on Broad Street, alone, which may explain the obesity rate in the City of Brotherly Love. I thought about making a pit stop for a powdered jelly, y'know, to take my mind off the possibility of being jobless and pregnant, but at that moment my cell rang. I knew I should have screened the call, only that would have entailed pulling over, and I was already running late.

"Why isn't your brother answering his phone?" my mother began, as if we'd been having a lengthy conversation about that very subject.

I lowered the volume on my Bluetooth and switched over into the right hand lane. "I don't know, Mom. He's probably busy at the club."

My brother, Paul, is part owner of a nightclub in Center City and (despite the occasional indiscretion involving the recreational use of a versatile natural fiber you can wear, smoke or bake) the pride of the Alexander family. In my mother's eyes, Paul is Superman who can leap tall buildings in a single bound, while I'm the worrisome wild-child in perpetual need of babysitting. I guess I should resent this characterization, but it's sort've true.

"Is there something I can help you with, Mom?"

"That's very sweet of you, honey. Drive over to Paul's and tell him I need to talk to him."

"I meant maybe I could help you with whatever you needed Paul for."

"Oh." She considered this. The thought clearly had not crossed her mind. "Well, I don't see why not."

Wow. She trusts me. I am so not going to let her down!

"Since your father and I can't fly in for your Cousin Marlene's daughter's wedding, I was going to ask Paul to represent us. But now that I think about it, he's so busy running his own business, you're right. You should go."

Crap. "Mom, you won't believe this, but I'm busy that day. What are the odds, huh?" Too late I realized she hadn't mentioned the date. "I'm busy the whole month of August," I added, to be on the safe side.

She exhaled so deeply I thought she'd pass out from lack of oxygen. "Have your brother call me."

I clicked off the call, feeling horribly guilty for having lied to my mother, (and so poorly) but the guilt was soon replaced by a major attack of nerves. With my heart slamming firmly against my chest, I pulled up to Dr. Claybourne's building and climbed out of the car.

*****

"I don't know if this is good news or bad, but you're not pregnant."

"I'm not?" I allowed Dr. Claybourne's words to sink in as my shoulders did a slow descent from up around my ears.

"But, the home test said—"

"Which is why we ran a complete diagnostic. Brandy, it's easy to make a mistake with those home tests."

"That's really nice of you, Dr. Claybourne," I said, feeling ridiculous. "But you pee on a stick and count to a hundred and twenty. How could I screw that up?"

Dr. Claybourne smiled. "You were probably nervous and might not have followed directions as carefully as you thought you had. It happens all the time. Are you disappointed with the results?" she asked kindly.

"No. It's—it's fine. More than fine. Really. I'm very relieved. But if I'm not pregnant, why am I late?"

Dr. Claybourne picked up my chart and looked over my medical history. Although my regular physician is only ten minutes from my home in South Philly, I'd opted out of the neighborhood. Doctor-patient confidentiality aside, news travels fast in that neck of the woods and gossip, even faster.

"I've seen the news reports on you, Brandy. It's not like you've had the most relaxing summer, so my best guess is stress. You're not that late. Go home, try to stay calm and call me next week if you're not back on schedule."

In the car on the way home, I was back on schedule.

*****

My dog, Adrian, greeted me at the front door carrying the remains of a Ben and Jerry's ice cream carton that he'd dug out of the recycle bin. I pried it out of his mouth and checked to see if there was any ice cream left. There wasn't. Disappointment swept over me. I had no idea I'd wanted ice cream so badly. I settled for a cherry Pixie Stick and sat down at the kitchen table to check my voicemail.

The first was from my mother. She'd called to read me my horoscope, but since she only shares the doom and gloom ones, I figured there was no rush in calling her back. The other message was from my friend, Vince Giancola, down at the D.A.'s office. I emptied the Pixie Stick into my mouth and called him back.

"I arranged that ride-along you wanted," he began, forgoing the usual amenities. "So, let me guess. You're reconsidering joining the force."

When I was a kid, I'd briefly entertained the idea of becoming a cop. I like to call it my "Charlie's Angels'" phase. I even went so far as to fill out an application for the academy, but that was before I realized you were actually expected to follow the rules you were hired to enforce. Rule following is not my strong suit.

"I'm working on an idea for a feature story on cops," I told him. *And it will be great and everyone will love me and then the station will be sorry they ever thought about letting me go and I'll be asked to run the entire news network and pigs will fly and everything!*

"Just make us look good," he said, and hung up.

Nick called while I was watching an old episode of *The Nanny*. It was the one where Mr. Sheffield told Fran he loved her and then he took it back.

"Hello, Angel."

"Hey," I murmured, suddenly shy. "What's up?"

"I was hoping you'd tell me."

"About what?" I asked, although I had a pretty good idea.

"About Fran's pregnancy test. So—is she?" he asked, lightly. I've learned not to let that fool me. Santiago's training in the martial arts has enabled him to appear calm, even in the deadliest of circumstances, whereas I couldn't keep my feelings a secret if my life depended on it, a theory that has been tested and proven on a daily basis.

I felt the blood rise to my cheeks. "No," I whispered, leaning back against the couch cushions. "She's not."

I waited a beat, and when he didn't say anything I added, "Nobody is."

And then I burst into tears.

Once the water works started I couldn't stop. "Eric's making me play Godfrey the Traffic Dog," I snuffled. "I'm very upset about it!"

"Apparently," Nick said, softly. "Brandy, I may be going out on a limb here, but I think something else might be bothering you."

"Nope. That's it. Um, listen, Nick, I've gotta go. I'm running late for my—uh—Intuitive Eating class." *Why did I say that? He knows I'm not a joiner.*

"See, I'm respecting my body. It's a temple, and, um, all that crap. Anyway, I'm supposed to bring dessert, and you caught me just going into the bakery. I'll take a dozen cannolis," I yelled across the room to my cat, Rocky. She was busy licking her girl parts and didn't bother to look up.

"I really have to go." I clicked off with Nick, and then I sat back and watched the rest of *The Nanny*, and cried some more.

*****

Officer Dave Wolinski is a twenty-five year old rookie cop with a passion for video games and nine-ball. He grew up at "F" & the Boulevard, attended Father Judge and married right out of high school. His ex-wife "is a bitch—no offense" and the new love of his life is an adorable, seven-month old Lab mix puppy.

I'd learned all this in the first ten minutes of my ride along. I also learned that working the beat is a lot like war—mostly boring, punctuated with sudden moments of sheer terror.

We'd been cruising around West Philly for a couple of hours, stopping briefly to grab some coffee and yell at an old guy who'd peed in the doorway of a laundromat. For some reason I'd been feeling kind of down, so it was nice to have something else to focus on.

As we climbed back into the patrol car, a late model, silver, m300 Chrysler barreled through the red light, going fifty miles an hour. The windows were rolled down and music blared from the radio. It was chock full of bass and expletives and seemed a tad on the hostile side, but maybe that's just me.

"Hey. Did you see that? The jerk almost ran over that woman in the crosswalk."

"It's show time," Dave announced. He pressed a button on the dashboard, setting off the flashing lights on the roof of the cruiser.

Okay! Now we're cookin'. We're gonna bust us some serious traffic scofflaws!

Dave hung a quick u-ie and followed the Chrysler. The driver caught sight of the patrol car in his rear view mirror, and Wolinski signaled for him to pull over. The guy slowed down, faked right and turned left, cutting off a couple of lanes of traffic, and sped away.

"So that's how you want to play it. Well, you're on, buddy." Dave glanced over at me. "Hang on tight," he yelled and tromped on the gas.

I started to get nervous. "Maybe you should just let me off at the Acme on the corner. I need to pick up a few things."

Dave grinned. "I thought you wanted the full cop experience." He radioed for backup and switched on the siren, while I clung to the door like a kid on a thrill ride, sure I was going to die. I hoped I'd remembered to put on clean underwear in case I got carted off to the morgue. I didn't want to embarrass my parents unduly.

We followed the guy for about eight blocks, and then he veered off onto a side street and zipped down the alley.

"Bad move," Dave said. "He just turned into a box canyon. We got him."

The driver sped up. He made it halfway down the narrow alley when he lost control of his vehicle and slammed into a dumpster.

Wolinski slowed to a stop and turned the patrol car sideways to block the exit.

We waited a beat, but there was no movement from inside the Chrylser.

"Stay put, and keep your head down," Dave ordered. He didn't have to tell me twice.

I scrunched down as he exited the car, gun drawn. Almost instantly, the crackling sound of gunshot pierced the air. Without thinking, I popped my head up over the dashboard and spotted Officer Wolinski laid out in front of the cruiser, blood oozing from his chest. The shooter hopped over the dumpster and fled down the alley.

Oh, shit.

I bolted out of the car and knelt beside Dave, pressing my hand to his chest to try and stem the flow of blood. He was out cold but still breathing. Blood seeped between my fingers. Frantically, I looked around for something to put pressure on the wound. I couldn't find anything suitable, so I yanked off my tee shirt, and shoved it against his chest, which left me sitting in the middle of the alley in my push-up bra.

Dave stirred and briefly opened his eyes, and I swear I saw a smile on his ashen lips.

While I waited for backup to arrive, a thought began to nag at me. Wolinski said the shooter had turned into a box canyon. Where had I heard that phrase before? And then it hit me. When I was a kid I used to watch old westerns with my dad. The bad guys always seemed to get trapped in box canyons—*places with an entrance but no exit.*

Oh, double shit!

Wolinski's gun lay inches away from me. I tried to grab it, but my hands were trembling so much it was tough to get a grip. Just as I was about to wrap my fingers around the handle, a shadow crossed my line of vision. In the next moment an enormous tennis shoe-covered foot stomped hard on my wrist, grinding it into the pavement.

Pain shot up my arm. I raised my eyes and saw the barrel of a .38 aimed directly at my head. The shooter stretched out a tattooed arm and pressed the gun against my temple. The only thought in my mind was that I was going to die, and everybody would know I wasn't really a 34C.

"Um, could I persuade you to rethink this?" I was beyond reason and figured there was no harm in asking.

The sound of sirens drew closer, only he didn't seem to notice. The man exuded arrogance. He pulled the gun away from my head and leered at me, his mouth forming a word so disgusting I wanted to wash my ears out with soap. Then he reached down and grabbed my boob. *Eeeww!*

"Party's over, asshole." I yanked my hand out from under his shoe, catching him off-balance. He stumbled backwards and I pounced on Dave's gun, aimed low and fired.

The bullet struck him in the thigh. He screamed and crumpled to the ground in agony, shattered bone poking through his skin.

"Cocksuckin' bitch," he screamed.

"Fuck you, you fucking jerk!" I screamed back and punched him hard in the testicles.

I kept on punching until suddenly I became aware of a pair of hands hauling me off the guy.

"It's okay," the cop said gently. "We'll take it from here."

"No, no. I've got it."

He threw a blanket around my shoulders and handed me off to his partner. "I think she's in shock," he advised her.

"No. Hey, I'm fine." The temperature was in the eighties, and yet I couldn't stop shaking.

Spectators were gathered on the sidewalk, some cursing the police, some videotaping the events. The EMT's flipped the shooter onto a stretcher while one of the officers cuffed him.

"Get this guy in the van before I kill him," the cop growled to the ambulance driver.

I looked around in a daze. Wolinski was being hoisted onto a stretcher. He was wearing an oxygen mask, which told me he was still alive. I walked over to him and squeezed his hand. My cheeks felt wet, and it took me a minute to realize I'd been crying.

I wandered over to the car. The front end was crumpled beyond repair, and yet the radio kept on playing, spewing shit that passed for music. Next to me stood another cop; a burly, middle-aged guy named McCabe. He looked like a seasoned vet, hard and cool and no one you'd want to mess with.

He reached a meaty hand in through the car window and turned off the radio. In the relative quiet I thought I heard someone whimper. McCabe heard it too.

"Stand back," he told me and grabbed the key out of the ignition. Cautiously, he approached the trunk and popped it open.

"Oh, for Christ's sake," he said, and I swear there were tears in his eyes.

CHAPTER TWO

"You don't want to see this," the cop warned. He was right.

I turned my head, but not before I caught a glimpse of two dogs—bloody and torn—one lying motionless, the other, eyes wide open, tummy heaving, whimpering in pain. It looked young and frightened.

"It's called 'trunking'," Officer McCabe explained to me, later, on the way to pick up my car at the station. "Takes dog fighting to a whole new level of torture."

"So—you mean this is like a real—thing?" It was hard enough to believe it was the brain child of one lone nut case, let alone a thriving business enterprise.

McCabe pulled his cruiser up next to my car and cut the engine. "It's a real thing all right. Gang Bangers love it because there's no overhead. They just throw the dogs into the trunk of a car and ride around town with music blasting to drown out the sound of them tearing each other apart. Whoever's left breathing at the end is considered the *winner*. Sick, fucking sons of bitches," he added. "Pardon my French."

Officer McCabe dealt with more horrific acts of inhumanity in a single shift than most people experience in a lifetime. I did not envy the man his job.

I opened the car door. "What's going to happen to the dog?"

"Depends. He's in pretty bad shape. He may have to be destroyed. And even if he makes it, who would want him? The poor bastard is so traumatized. Listen, you gonna be okay?" he asked as I hopped out of the patrol car.

"Absolutely. Thanks for the ride."

I watched him head into the police station, and then I walked over to the nearest bush and hurled.

*****

"Pass the beer nuts."

"You've had three bowls already, Sunshine."

"Yeah, I know. It's the only thing I can keep down. There's just something about witnessing the decline of western civilization that wreaks havoc with the digestive system."

My friend John and I were seated at the bar at DiVinci's, a local pizza joint. We were waiting for my Uncle Frankie and his girlfriend, Carla, to arrive. For some reason, they thought I needed "emotional support." Personally, I'd rather forget the whole thing, but they weren't about to let that strategy fly.

John shoved the bowl of beer nuts toward me and gave me a look I knew only too well.

"Uh, oh, here it comes," I mumbled.

"Bran, would you stop minimizing what happened to you? I thought the one and a half sessions you spent in therapy last month cured you of that."

"It was three sessions, and the issue never came up."

"I saw you being interviewed at the scene," he continued, ignoring my response. "It was all over the news. You were covered in blood from head to toe."

"Yeah, well, it's not like it was mine. I wasn't in any real danger." Okay, so I glossed over the part where psycho-man pulled the gun on me before I blew his leg to smithereens. My friends didn't need to know it could have been *me* they were hosing off the pavement. And to be totally honest, I wasn't in love with the thought either.

Thank God John knew better than to bring up the dogs. It had been a week, but I'd only just stopped crying.

"Johnny, could we just drop this, please? I have bigger things to worry about. The news crew got there so fast I didn't have time to clean Wolinski's blood off me, and now everybody down at the station is calling me *Carrie*. So, anyway, where's Garrett? I've barely seen you since you started going out with him. Hey, why don't you guys come over for dinner tomorrow night? I could order in from that new Thai place."

I'd hoped the switch to John's new favorite subject would let me off the hook for a while. John had been peering at me, trying to discern my true frame of mind, which was fragile, at best. Now, he glanced away, inspecting his manicured nails.

"I'm working at the gallery tomorrow night." The gallery being *Lucinda's on South.*

"Oh, well, what about Sunday? I want to get to know Garrett better. I only met him twice, but he seems really nice."

"Sunday, Sunday. Let me think. Oh, we've got tickets to the Annie Leibovitz exhibit. I'd invite you along, but it's sold out. Sorry, doll face."

"Get out! I love Annie Leibovitz. I'm sure I can get in on a reporter's pass. What time should I be at your place?"

"Ah, well, here's the thing, Bran. Garrett's kind of... shy. I want to wait a while before bombarding him with everybody. Oh, hey, here come Frankie and Carla."

Frankie is my mom's much younger brother, and one of my favorite people on Earth. My uncle, the manager of a boxing gym, graduated from State Pen U. He and Carla met when he sobered up and stopped knocking off liquor stores to feed his habit.

Frankie walked over to me and kissed the top of my

head. "How ya doin', kiddo?"

I flashed him two thumbs up and reached for more beer nuts.

Carla brought up the rear. She was wearing half a tube of eye shadow and balancing her signature five-pound beehive on her head. She smothered me in a "poor baby" embrace and then leaned across the bar to talk to John.

"We had a blast at Garrett's the other night. What a great guy."

John rolled his eyes in my direction. "Ixnay Arla-cay" he hissed out of the corner of his mouth. Carla glanced my way and blushed, and began picking invisible lint off her halter top.

"Wait," I said. "You guys went over to Garrett's?"

"No." Carla sputtered. "And neither did Paul."

An awkward silence ensued. I tried to cut John a "WTF," but he was busy taking inventory of his feet.

Uncle Frankie ordered a coke and sat down on the bar stool next to me. "I hear Dave Wolinski's expected to make a full recovery. I can't believe the numbnuts wasn't wearing a vest. Said they're too hot and uncomfortable, but I'll bet it beats a bullet in your chest."

"How do you know Dave?"

"He works out at the gym. Word has it you saved his life."

"It was the least I could do. He let me play with his siren."

It was easier to make a joke than to dwell on what might've happened if I hadn't been there. Dwelling's for losers. I'm all about denial, baby!

The door opened and homicide detective Robert Anthony DiCarlo walked in. His handsome, Irish-Italian face was edged in five o'clock shadow, his mouth upturned into a killer grin. Bobby DiCarlo's got dimples a girl could get lost in. I should know. I navigated the depths of that smile for ten years. Now we're strictly friends, but it still manages to give me a thrill.

I was about to wave when I noticed he had company. He was talking to a uniformed cop; tall, blond, cute, and female. She leaned in close and whispered something in his ear which, apparently, was the funniest thing he'd ever heard, because he threw back his head and guffawed so hard everyone began to stare. (Okay, just me.) He even punched her arm the way eleven year-olds do when they want to touch a girl but are trying not to be obvious about it. She eyed him coyly and punched him back. Funny, I felt like punching him, too.

DiCarlo watched her grab a to-go menu and head back out the door. He was still smiling when he reached the bar. He gave me a quick peck on the cheek and sandwiched in between John and me.

"Who's the uniform?" John asked, thrusting his chin toward the take-out counter.

DiCarlo followed his gaze. "Nobody. Just someone from work."

"She's pretty," I said.

Bobby shrugged. "Really? I hadn't noticed."

Oh, gimme a break, you big fat liar. "Well, trust me, she is."

A seat opened up on the other side of me and Bobby nabbed it. "So, how're you holding up, Sweetheart?" He reached for the bowl of nuts, but I beat him to it and grabbed the last handful.

"Good. Great," I told him. "I'm always so invigorated after I shoot someone." I didn't mean for it to come out bitchy. It just did.

John and DiCarlo exchanged looks.

"What?"

"Are you mad at me?" he asked.

Why, yes. Yes, I am. How dare you move on in your life and be all flirty with someone new, even though we mutually agreed we're not meant for each other and I'm in love with Nick?

"No," I sighed. "Sorry."

He nodded and ordered us a couple of Rolling Rocks, tipping the server more than the price of the beers.

Frankie and Carla wandered down to the other end of the bar to watch the Phillies' game, and John had to take a call from Garrett, (for some reason that Garrett was really beginning to bug me) so that just left Bobby and me.

Bobby took a slug of his beer. "I got some news about the shithead that fired on Wolinski," he told me. "He's a twenty-seven year old gang member from North Philly, named Mario Lewis, with a laundry list of felony charges including assault, dog fighting, and drugs. When they picked him up he was high as a friggin' kite, which explains why you were able to take him down when he pulled the gun on you."

"Oh, you heard about that."

"Did you really think I wouldn't? Why didn't you tell me yourself?" he added quietly.

"I, um..."

"Forget it. I know why. I'm just glad you're okay...you are, aren't you?"

I blinked back a fresh set of tears and downed my beer.

"Brandy, this wasn't your fault. You shot that guy in self-defense. He would have killed you."

I shrugged, swallowing hard.

"You wanna talk about it?"

"Not yet."

"*Not yet* like in *never*?"

"Yeah, probably. Listen," I said instead. "I need to ask you something, and I'm serious, so don't make a joke out of it, all right?"

"Okay, shoot."

"Well, yesterday at work, I was talking to Eric, and he said something, just kidding around, but—well, do you think I'm some sort of—death magnet?"

"Death magnet? Get outta here."

"Listen, I've been back in town for what—less than a year, and I've spent the entire time either being shot at or shooting someone else. I'm like that kid from Peanuts, the one with a cloud of dust that follows him everywhere.

Only in my case it's dead bodies. I just don't know why I can't live my life like a normal person."

Bobby stared at me for a beat, and I stared back, taking note of the deep circles under his eyes. He should've been home sleeping or spending time with his kid instead of sitting there comforting me.

"Bran," he said, taking my hand, "I don't know about normal, but you're the best person I know. Most people run the other way at the first sign of trouble, but you're not wired that way. I wish you were," he added, quietly. "Listen, if you're getting more than your share of the ugly side of life, it's because you're one of the few people with the guts to take it on."

I looked into Bobby's smokey blue eyes and smiled. "Thanks for not making me feel like a freak, Bobby."

"Hey," he grinned and whispered in my ear. "You want me to take care of this Eric character? I got friends in high places. I could arrange to have his car booted."

It was the first laugh I'd had in days.

"Speaking of the ugly side of life," DiCarlo said, his voice turning unexpectedly sour, "Mike Mahoe picked up a friend of yours the other day on a weapons' charge."

"Who?"

"Raoul Sanchez. He was hauling around a load of semi-automatics in the trunk of a stolen car. They also found three cases of hollow points in the back seat. You keep some rough company, Sweetheart."

Raoul Sanchez was not a friend—an acquaintance, at best, if you count the time I ran over his hand. (It was an accident…more or less.) Anyway, Bobby wasn't talking about Raoul. He meant Sanchez's sometime employer, Nick.

I didn't take the bait, so Bobby pressed. "So what's going on with you and Santiago these days? You guys an item?"

"Well, it's not like I'm upgrading my Facebook status to "In a Relationship" or anything…"

It was awkward talking to DiCarlo about Nick. First off, Bobby and I share a lot of history and residual feelings that, once acknowledged, we tacitly agreed to ignore. And secondly, it was way too soon to tell if Nick's declaration of love would actually translate to us being the aforementioned item. Then there was the whole "opposite sides of the legal fence" thing they had going on. DiCarlo was pre-disposed to believe the worst about Nick, and I didn't have the energy to challenge him. Luckily I didn't have to.

"Hey, look who's back," I said, nodding toward the door. The blond bombshell cop had reappeared this time sans uniform and sporting a thigh high mini skirt.

DiCarlo jumped to his feet. "I'll be right back. She must've forgotten something."

I'll say. The rest of her skirt, for starters.
*****

Try as I might, I could not stop thinking about the dogs in the trunk of Mario Lewis' car. One was dead; the other so physically and psychically traumatized it might as well be. So, against my instincts for emotional self preservation, I decided to go see the surviving puppy.

He was being housed at Jacob's Place, a pit bull rehab center located in Ambler. I'd called ahead and spoke at length to Eunice, a volunteer at the center. She told me I'd be more than welcome to visit, but the news wasn't too encouraging. The dog had lost an eye in the fight, and he was still very weak.

I'd almost changed my mind after hearing that, but since I was the one who'd discovered him, he felt like my responsibility. I mean once someone touches your life, you can't just walk away. That's the rule. Well, *my* rule, anyway. Besides, they opened a retro hoagie shop on Plymouth Road, and I promised Uncle Frankie I'd bring him back a "Bobby Rydell with 'the works'."

Jacob's Place was located on ten acres of farm land donated by a local philanthropist, in memory of his rescued Pit. The facility housed between 100-150 abused and abandoned dogs, and, due to the rising popularity of breeding pit bulls for sport, the numbers were growing.

I learned all this from the Facilities Director, Judy Harrison. Judy was a tall, pretty woman in her late forties.

"These dogs are the lucky ones," she said, stopping in front of a kennel full of canines. "I could tell you stories that would make your hair stand on end, and then just when you think it couldn't get any worse, you hear about some fresh, new horror. It's just beyond me that people are capable of such intense cruelty."

"How do you do it?" I asked. "How do you keep going day after day?"

Judy shrugged. "You take it one dog at a time. The reward is in helping the ones we can get physically and emotionally healthy enough to be placed in good, loving homes. I have to warn you, though," she said, her look turning somber, "sometimes the damage just goes too deep, and that may be the case with Popeye."

"Popeye?"

"That's what we call the little one you found. Since the operation to remove his damaged eye, he has this funny little squint and he looks just like--"

"Popeye," I finished for her.

Her smile was disarming. "He's become a favorite of the staff. He's a beautiful puppy with the most unusual markings. Would you like to see him?" she asked.

I nodded, although I knew this was an invitation to heartbreak.

We walked up to the onsite veterinary clinic, past a long line of cages filled with dogs in various stages of recuperation. Judy stopped in front of a small dog. He was cream colored, with a pinkish nose and belly. On his left hind leg there was a large, distinctive, brown spot in the shape of a near-perfect heart.

Popeye's head was swathed in bandages. A plastic cone collar had been placed around his neck to keep him from tearing at his wounds.

The puppy didn't look up when Judy called to him. In fact, he didn't seem aware of our presence at all.

"This little guy is in bad shape. If he doesn't start eating soon, we're going to have to feed him intravenously. Then there's the risk of infection from the puncture wounds he suffered. The saddest part," she added softly, "is he hasn't connected with anyone here. We have people working with him around the clock but trust is a fragile thing."

Judy stopped for a moment, and when she continued, her voice was laced with bitterness. "We do the best we can to help every dog that comes through our doors, but sometimes it feels like a lost cause."

I tried not to turn away, but the look on Popeye's face was too much to bear.

On my way out I stopped to make a donation. I didn't think I'd be back. I just didn't have the stomach for it.

*****

"Somebody's here to see you, Ms. Alexander. Says he's a friend of yours."

I was at work, looking up information on dog fighting when Al, my buddy from security, called. "He looks like a gangster," Al whispered into the phone."

Well, that could be anyone. I had an eclectic mix of friends, some of which were, in fact, actual gangsters. "What's his name?" I asked.

"Alphonso Jackson."

Alphonso. I smiled to myself. "Send him up."

Five minutes later there were audible gasps from my co-worker, Shelley, as Alphonso entered the room. Tall, dark and gorgeous, in a totally gang-banger kinda way, Alphonso epitomizes the word cool. He freelances for Nick and is a sort of Jack of all things bad-ass Trades.

He cut me a full-watt smile. "Hey, Sweetcakes. Nice digs." Then he turned a smoldering gaze on Shelley, who didn't know whether to run for her life or drop her drawers.

"Okay, rein it in there, cowboy."

Alphonso let out a full throated laugh and settled into the chair opposite my desk. The *Alphonso Show* over, Shelley made a wobbly exit.

"So what are you doing here?" I asked. Alphonso and I are friends, but not the "Let's do lunch" kind. If he showed up at my work, it was for a reason.

I started to get nervous. "Is Nick okay?" Nick was away on business, and was *in communicado*—at least with me. He says he doesn't like mixing business with pleasure, but I suspect it's his way of keeping me safe. The less I knew about his business dealings, the less likely I could be used as a pawn somewhere down the line.

"Relax. Santiago's okay."

"Do you know if he's up on the local news?"

Alphonso peered at me over his shades. "If you're asking does he know about you almost getting taken out by that fuckwad, dog-abusing tweaker, he might've heard something about it."

"Oh," I smiled. "That explains it. You're here to check up on me. Well, I'm happy to report I'm fine. So when you talk to Nick, tell him there's nothing to worry about."

"Ah, how do I put this gently, Sweetcakes? You're not fine. Not by a long shot."

"Well, that's a little judgmental," I sniffed.

Alphonso leaned in close and tapped my computer screen, leaving a thumbprint on Mario Lewis's acne-scarred face.

"I'm not talking about your mental health here, although that may be up for debate. Word on the street is when you shot this asshole, you pissed off about thirty of his closest friends, AKA The Junk Town Gang. Ring any bells?"

"Aren't they the ones who trashed a Seven-Eleven last month, because they ran out of Big Gulp cups?"

"And set the clerk on fire. Listen, Santiago thinks it might be a good idea if you stayed at his place—just until things settle down."

"Oh, c'mon, Alphonso. You really think the Junk Town Gang is going to come after me just because I shot one of their own? What babies. If they can't stand the heat, they should stay out of the kitchen."

Alphonso shook his head. "Nick said you'd start talkin' crazy. You always do when you're scared. Don't give me a hard time about this, okay?"

I was about to go round two with him when my phone rang.

"Brandy Alexander," I said tersely. "Oh, hi…uh huh… yeah, okay then…thanks for letting me know."

I turned back to Alphonso. "So, on a scale of one to ten, how pissed off do you think the Junk Town Gang would be if Lewis uh, y'know—died?"

CHAPTER THREE

Thanks to some rather spectacular gang-inspired nightmares, I awoke the next day before dawn too afraid to go back to sleep. Rocky and Adrian had crept off the bed in the middle of the night, (probably driven away by all my thrashing about) leaving me all alone. Suddenly, I missed Nick so much that I wanted to cry. Instead, I got dressed and headed for the shooting range. There's nothing like playing with high tech ammo to chase away the blues.

The place was already packed, but I ran across Vince and he offered to share his space with me. I was taking a chance. Vince is not a morning person.

"Your aim is all off," he scowled and tightened the strap on his protective goggles, making his naturally chubby cheeks stick out more than usual. He looked like Rocky the Flying Squirrel.

"Well, how am I supposed to concentrate? I pop a guy in the leg and the next thing I know he drops dead in his hospital bed."

"You have nothing to feel guilty about, Brandy. You did what you had to do."

"Yeah, I know." The trouble is it didn't help.

Rationally, I understood that Lewis had left me with no choice, but emotionally—not so much.

I shot off another round and missed by a mile.

"You're flinching on the recoil. Try taking a deep breath before you shoot." I did as I was told, aimed and fired. Not bad.

"It's just sort've a shock, y'know?" I said, as I reloaded my gun. "I mean Lewis seemed to be on the mend and then, boom, he's gone. So, what happened to him, anyway? Did he develop an infection or something?"

Vince shrugged. "We'll know more after the autopsy."

"Autopsy? But if he died of natural causes, why would they perform an autopsy?"

Too late, Vince realized his mistake. The corner of his mouth began to twitch. "Just routine. So anyway, did you catch the Phillies' game the other night?"

"Vincent." I fixed him with a stare. "Autopsies haven't been routine since the 1950's. They wouldn't have ordered one unless the family wanted it, in which case they'd have to pay for it—unless the death was suspicious…that's it, isn't it? The death was suspicious!" I yelled, waving my 'shootin' arm in the air.

"Hey, hey! Put that thing down, ya maniac. It's loaded."

"Oops." I put down the gun and took off my goggles. "Vince, are you saying my shooting Lewis may not be what killed him?"

"Brandy, I'm not saying anything. Would you please just give it a rest?"

"Look, if there's a chance I wasn't responsible for Lewis' death, I have a right to know. And if he was murdered, well, that's the public's right to know."

Had he been physically able to, Vince would have kicked himself in the butt.

"Will you keep your voice down? Nobody said anything about murder. We're still looking into things."

"So you admit there's something to look into."

"Jesus, you're a pain. And to think you were once my

girlfriend."

"Oh, please. We were in the third grade. And don't change the subject."

"You're not gonna let this go, are you, Alexander?"

"Vincent, I shot the guy. Now he's dead. I was willing to accept responsibility for that, but now you're saying you don't know for sure if the two are related. Only some people might get the idea that they are and be kinda—y'know—homicidal about it."

Vince's ears perked up. "Has someone threatened you?"

"No." I answered honestly. It was all rumor, and I refused to live my life in fear, which was why I'd declined Nick's offer to let me stay at his place while he was gone. (Well, that, and because for reasons I couldn't fathom, I was feeling upset with him. My mother would chalk it up to hormones. Then again, my mother chalks everything up to hormones.)

Vince took off his goggles. "Look, Bran, I can't tell you what I don't know, all right? I don't have the final report. But mistakes get made, y'know what I mean? So until we get the results of the autopsy I've got nothin' to say."

"But—"

"Nothin.'"

*****

Two days later, I drove over to the hospital cafeteria to pick up some lunch, because as everyone knows hospital food is the yummiest! Oh, and as long as I was there I figured what would it hurt to ask a few questions about Mario Lewis? I polished off my pudding cup and headed for reception.

A couple of uniformed guards stood at the desk having a heated discussion over the cancellation of *Jersey Shore*. They stopped talking as I approached. The female guard stared at me curiously. She appeared to be about my height, (5'2" give or take an inch) but broader in the shoulders. Her name tag said Edie Wyncote.

"Can I help you?" she asked.

"Thanks." I whipped out my Press I.D., attempting to channel the cocky assurance of, say, Geraldo Rivera. *I'm a very important person, and I need my questions answered, stat!*

"My name is Brandy Alexander."

"I knew it!" she shouted. "High five, girl!"

I stuck a reluctant hand in the air, truly hoping her enthusiasm was due to my in-depth reporting on Skinny Jeans, but she burst that bubble in a hurry.

"You are my hero. What you did to that douche bag was awesome." Edie whipped her head back around to her colleague. "You know who she is? She killed the guy who shot the cop."

"Woah," I said nervously. Sitting in the lounge a few yards away, a group of young men in baggy pants with matching red streaks in their hair puffed away under the "Positively No Smoking" sign. One of them looked up at the reference to Mario Lewis. He cocked his finger at me, gun style, and blew a smoke ring in my direction. The hostility packed in that small gesture made my skin crawl.

I turned back to the guards. "Let's not jump to conclusions here. I mean I don't want to take credit where it isn't due."

The male guard gave me the once-over. He was white, with a crew cut and a scar over his right eyebrow that sliced it in two. Tats peeked out from the collar of his uniform. "What'd you say your name was again?"

"Brandy. Look, whether or not I actually killed this guy is subject for debate, and I'm afraid I don't have time right now. Could you just direct me to the floor he was staying on?" I was going to make up an elaborate ruse for going up there, but it turned out not to be necessary.

"Fifth floor," Edie directed me. "Ask for Suzanne Dunham. She's the floor nurse. I believe she was on duty that night."

"Thanks."

I could feel the heat of several pairs of eyes on my back

as I headed for the elevator.

Nurse Dunham wasn't there. However, I did run across a brash, young orderly in the elevator on the way back downstairs. His hair was black and massively curly. He bobbed his head and eyed me with unreserved glee. "Hey, aren't you—"

Oh, great. Here we go again. "Yes," I huffed with all the impatience I could muster. "I am the one who shot Mario Lewis. But that doesn't necessarily mean I killed him, so let's not go around spreading rumors. Okay?"

"*O-kaaay.* I was going to say, aren't you the girl who played the alien in last week's episode of Star Fleet 2110. But this is cool too." He leaned into me with a conspiratorial whisper. "Y'know, I was here the night Lewis went Code Blue."

"*Really.* So, Mohindar," I smiled, reading from the plastic name plate attached to his scrubs. "Let's talk."

We got off at the next floor, and I followed my new best friend down the hall. He paused in front of a corner room at the far end of the corridor, adjacent to a utility closet.

"This was Lewis' room," Mohindar announced with the jaunty air of a Disneyland tour guide. "Admin tried to isolate him as much as possible because it freaked out the other patients seeing the guard at his door." Mohindar shrugged. "I don't know what people were so upset about. I mean it's not like he was going anywhere."

We rounded the corner and ran smack into a large area sectioned off with sandwich board caution signs and bright yellow tape. Tiles were piled high next to a gaping hole. Construction workers cruised the hallway wearing hospital-assigned guest badges pinned to their shirts.

"What's all this?" I yelled over the din of machinery.

"They're renovating the wing. They had to combine two units because of all the construction, so it's been pretty crazy." Mohindar slumped against a wall. "It's hard enough keeping track of the doctors and nurses I already work with, and now we've got all this new staff here. Between you and me, this job is getting to be too much. I'm thinking of quitting and going to work for my brother-in-law. He has a dry cleaner's in Hatboro."

*A thought started percolating in my brain. With all this chaos, it would be fairly easy to get to Lewis without being noticed. The regular staff wouldn't necessarily keep track of contract construction workers and, add to that, unfamiliar doctors and nurses from another unit…*I cut my eyes to the blue plastic tarps that were strewn all over the floor. They provided ample space for someone to hide.

"Mohindar, how long has the renovation been going on up on this floor?"

"Let's see, about a month now."

Which meant Lewis was there during the construction.

"Listen, do you remember anything in particular about the night Lewis died?"

Mohindar crammed a wad of gum the size of a fist into his mouth and started chewing vigorously. After a minute he blew a large bubble and said, "Yeah."

I waited but he didn't elaborate. "So, what happened?" I prompted.

"It was around 10:30 p.m. when the electricity cut out."

"It cut out?"

"Oh, yeah. It happens all the time. And for some reason, the back up generators didn't kick in. The construction has really messed with the electrical wiring. Sometimes the lights go out, or alarms go off for no reason. We've even lost power to monitors. Y'know, stuff like that."

"So what happened that night?"

"Some people got stuck in the elevator. The maintenance crew was working on another problem, so one of the nurses called to the cop that was stationed outside of Lewis' room, and he went to check it out. He couldn't have been gone for more than ten minutes or so, but when he got back, Lewis was gone."

So that's what Giancola was trying so hard not to tell me. Lewis died while the cop was off helping the people stuck in the elevator. Did the electricity go off by accident, or did someone cut the power in order to create a diversion? No wonder the authorities deemed his death suspicious.

I resisted the urge to call Vince, figuring he'd be more inclined to lecture me than provide me with a detailed report. I guess some people just have a hard time sharing.

*****

After dinner I settled down in front of the TV to watch *The Antiques Road Show*, (because my mom was sure those hideously ugly ceramic lamps with the cherubs on them that my grandmother bought at Lit Brothers a million years ago and now reside in my basement, under the wine making kit—another sure-fire money maker—are "worth their weight in gold now") and shared a turkey pot pie with the dog, when John called.

"Hey, Sunshine, you busy tonight?"

"Why? What's up?" The last time I blindly confessed to having no social life I ended up babysitting for Bobby's little girl while he went out on a date.

"It's prime rib night at Henry's Bar and Grill, and I've got a two-for-one coupon. Do you want to go?"

"Why aren't you taking Garrett?"

"I miss you."

"Garrett busy?"

"God, you're so cynical. Can't a guy take his best friend to dinner?"

Okay, now I felt bad. He was probably just trying to make it up to me for not including me in Garrett's little soiree. I can't say that I blamed him. John's boyfriends love me, and sometimes John can feel a little left out. Well, I'd just have to show him there's nothing to worry about.

"I already ate, but how about you and Garrett and I go to dinner next Friday?"

"Next Friday?" he repeated. "The three of us?"

"Yeah. And listen, John, no matter how great Garrett

and I hit it off, nobody could ever take your place. You know that, don't you?"

"Um, Bran?"

"Uh huh?" Only I wasn't really listening. Adrian had swiped the turkey pot pie and was trotting off toward the kitchen. "Listen, I've got to go. I'll see you guys next Friday."

Ten minutes later John called back.

"Hey, John."

"It's one meal."

"Okay, okay, if it means that much to you, we can go out tonight too. Who am I to say no to free food?"

"C'mon, don't be like that…"

"What are you talking about? I just said I'd go."

"I'm trying, I really am," replied a new voice, "but, frankly, I find her insufferable."

"Yo," I said, a little louder. "Who's insufferable?"

"You're not being fair, Garrett."

Garrett? Oops. John must've butt-dialed me by accident. Sounds like he and Garrett are having a fight. I should really hang up…

"I know she's your best friend, John, but—"

Best friend? Hey! That little twerp is talking about me. I held my breath and pressed my ear to the receiver.

"Look, Garrett, Brandy may appear a little…self-involved at times, but once you get to know her—well, she'll still seem self-involved, but—"

But that's part of her charm…I mean my charm. Jeez, John, tell him.

I'm sure he did, too, only at that point the call disconnected, so I didn't get to hear him say it.

I called Franny. "Am I self-involved?"

"Can I call you back?" she whispered. "The baby finally fell asleep, and Eddie and I are—y'know, taking advantage of a little *alone* time."

"Yeah, sure. But just tell me if you think I'm self-involved. I overheard John talking to Garrett and—"

"You're not self-involved. I'm hanging up now."

"But why would he say that? I mean, really. That makes no sense at all, Fran...Fran? *Unhh!*"

*****

I knew it was stupid the minute I turned left instead of right. The right turn would have taken me home. The left took me through Mario Lewis's old stomping grounds. I knew it and yet I kept on going because I just couldn't leave it alone.

The entire week had passed without incident. No phone calls from Lewis's disgruntled family threatening to kill me in my sleep. No emails from outraged do-gooders who'd caught the video circulating around the Internet of what appeared to be me shooting a defenseless Mario and punching him in the nuts for no apparent reason, (the part where he'd shot the cop, conveniently, having been edited out). And, best of all, not a peep from Mario's posse. So why, in the immortal words of Bubbie Heiki, was I "borrowing trouble?" The truth is I had no friggin' idea.

I guess I was looking for exoneration. The reports on Lewis' death came back, and as it turns out, shooting someone in the thigh can be fatal. Who knew? Seems the blood vessels in the thigh are huge. The break in his bone could have caused fatty deposits to loosen and go into the blood stream, which might have caused a pulmonary embolism.

Might have. The initial findings were "inconclusive," Vince had informed me, after reading the report. And that, apparently, was about as much closure as his death warranted.

"But what about the guard leaving his post? Someone could have slipped in and killed Lewis while he was gone. And, by the way, how come you didn't tell me about that?"

"Let me remind you of something, Alexander. You're not a cop. I'm not required to tell you. In fact, I'm required by law *not* to. Look, the autopsy may have been inconclusive, but as far as the police are concerned, Lewis died of natural causes. What the cop did was unprofessional, and he's been disciplined, but it didn't change the course of history."

"Okay, let me get this straight. It's possible that he *didn't* die from the gunshot wound, but, for the sake of convenience they're just going to say he did. So much for justice for all."

Vince muttered something under his breath that sounded like *God help me.*

"Brandy, will you get off your high horse? The authorities did their job. Look," he said, his voice softening, "I know you feel bad, and I'm sorry for that, but I can't continue this investigation just to assuage your guilt."

"Well, I just think it's weird, is all."

"Oh, Jesus, what now?"

"Vince, the fact is Lewis was recovering nicely. By all accounts he was expected to be released soon. But you know as well as I do there were a whole bunch of people who wished he'd never survived. Animal Rights' activists had been outside the hospital for days, chanting 'Death to Lewis.' Plus, emotions run high any time a cop gets hurt in the line of duty. Maybe some nut couldn't stand the thought of Lewis shooting Wolinski and decided to return the favor out of some kind of misguided vigilante justice. Not to mention Lewis was a gang member with a history of violent crimes. Any number of people probably wanted him dead."

Vince chewed on his lower lip, blowing a soft puff of air out of the side of his mouth. "Okay, okay, I get your point. Look, the truth is nobody gives a crap about this piece of shit cop-killer. And if I could've dumped his dead ass in the Delaware River, I would have done it without a backwards glance. But we did everything by the book, and there just wasn't enough evidence to indicate there had been foul play."

Great. Only he didn't have to live with the guilt. Well, if there was a chance that someone else was responsible for

Lewis' demise, I owed it to myself and to his family to check it out.

According to public records, Lewis lived on a side street in the heart of Junk Town, a section of Erie Avenue famous for heroin trafficking and gang related homicides. The streets were surprisingly empty. I guess all the killers and drug dealers were on a dinner break or something. I passed an array of row homes, duplexes and federally funded apartment buildings in various stages of decay, and turned right on a filth encrusted street named Garland.

Even the air smelled different here. Like garbage. Hot, rotting garbage.

I checked the address and squeezed into the one available spot across from an ugly, faded, brown duplex. Bags of trash, filled to overflowing, sat on a tiny, lopsided porch. The foundation had eroded eaten away by time and termites. There were bars on the windows and door.

Next door to the Lewis house stood a big wooden fence topped with barbed wire. Hidden from view, a couple of dogs snarled, making deep, rumbling noises that sounded suspiciously like, "Yum, lunch!" If their intent was to scare the crap out of me, mission accomplished.

Someone had hauled an old floral couch out onto the sidewalk. A toddler in a diaper and dirty tee shirt straddled the back, riding it like a hobby horse. He looked dangerously close to toppling onto the hard pavement, so I opened the car door and crossed over to the other side of the street.

Fixing round, wide eyes on me he looked up and smiled; a smile so full of innocence, trust and delight it made my heart hurt. And in that moment, I knew why I was there. Because Mario Lewis hadn't started out his life as a monster.

A little girl, no more than six or seven, came out of the house and dragged the baby off the back of the couch. She stared at me with the same round, wide eyes.

"Is he your brother?" I asked.

The screen door opened again, and a woman in her early twenties walked out. Her hair was stuck out at strange angles, like she'd slept on it funny, and her eyes were puffy and red, as if she'd been crying.

I got a sudden, sick feeling in the pit of my stomach. Did those kids belong to Mario? Was the crying woman Mario's wife, his girlfriend, his sister? Was she mourning his loss? Well, tough. I'd been seconds away from dying at the hands of that creep, and if I hadn't stopped him, my family, my friends would be the ones in mourning.

I refuse to feel sorry for them. I refuse. I repeated it to myself like a mantra.

The woman glared at me and started down the sidewalk. The little girl met her halfway, instinctively ducking as the woman reached out and slapped her on the side of the head. A quick assessment of the situation told me she was a little on the crazy side. I scooted back across the street and headed for my car.

A middle-aged woman had come out of her home and was hosing down her sidewalk. She watched with guarded interest the younger woman came up behind me and grabbed hold of my tee shirt, jerking me backward. I could feel the material give way as I spun out of her grasp.

She stood there, eyeballing me. "Why you messin' with my kids?"

"I wasn't—"

"You from DHS, ain't you? Well, you ain't gettin' my kids. Their daddy's gone, and they's all I got."

"Look, I'm not here to take your kids away—"

"Then you must be a damn reporter," she muttered. "You people hounding me all hours of the day and night. Wantin' to know things that ain't your business. Get the fuck outta here."

My thoughts exactly. I started to back away, happy to leave in one piece, when she made a sudden leap to the rage of recognition.

"Hey, you the bitch that shot my Mario."

Without warning she lunged for me. I dodged, and she ended up doing a face plant onto the hood of my car. I ripped open the door, but she had already peeled herself off and charged after me again.

This time she went for the throat. My hand shot up between her arms and I popped her in the nose. She let go of my neck, and clawed at my face with strong, bony fingers. Luckily, she was a nail biter, so they didn't do much damage. Unfortunately, her fist did.

"Ow!" I cried, landing on my butt on the pavement.

"Roger! We got trouble." The lady with the hose shouted. "Come out here and bring Junior!"

"Forget Junior," I howled. "Call 911."

Two beefy men appeared, just as Mario's lady friend jumped on top of me and pounded my head into the ground. The older woman turned the hose on us, attempting to shock us into civility, or at least stop making a mess on her sidewalk. Junior grabbed Mario's girlfriend, and pulled her arms across her chest, like a straight jacket.

"Calm down, Sherese."

Sherese kicked and cursed at him, but it seemed more obligatory than anything else. All the fight had gone out of her.

"We're not done, bitch," she spat, as Junior guided her across the street and back into her house.

My head ached, and I felt a little trickle of blood on my right temple. I ran my tongue around the inside of my mouth, doing a quick assessment of my teeth. They all seemed to be intact.

Roger offered a hand to me and I took it gratefully and struggled to my feet. I was dripping wet, and my face was beginning to swell like a hot air balloon.

"You're bleeding," Roger observed. "Come on into the house and my wife will fix you right up."

I shot a quick glance at Mario's place and shook my head. "I really appreciate what you did for me, but I think I'd just better go."

Roger's wife threw a supporting arm around my shoulder. "Don't worry about her, honey. She's probably passed out on the couch by now. I'm Candice. Let's get some ice on your cheek. You don't look so good."

Their house was worn but spotless. Pictures of children and grandchildren graced every available bit of space.

"That's our grandbaby, Kendra," Roger explained, pointing to a photo of a beautiful, young woman in a cap and gown. "She just graduated school this year. She's going to be an R.N, like her grandma."

Candice emerged from the kitchen with a bag of ice and some homemade chocolate chip cookies. She followed my gaze to her granddaughter's photo.

"That girl was raised right here in this house," she stated with pride. Thrusting her chin toward Mario's, she didn't bother to hide the contempt that crept into her voice. "There are a lot of decent people in this neighborhood. It's trash like them that ruins it for the rest of us. Tell me, is what she said true? Are you that reporter gal who shot Lewis?"

I nodded, not trusting my voice.

"You did the world a favor, far as I'm concerned," Roger stated flatly. "Course, not everybody sees it this way." He gave his head a rueful shake. "For the life of me, I can't understand it. Folks like him bring drugs and violence into our neighborhood and half the town treats him like some kind of damn folk hero."

Candice took my swollen face in her hand, inspecting the damage. "No offense, honey, but it wasn't too smart coming here."

"Yeah," I agreed. "That's a real problem of mine. Not thinking things through, and all that. I'm working on it."

"Well, why exactly did you come?"

I debated whether to confide in this nice couple. There certainly wasn't any love lost between them and their former neighbor. I opted for the truth.

"So, you think Lewis could have been murdered,"

Candice said when I finished. "Makes sense to me."

"Yeah? Why's that?"

She handed me the bag of ice and a couple of cookies. I took a bite of cookie and winced. My cheek was killing me, but, not one to waste perfectly good dessert, I pressed the ice against my face and kept on chewing.

"There was constant commotion going on in that house. Lewis and Sherese fought all the time. He was a crazy bastard. He actually chased her down the street with a carving knife one day because she let the kids eat his chocolate bar."

Well, that would piss anybody off.

"I just prayed those babies would get taken away before something awful happened to them."

"People would come and go at all hours of the night," Roger supplied. "There'd be music blaring, dogs barking. It was impossible to sleep some nights."

I thought back to the last time I'd heard music blaring. Lewis had used it to mask the sounds of something far more disturbing in the trunk of his car.

"Who owns the empty lot next door to Lewis' house?" I asked.

"They do. It was Mario's grandfather's place. The house burned down a few years ago, and they finally got it all cleared out."

"Could they have been using the property to stage dog fights?"

"Couldn't say for sure. But I'll bet there'd be upwards to fifteen dogs in that lot at times. They treated them something awful, too. Once, Junior found a dead puppy, stuffed in our trash. It couldn't have been more than three months old. That puppy had been mauled so bad there was practically nothing left."

"Bait dog," I thought, and almost threw up.

"Did anyone ever call the cops on them?"

"All the time," Candice said. "But it never did any good, and after a while, they just stopped showing up.

There was no point to it. Anyway, you learn real quick around here to mind your own business. It's safer that way."

Half an hour later I thanked Roger and Candice King for their kindness and then reached into my bag for a pen and paper. I wrote down my name and number and laid it on the coffee table. "I'm probably just grasping at straws," I apologized, "but if you can think of anything else, please give me a call."

Roger cast a hurried look in my direction and then cut his eyes toward his wife. "How about getting Brandy some cookies for the road?"

"I would," Candice laughed, "but she ate them all."

I followed the Kings to the door, taking note that Roger picked my number off the table and pocketed it.

"You take care," Candice told me, as she gave me a hug.

"Thanks for everything," I said, "and sorry about the cookies." I left with a sore jaw and a heavy heart.

Okay, Brandy. Just accept the fact that there is no mystery tied to Mario Lewis's death. You shot him. He's dead. Your fault. Move on.

I got into my car and pulled away, catching sight of Lewis' kids standing on the porch. They were scowling at me. Even the little one. Fabulous. First I shoot their father, and then I deck their mom. I hate for anyone to think ill of me, but at the rate I was destroying family members, who could blame them?

CHAPTER FOUR

On the way home, I stopped at a liquor store to pick up some lottery tickets. I figured in the past week, I thought I was pregnant but wasn't, I almost got laid off but didn't, and Mario Lewis tried to kill me but couldn't. Plus, I didn't lose any teeth when his girlfriend punched me, so, obviously, I was on a lucky streak!

A girl in line ahead of me cradled a six-pack of Budweiser. She looked about fourteen. When it was her turn she sidled up to the clerk and hoisted the beer onto the counter. "I'll take a carton of Pall Malls," she told him.

"I need to see some I.D."

"No problem." She reached into her back pocket and laid a driver's license on the counter.

The clerk took a look and laughed, and handed it back to her. Then, he scooped up the beer and placed it on the counter behind him.

"Sorry, I don't sell to minors."

The girl leaned over the counter and jabbed the card with her index finger. "But it says right here I'm over twenty-one."

"Yeah. It also says you're a man."

"So, what's the problem? It says I'm twenty-one."

"A twenty-one year old *man*."

She let out an exasperated sigh and turned around to me. "Hey, will you buy me some beer?"

The clerk leaned across the counter and tapped her on the shoulder. "Uh, you know I can hear you, right?"

I figured anyone with that kind of chutzpah didn't deserve to go away empty handed. I bought her some string cheese and a Red Bull and headed back to the car.

As I climbed into the driver's seat, I spied a thirty-ish looking guy with a crew cut rounding the corner. He was wearing shorts and flip flops and a tee shirt that said, "I'm great in bed." A spotted boxer- terrier mix puppy with big dark eyes, and ears that stuck out like a bent antennae trailed along beside him.

I whipped out my cell phone and called Janine. "There's a guy wearing a tee shirt that says *I'm great in bed*," I reported.

"Is he cute?"

"If he was cute, would he have to wear the tee shirt?"

"Good point. Well, at least he's confident in his abilities. Do you think I'd like him?" she asked.

Janine's great, but her taste in men is borderline icky. The last guy she went out with asked her if she'd be cool with a ménage a trois with a stripper he'd met at a bachelor party (she wasn't). Fran and I are trying to wean her off the weirdos.

The puppy stopped about two yards from the car and began sniffing the ground, then squatted to do her business. The guy looked away, like he had no idea in the world there was a dog attached to the other end of the leash and that he would be responsible for what came out of it.

The puppy finished up, and the guy yanked on her leash and kept walking, ignoring what the dog had left behind.

"Hang on, Neenie." I rolled down the window and leaned over curbside. "Yo! Pick that up, ya yutz."

Mr. "Good in Bed" flipped me the bird and kept walking. How rude was that!

The guy reached the liquor store and tied the leash to a lamp post. The puppy lay down and began to whimper.

"Shut the hell up," her owner muttered, and punctuated his words with a vicious kick to the dog's hind quarters. The puppy yelped in pain.

My heart stopped. "Are you insane?" I screamed.

Ignoring me he turned and went into the store.

"Bran, what's going on?" Janine yelled through the phone.

"I'll call you back."

Without thinking, I scrambled out of the car and ran over to the puppy. "Hi Baby," I soothed.

She licked at her injured leg, but stopped to lick my hand, instead. I could see her owner standing at the counter, talking to the clerk. In a flash, I untied the leash and coaxed the dog to her feet. She began moving forward with a slow, painful limp. I bent down and scooped thirty-five pounds of puppy in my arms, waddled back to the car, and shoved her into the back seat of the LeSabre. Then I climbed into the driver's side and locked the doors, shaking with rage.

At that moment, the jerk came barreling out of the store and ran full steam toward my car, only he stumbled and tripped on his flip flops. He yanked them off and threw them at my windshield. They bounced off into the street. I scrambled to start the engine, but sometimes it stalls in the heat and this was one of those days.

The guy reached the car and pounded on my window, his face turning the color of cooked lobster. Any minute I expected his fist to come flying through the glass. I prayed for a miracle and tried the key again. This time it worked.

"Give me my God damn dog!" he roared.

"Bite me!" I stomped on the gas and took off.

Oh my God. What have I done? I just stole a dog! I called Janine back. "I just stole a dog."

"Oh. Um, congratulations!"

"Neenie," I huffed, swerving out of the way of a van, "I could be in real trouble here."

I glanced in the rear view mirror. The dog kicker appeared out of nowhere and was following me in a black Ford pickup. He was about five cars back and gutter sniping to close the gap.

"Oh, shit."

"What?"

"He found me."

"Who?"

"Jeez, Neenie. Keep up. The guy with the dog. I gotta go."

He gunned his engine and tried to squeeze in right behind me. Luckily, the friendly drivers of Philadelphia didn't care much for this yahoo bolting the line. They closed ranks and locked him out. I took the opportunity to hang a left on South Street and prayed he didn't notice. Unfortunately, he did. Three blocks later he was two cars back. *Great. What now?*

I was only a few blocks away from Uncle Frankie's gym. Now, normally, I don't like to involve my friends and family in my petty problems. But so far, the day really sucked, and I was tired of fighting my own battles, even if I was the one who'd started them. I hit speed dial and called my uncle.

"I'm in trouble," I announced. "Could you meet me outside the gym in about a minute?"

"You got it, hon," he said, no questions asked.

I looked in the rear view mirror again. The guy was practically riding my bumper. He looked really mad. "Oh, and Uncle Frankie, you might want to bring some friends."

Half a block later, I pulled into South Street Gym's parking lot, the Ford pick-up riding my bumper the entire way. Uncle Frankie was standing there waiting for me, flanked by three giant gym rats with muscles to spare. I pulled up next to them and jumped out of the car.

The dog kicker had gotten out of his truck and was headed in my direction. He was so focused on me he didn't seem to notice my steroid enhanced entourage.

Frankie gave me the once-over. "What happened to your face?" Without waiting for an answer, he added, "Did he do this to you?"

My uncle has a soft spot for me and a short fuse when he thinks someone has done me wrong. Before I could set him straight, he broke ranks and was on the guy like Whiz on a cheese steak.

He grabbed him by the front of his shirt, stretching the collar all out of proportion. "You're a real big man, beatin' up on a girl, aren't ya?"

"Whoa," the guy said, stumbling backwards. "I didn't lay a hand on this whack job. She stole my dog."

"Hey, watch your mouth." Frankie turned to me. "D'jou steal his dog?"

"I had to. He kicked it."

"You swear he didn't hurt you?"

I nodded.

Frankie smoothed down the guy's tee shirt, and shoved him backwards toward his car. "Get the hell outta here, you creep."

"What about my dog?"

Frankie snarled at him. "What dog?"

"Yeah, what dog?" The gym rats echoed like a Greek chorus.

He stood there for a minute appearing to weigh his options. "Ah, you're all nuts. You can keep that pain in the ass hound. I'm tired of her pissing on my rug, anyway."

We watched him as he drove off. "So, Uncle Frankie, you want a dog?"

*****

Halfway home, my breathing began to return to normal. The puppy had settled into the back seat and was busy gnawing on a bag of beer pretzels I keep on the floor of the car in case I'm ever lost in a snow storm and have resort to cannibalism in order to survive—but, wait—no, I don't, because I had the foresight to pack a bag of pretzels!

"Don't make crumbs," I told her and reached for my phone to call Paul.

"I found a puppy," I announced.

"Yeah? Where?"

"Right on the street. It followed me home. I put signs up and all, but nobody's come to claim her, so I was thinking maybe you'd want her."

"Brandy, you know I've got asthma. How am I supposed to breathe?"

"I'll pick up some Benadryl on the way over. Please, Paul. Just until I find a permanent home for her. I'd take her, but I've got a lot on my plate right now."

"I k-know," Paul said, his stress stutter kicking in, "I've b-been w-worried about you."

"No need, Paulie. I'm fine. Honest. Listen," I said, feeling warm, wet, puppy breath on the back of my neck. "You don't have to give me an answer now. Just think about it, okay? I'll call you tomorrow." I drove the rest of the way home with the puppy's head on my shoulder.

*****

I woke up at 6:00 a.m. to a ringing phone and the combined weight of two canines sitting on my chest. Rocky was stretched out on the pillow next to me, unfazed by the puppy's unexpected arrival. I shoved the dogs off me and grabbed the phone.

"Brandy?" The voice was vaguely familiar.

"Yes?"

"It's Roger King."

I have found that early morning phone calls generally fall into two categories. Either someone died, in which case you probably didn't need to be woken up, they'd still be dead at a reasonable hour, or the occasional time zone mix-up. Since we lived on the same coast, I went straight to the worst case scenario.

"Is Candice okay?" I asked, slightly panicked.

"She's fine. Listen, I'm sorry about calling so early, but I've got to get to work, and I didn't think I should wait on this."

"Wait on what?"

Roger lowered his voice. "Something happened about a week before Lewis got shot. Candice doesn't know about it, and I want to keep it that way. Can you meet me at the McDonald's at Broad and Snyder in an hour?"

I had to be in Horsham by nine to cover their annual Police VS Firefighter softball game. I was throwing out the first pitch. I did a quick mental calculation. It would take me twenty minutes to shower, throw on some clothes, and feed and walk the dogs. No time for breakfast, but I could grab a bite at Mickey D's. *Oh boy, breakfast fries!*

"I'll be there," I told him. "Can you give me a hint as to what this is about?"

Roger hesitated. "I can't say now," he whispered, and hung up.

Forty minutes later, I slid into a booth across from Roger King, balancing a tray of Egg McMuffins and coffee. He waited until I settled in, and then he turned an earnest eye on me and cleared his throat.

"A couple of weeks ago, Candice spent the night at her sister's, and I had a boys' night out."

"Oh." I said, squirming uncomfortably in my seat. "Listen, Roger, I barely know you. Don't you have a friend or someone more appropriate to confess that sort of thing to?"

Roger laughed so hard that he choked on his coffee. "Candice is the only woman for me, and she knows that. This is about something I saw that night. I'd been over to a friend's place for a poker game. It broke up at around two, and I came home and parked in front of the house. I'd just shut off the engine when a car turned the corner and cruised down the street. I got a little suspicious because they didn't have their lights on, so I sat there waiting to see what they were going to do."

"Could you tell the make of the car?"

Roger shook his head. "It was too dark out. I guess the city don't want to spend money on street lamps. All I know is it was some kind of SUV, but I couldn't tell the make. Anyway, it pulled up in front of Lewis' house and this guy got out. He made a phone call and a few minutes later, Lewis came out of his house. He wasn't wearing nothin' but a pair of shorts, and it looked like he'd just woke up.

"The next thing I knew, two more fellas piled out of the car. Can't be sure, but I think one of them was white. The other one was black. The black guy was holding a bat, and the white guy grabbed Lewis as he tried to run back into the house. The one with the bat started swinging at Lewis' head. Lewis raised his arms up and tried to protect himself, but they wouldn't let up. I could swear they was gonna kill him, but they just messed him up a whole lot."

"Could you hear what they were saying?"

"Clear as can be. He was laid out on the sidewalk, moaning the same name over and over. Donte. That's when the guy with the phone went over to him, and Mario started blubbering something about blood. I thought he meant he was bleeding, but then Donte went off on him. He said, 'Yeah, we blood, but this is business, bro. You fuckin' up. You fuck up again, you dead.' Then he said he blew the whole deal with the dogs."

"The dogs?"

"That's right. Then the white guy pulls out a gun and says he don't wanna wait. He just wanna cap his ass. So that guy, *Donte*, said he'd see to it that Lewis wasn't any more trouble. That's when the guy with the bat looked over to my car and saw me sitting there.

"I'll tell you, my heart just about leaped right out of my chest. He crossed the street and threatened to smash the window if I didn't open up. I thought about leaning on the horn to scare him off, but in this neighborhood it's unlikely anyone would pay much mind. So I started fumbling around a bunch, pretending I was drunk and he finally walked back to his car.

"I thought I was in the clear, but a minute later he came back, and damn if he wasn't holding a blow torch. He fired it up, and said I'd better mind my own business or he'd burn my house down. Then Donte yelled for him to come on. He said, 'Hey, Torch. Stop fuckin' around, man.'

"After that, Donte helped Lewis off the ground and got him back inside, and they all piled back in the car and took off. I waited until they turned the corner and then I got in my house real quick. The next night when I came home from work, the dogs were gone."

So, Mario was in business with a relative named Donte, some white guy with anger management issues, and a gentleman named Torch who liked to set people on fire. Rough crowd.

"Roger, do you think you would recognize these guys if you saw them again?"

Roger shook his head. "Honey, I made it a point not to. If they thought I had the potential to identify them in a line up, they might've killed me on the spot."

I put down my sandwich mid bite. "Wow. No wonder you don't want Candice to know."

"Look, this may amount to a whole lot of nothin', but I wanted someone to know—just in case…"

*****

"You wanna keep them pearly whites? Tuck in your chin and get those hands up."

I did as I was told and fended off a couple of sharp jabs. I even managed to throw a quick counter punch. Although it never actually landed, Danny Jenkins, my sparring partner, winked and assured me I was "doin' just fine." Danny works at my uncle's gym. He's old enough to be my grandfather, but he's the best trainer in Philly, and I needed all the help I could get.

After my talk with Roger King, I'd resigned myself to the fact that I wasn't going to let this thing with Mario

Lewis go. Something fishy was going on, and whatever it was, it put King and his family in jeopardy. So, if I was going to stick my nose in other people's business, I had to learn how to protect it.

"I'd be careful, Danny. She's short, but she's scrappy," a familiar voice teased from ringside.

I peered over my shoulder and found DiCarlo watching me. He looked damn good in new boxing trunks and a fresh, white tee shirt that showcased tanned, sculpted arms. Bobby had shaved. It was a departure from his usual scruffy look. Plus, I couldn't be sure, but I thought I smelled cologne.

"Think I'll take a break," I told Danny and hopped out of the ring.

Bobby gave me his usual greeting. "Yo."

"What's the occasion?" I asked, taking in a whiff of *Polo Extreme Sport*. I recognized the scent from a shopping excursion with John, pre-Garrett, when he was looking to "exude a manlier image" for some guy he'd met at a shoe sale at Barney's.

DiCarlo shrugged. "No occasion. Can't a guy smell nice every once in a while?"

Before I could come up with a clever retort, he asked, "What happened to your face?" I guessed that was going to be the question of the week.

"Tripped over the cat. Listen, I need to talk to you about something. Got a minute?"

Bobby glanced at the front door. "Sure."

We walked over to the bench, and he untied my gloves while I filled him in on my conversation with Roger King. DiCarlo listened with the ear of a cop, taking mental notes, and interrupting only to ask the occasional clarifying question.

"Mario and those guys were involved in some kind of business, probably something to do with dog fighting," I concluded. "And Mario screwed up the operation somehow, so they killed him."

"I don't know, Brandy. That's a really big assumption. Look, if they'd wanted him dead, why would they wait until he was in the hospital with an armed guard standing outside his door? They would have killed him that night. If anything, they were just trying to scare Lewis."

"They *would've* killed him that night, Bobby, if it hadn't been for the one guy speaking up for him. Something else must've happened to make them change their minds. But what?"

"Beats me. But I see where this is heading." DiCarlo set his smoky blues on me. "Cut yourself a break and stay out of this. And if your pal, Roger King, is so concerned for his safety, he needs to talk to the cops."

"Yeah?" I challenged. "Well, who's gonna speak for the dogs? Listen, I've got a gut feeling about this, Bobby. I saw with my own eyes what Lewis did to those puppies. What if there's more to that story? What if Lewis was only a small part of a much bigger operation? What if—"

DiCarlo cut me off. "Okay, okay. I get it. Look," he sighed, "if it was anybody else talking about 'gut feelings' I'd say they were crazy. But it's you, and I've never known you to be wrong."

Bobby ran his fingers through his hair, messing up the perfect "do" he had going.

"Listen," he said, finally. "I heard from a buddy that's working the case that the night Lewis died, there was some sort of distraction on the floor. And the cop watching his room left his post for a few minutes."

I considered playing dumb, but if DiCarlo was willing to be honest with me, I had to do the same. "I know," I confessed.

"How the hell did you—ah, never mind."

"According to my source (Mohindar, the future laundry mogul), it was an officer named Carl Abrams. Can you get him to talk to me? Off the record, of course."

"Not on a bet."

"Don't you mean you'll think it over and get back to

me?"

But Bobby had checked out. "Listen, Bran," he said, standing up, "my, uh, sparring partner's here."

I followed his gaze and spotted the blond cop from DiVinci's headed our way. Oh. Now the cologne, the shave, and the haircut all made sense.

"I'll see ya later, okay?" And he was gone like a shot. *Crap.*

*****

"My life sucks."

"True," Franny agreed and handed me her baby. "But this should cheer you up."

Gazing down at my beautiful goddaughter lying in my lap, I watched in awe as she grabbed my thumb in her tiny little baby hand.

"You are the sweetest thing ever," I cooed. "How can people like Mario Lewis exist in the world alongside someone as precious as you? Oh, look, Fran, she loves me. See how she's smiling?"

"That's gas."

"Oh…are you sure?"

"Yeah. But she really does love you, hon." Franny wiped some spit-up off my sleeve and tossed me a burp cloth. "You should feel honored. She doesn't spit up on just anyone."

I suspected she did, but being desperate for approval, I didn't argue the point.

We sat outside on Fran's stoop slurping Italian ice and watching the neighborhood kids play tag in the street. It was 90 degrees out, and the public pool was closed for repairs, so someone had taken pity on them and opened up the fire hydrant.

"What kind of moron would open the hydrant?" Fran grumbled. "No wonder there's no water pressure in the house."

I shrugged. "It was probably the guy up the street with the spider monkey. It just seems like something he would do."

A barefoot kid in knee-length swim trunks moved toward us. Discreetly I tried to shoo him away, but he kept on coming. Maybe he was dyslexic and thought I meant "come closer." He stopped in front of me, one arm extended. "Hey, Lady. Here's your pipe wrench back. Thanks for the loan."

Franny eyed me. "You're such a pushover."

"Well, it's hot out. And look how much fun they're having. Besides, it's only slightly illegal." I put the wrench down next to me and handed the baby back to Fran. She placed her in her infant swing and gave it a gentle shove.

"So where were we?" she said. "Oh yeah, your sucky life. By the way, I'm with Vince and DiCarlo on the Lewis thing. Your life will suck way less if you just stay out of it."

"It's not just that, Fran. It's everything. Instead of moving forward in my career, I'm stuck doing traffic reports dressed as a St. Bernard. And now John is so wrapped up in Garrett, he doesn't have time for me anymore. Plus, his boyfriend hates me—for no good reason at all."

"And don't forget the whole 'Bobby dating someone else' thing, and you feeling jealous."

"I'm not jealous."

"Right."

"I'm not."

"If you say so."

"Shut uh-up. I'm very happy for him…really." I slumped forward and took a large bite of water ice. *Oh great, brain freeze. Well, that's just fabulous.*

"Brandy," Fran said, not without sympathy, "all these things are a drag, but you've been through worse. There's something else going on here, so why don't you just spill it?"

"I don't know," I confessed. "I've just been so down lately." I rubbed my hands over my face and winced. The bruising on my cheek had mostly subsided, but it still hurt to the touch. "I can't believe I walked right into that flag pole."

Fran leaned in close to me, her nose practically grazing my forehead. "Wait a minute," she said, thinking. "You told me you got hit with an air hockey puck at the arcade…oh my God, Bran. Did Nick do this to you? *He did, didn't he? The bastard!"*

"No! Franny, have you completely lost your mind? As if I'd ever put up with that shit! Besides, Nick would never hit me. And anyway, I haven't seen him in weeks." The words caught in my throat, and I stopped this short of bawling my eyes out.

"Oh," she said, as if I'd just unlocked the secrets of the universe.

"I haven't seen him in weeks," I repeated. And then I completely lost it. Pent up tears rolled down my cheeks and splash-landed in the Italian Ice.

"Franny, I thought that when he told me he loved me—"

"Birds would sing, flowers would bloom, and you'd walk off into the eternal sunshine of your fantasy-driven life?"

"Pretty much," I admitted miserably. "But if you tell anyone, I *will* have to kill you—and I'm not without practice."

"My lips are sealed."

I reached into my jeans and fished out an old Kleenex, and blew my nose. "Okay," I began. "I know Nick isn't purposely avoiding me or anything. I mean if it's anyone's fault it's mine. He tried to talk to me after my—uh, 'scare,' but I just wasn't ready. And then he took off on business and—jeez, Fran, I don't even know where he goes…or what he does…or who he's with. I mean, I love the guy—but who the hell is he? I have no friggin' idea."

"And maybe you're just a little afraid to find out."

"Yeah. Maybe." In truth it was more like if he had time to think about it, maybe he'd change his mind about me.

But I just couldn't admit that. Not even to Fran.

We hung out the rest of the afternoon watching Dora the Explorer and pretending we'd put it on for the baby. I just love that Dora. She's a little spitfire!

The sun had already set by the time I left Fran's. She walked me to the door, hesitating as I stepped outside.

"I know it won't do any good to ask you to stop your investigation," she said, "so just be careful, okay?"

"I will. Thanks. And, uh, thanks for talking to me today. I really don't know how to repay you. Say! Would you like a puppy?"

*****

Two nights later I was headed home, having just wrapped up the latest humiliating effort to hang onto my job, doing a promo as the ever-popular Godfrey. *("This rush hour traffic report is brought to you by Doggie Donuts. So good, you may be tempted to dunk them in your morning coffee—but save them for your canine pals!")* The costume weighed about twenty-pounds. It's a bitch to take off, so I didn't bother to change back into my street clothes. Plus, it was kind of fun to see the looks on people's faces when I pulled up next to them at red lights.

I turned onto my street and immediately tensed as a slew of police cars came into view; their rotating lights making my head ache. They had converged on a house at the other end of the block. Upon closer inspection, I realized it was my house.

Oh, crap! The dog's owner must've changed his mind about wanting his dog back, and now they're here to arrest me...is dognapping a federal offense? I could go to jail... I can't go to jail! I'm claustrophobic...I hate sharing a bathroom...Prison jumpsuits only come in orange... What do I do? What do I do? I'll keep driving. I'll just cruise on down past my house, real nonchalant, check it all out...

As I got closer, I panicked and tried to cut a u-ie in the middle of the road, only my street is so narrow I grazed my neighbor's bumper and set off his car alarm. As Mr.

Yong came out of the house to see who was trying to make off with his Ford Fiesta, a uniformed cop stuck his head in through my car window. Fortunately, it was Mike Mahoe, a friend of mine.

"Brandy?"

I reached up and removed the top of the costume, revealing my sweaty, prison-bound head. "I don't want to go to jail, Mike. I can explain about the dog." I started to blurt out the whole story, but Mike drowned me out.

"Brandy. It's not about some dog. It's—ah, hell, just try not to freak." He stepped away from the car and I squinted into the growing darkness and freaked.

CHAPTER FIVE

I scrambled out of the car and thrust Godfrey's head at Mike's chest. "Hold this,"

I yelled and bounded toward my house. A crowd had formed, and I battled my way through. Mahoe trotted along behind and yelled for me to wait up.

Shards of broken glass lay strewn on my front porch, carnage created by a spray of bullets that splintered the front door and shattered every window facing the street. I reached the yellow tape that marked off the crime scene and ducked under it. A hand shot out, grabbed me by the collar and yanked me back.

"Let go, Mike. Rocky and the dogs are in the house. I have to get in there."

"You can't. They haven't finished checking out the premises yet."

"But they could be hurt—"

"All right, give me a minute, and I'll talk to the officer in charge." He handed back Godfrey's head. "Stay put," he ordered.

"Yeah, I'll do just that." Hysteria made my voice hoarse. I turned and stormed back toward my car.

"You know, I'm not the enemy here," he shouted after

me.

I waited for about a nano-second, and then I marched back to the police barricade and ducked under the tape. A rookie cop stood guard at what was left of my front door.

"Hey, get back."

"I need to get inside." I shoved past him which, in retrospect, probably wasn't the best move. He grabbed my furry arm and pinned it behind my back.

"Ow! Look," I shouted and tried twisting out of his grasp, which only made him hang on tighter. "This is my house, and my cat and dogs are in there, and they need me. So I'm going in, and not you or anybody else is gonna stop me. Now let go!"

"Just calm down, Ma'am."

"I'm not gonna calm down. Look, you little pisher—"

Mike came up next to us. He didn't seem surprised to see me there.

"Skip," he interrupted. "This is Brandy Alexander. She's the one who saved Wolinski. Cut her a break, okay? She's had a rough couple of days. I'll escort her in."

"She's all yours," Skip muttered and let go of my arm. He stepped aside, and Mike and I entered the house.

The forensics team was just leaving. There was glass everywhere but, the house looked pretty much as I'd left it. Well…except for the bullets that decimated a lamp and left gaping holes in my brand new sofa.

I galloped up the stairs two at a time and found the dogs and Rocky huddled together in Paul's old bedroom closet. I shut the door, went downstairs, and returned with some leftover lasagna for them to share. Any good psychologist will tell you that you can't solve your problems with food, but they're wrong. I ate a TastyKake and felt tons better.

"Mike, I know this looks bad. But, maybe it was just some guy who was excited about the new assault rifle he got for his birthday, and he just happened to pick my house to practice on."

"I don't think so."

"But—"

"Brandy, someone actually took the time to get out of their car and spray-paint 'Bitch-ho' on your front step. This was personal."

"Y'know, my neighbor, Mrs. Gentile isn't the easiest person to get along with. Maybe it was meant for her." Okay. That's unlikely. Mrs. Gentile is in her eighties. She may be a bitch, but I seriously doubt anyone would mistake her for a 'ho.

I walked back outside and found her holding court with the neighbors. She had a clipboard which she circulated among the crowd. Mrs. Gentile's been trying to get preferential parking for our block, which I think is downright unfriendly. But I felt like I owed her one because of recent events. I strode over to her.

"Uh, Mrs. Gentile, I'd be happy to sign your petition."

Grace Romano, my mother's oldest and dearest friend from the neighborhood, cut me a guilty look. She handed the clipboard back to Mrs. Gentile and slunk off toward her house. I craned my neck to read the upside down words (a skill I cultivated from years of cheating in high school math class). All I could make out was my name before Mrs. Gentile snatched it way, pressing it to her scrawny chest.

"You're a menace," she squawked, wagging a bony finger at me. "This neighborhood is for decent people. We want you out of here."

"What?"

She turned the clipboard around so I could read it. A dozen or so of my neighbors had signed the petition. Some of them, twice.

Mike waited while I spoke to a Detective Cabot, who suggested that someone might have a vendetta against me.

"Gee, ya think?"

Mike elbowed me in the ribs.

"Sorry. I'm a little stressed."

I thought for a minute and then rattled off a rather lengthy list of people I might have annoyed to the point of using weapons of mass destruction against me. Then I collected the dogs and cat, packed a bag, and called my friend Taco, whose dad owns a lumber yard. Taco arranged to have someone come by and board up the windows and door. The thing that bothered me the most was what they'd written on my front step. I mean, that was really uncalled for.

"Brandy, I hate to leave you here like this," Mike said, "but I've got to get back to the precinct." He took a few steps and stopped, the corners of his mouth forming a grim smile. "Are you gonna be okay?"

"Peachy."

"Do you want me to call DiCarlo?"

My brain flashed back to Bobby and the blonde at the gym and I shook my head. "I'm fine, Mike. Really. Thank you for all your help tonight."

Mike gave my shoulder an awkward pat and climbed into his patrol car. The neighbors had moved back into their own homes, satisfied that the Brandy Show was done for the night. I sat down on the front step and considered my options.

I could go to John's, but I didn't want to risk running into Garrett. Uncle Frankie was still at the gym, and Fran and Janine were having dinner at their mother's. Paulie? He'd only get upset and blow things all out of proportion. After all, nobody died, and the house is still standing. In the scheme of things, this was no big deal.

The rain that had threatened for days began to fall in hard, fat drops. It ran in rivulets down my face and saturated the fake fur from the Godfrey costume. It clung to my body, emitting an odor akin to raw sewage.

I reached up and swept my sopping wet bangs off my forehead. Too late, I remembered the temporary color Carla had put in my hair to give me a "saucy little lift." She'd promised it would wash right out with water, and it did, leaving splotches of brown dye on my cheeks and hands. Icing on the cake.

The puppy nudged up against my leg, settling in next to me, and nuzzled me with her warm, wet nose. She trusted me to take care of her, and I was failing her miserably. I'd never felt more frightened or alone in my life.

I slumped against the back of the step and closed my eyes. And in the next moment, the voice of a slightly fallen angel caressed my soul.

"Hello, Darlin'."

My eyes flew open and Nick stood in front of me. He wore a dirt-encrusted, sandy-colored tee shirt and desert-camo pants. His wavy, dark hair was tucked behind his ears, and the rough beginnings of a beard graced his normally clean shaven chin. Dried mud was caked to the sides of his boots, and he had a deep gash over his right eye that said his time away hadn't been all fun and games.

"Oh!" I yelped and leaped to my feet knocking Godfrey's dismembered head clear into the gutter. Nick stretched out an arm to steady me. Even in the limited light from the moon I could tell that his sinewy biceps were a sun-soaked brown.

"I didn't mean to scare you, Angel." His eyes were tired but he cut me a smile that was so damn sexy I could've done it with him right there on the lawn, in front of God and Mrs. Gentile. As if on cue, he cupped my face in his hands like I was the most precious thing on the planet and kissed me.

I swooned. How corny is that? But that kiss was the first good thing to happen to me in weeks, and I was determined to enjoy it.

A minute later, Adrian started barking and snapped me back to reality. I took a deep breath striving to appear confident and in control, which was difficult enough dressed as a St. Bernard with hair dye running down my face. Only now, the puppy had gotten up and was walking in concentric circles around me, her leash expertly trapping my legs. I pitched forward and Nick tightened his grasp on my arm, and pulled me back toward him.

"Who's your new friend?"

"Long story," I said, tugging on a stray tuft of fake dog fur. "I, um, actually had a different outfit planned for your homecoming, but then I decided to go with this."

"Ah, furry porn chic, an interesting choice," he joked, but his eyes were trained on the wreckage that used to be my front door. "I'd heard you had some unexpected company tonight," Nick continued. He kept his voice calm, but I felt an almost imperceptible shift in his energy as he assessed the damage.

"Oh, that," I shrugged, as a kernel of resentment sprung up in my throat surprising the crap out of me. I swallowed hard and shoved it back down. "Nothing to worry about. Just your typical evening at Chez Alexander."

Nick eyed me as he knelt down to unwind the puppy's leash from around my legs. "Come on, Angel. Let's get out of here."

A million questions raced through my brain. Like how did Nick manage to turn up just when I needed him most, and why was he dressed like Rambo? But the question that loomed above all others was why I suddenly felt so pissed off. And more confusing was the fact that the target of my anger wasn't the schmuck who'd shot up my house.

We piled my rapidly growing menagerie into the back of the truck, and I began to climb in after them. Nick caught me around the waist and deposited me in the front seat. He seemed singularly unconcerned that I was dripping water all over his leather upholstery.

"Are you sure you want me up front? I don't smell too good," I announced as if it were Breaking News.

Nick tucked me in close to him. "I'll take my chances," he said, and the anger I'd felt dissolved as suddenly as it had come. I leaned my head back against the crook of his arm and promptly fell asleep.

*****

"I don't care that the cheese is imported," I insisted, awaking with a start. "I don't like frittatas."

Nick laughed quietly. "I'll make a note of that, Angel."

"What?" I rubbed my eyes and looked around. We were parked in the loading zone in front of an understated, yet elegant apartment building located across the street from Rittenhouse Square. Nick's place.

Nick gently disengaged his arm from around my shoulders and turned off the engine. He unloaded Rocky's carrier and unlocked the front gate, while I coaxed the dogs out of the back seat and into the pouring rain.

We rode the elevator in exhausted silence. Butterflies slammed against the walls of my insides as Nick led me down the hall to his apartment. He'd only been gone a few weeks, but my insecurities were back in full force. And it didn't help that I was walking around in a smelly dog suit looking like a sorority pledge's worst nightmare.

Inside, the apartment was hot and steamy like a tropical rain forest. A faint smell of coffee lingered in the air. The living room window had been left open a crack, and a small puddle of rain had collected on the hardwood floor near the baby grand piano in the corner.

Nick put down Rocky's cat carrier and closed the window. Then he crossed back over to me and held me in his arms. "I've missed you, Brandy Alexander."

"Is that why I haven't heard from you?" I murmured into his chest. "Because you missed me?"

Oh, shit. I didn't mean to say that. Okay, I was thinking it, but I definitely did not mean to say it.

Nick raised an eyebrow. "You're mad at me."

"Don't be ridiculous." I was so mad at him! How could he run off and leave me when we hadn't had our talk that I didn't want to have in the first place and avoided like the plague? Doesn't he know how this works?

"It's just been a long couple of weeks," I explained.

Nick lifted my chin until our eyes met, and I studied, with growing apprehension, the gash on his brow.

"We both have a lot of catching up to do, Angel," he said as if to ward off my inevitable barrage of questions. "But maybe we can put all that on hold just for tonight."

Perhaps I was finally learning some self control—or maybe it was the way he ran his fingers lightly down my spine as he slowly unzipped the back of the dog costume, that made me see the wisdom of his suggestion.

"Um, okay."

Santiago led me into the bathroom and shut the door. He lit a candle and filled the tub with bath bubbles left by a former overnight guest. I suppose I should've been jealous, only the practical side of me took over, and I figured, "I'm here, she's not, why waste perfectly good bubbles?"

Nick stripped off his wet tee shirt, and I was surprised to find the bandages had been removed. Gingerly, I touched the length of his scar. "Does it hurt?" I whispered as if by keeping my voice down that would somehow mitigate the pain.

In response, Nick took my hand and held it palm up, brushing his lips over the fleshy, most sensitive part. "This is called the Mount of Venus. It was named after the Roman Goddess of Love," he said and bit down just hard enough to send a current of electricity straight to my lower belly and then some.

"Mount of Venus," I repeated. "I've always wondered what it was called." *I've never wondered what it's called. I'm making shit up. I'm just so nervous!*

Nick looked me up and down as if he wanted to devour me. "Some people believe that a fleshy palm is the sign of a great lover."

"Really? Y'know, my grandmother had the fattest palms…" *Unh, way to go, Brandy. Bring your grandmother into it. Super sexy.*

"Listen," I said, feeling like a big, fat, romantic zero, "I think I can take it from here. Why don't you go check your mail or something, and I'll get cleaned up and be with you in a jiffy."

Nick slipped his arms around me, his hands riding low on the small of my back. "Or," he suggested in a voice so husky it made my knees wobble, "I could just stay here with you."

"Oh, but—"

"Shh, mi amada," he said and kissed me full on the mouth.

With agonizing slowness he peeled the costume off my shoulders, inching it down my body. I was soaked through to my bra, which, much to my chagrin, was the one I wore on Laundry Day and looked like a family heirloom. I didn't have to worry though, because Nick unsnapped it one handed, and it fell to the floor. I kicked it aside and unbuckled his pants.

I couldn't help but look down. Nick's time away must've been all business because he sure looked ready to play. I reached down and cupped his balls. They were full, and tight. He smiled and pulled me close, and all the fucked up shit of the past few weeks melted away as he pressed himself against me.

"Did you miss me?" Nick whispered. Rubbing his thumb roughly over one nipple, he sucked on the other, until they peaked with desire.

"Oh, God, yes," I moaned, arching my back. My pulse quickened and my stomach turned to mush as he insinuated himself between my legs. Every nerve ending was on heightened alert.

Uh, oh. I need to slow down. At the rate this is going, the night will be over before it even gets started.

I distracted myself by mentally reciting the twelve times table and the entire 2012 Phillies lineup.

"Stop it, Angel." Nick swatted me on the ass, just hard enough to let me know who was in charge. I would have been mad as Hell, if I hadn't been so damn aroused.

"Stop what?"

"Stop thinking."

I felt my face flush. "How did you—?"

"I pay attention." Santiago picked me up and I wrapped my legs around his waist as he carried me into the bedroom. He set me down on the bed and stretched out beside me. "There's no need to try to prolong the pleasure, Darlin.' We have all night, and I plan to use every minute of it pleasuring you—again—" he paused to kiss the nape of my neck—"and again—" he moved down my stomach and licked at my belly button before dipping his head lower still—"and again."

*****

My dad always says the best way to forget your troubles is to throw yourself into your work. Unfortunately… as of ten o'clock the next morning, that was no longer an option.

"You're firing me? On what grounds? Look, if this is about the graffiti in the women's bathroom, I want to go on record as saying I did not write, "Eric smells like farts." (Although at the moment, I was in total agreement with whoever did.)

Eric sat at his desk fumbling with a rubber band. He wouldn't make eye contact… the little weasel. "Brandy, this is coming from upstairs. They think your life is a little too—complicated right now, and it's hurting the station's image."

"Are you freakin' kidding me? WINN is a news station. I am the news. If it wasn't for me, you people wouldn't have anything to talk about."

"That's the point. Our viewers tune in to your segment to get away from all the lousy things that happen in this city. You're supposed to be the comic relief."

Okay, I could see where he was coming from, but still…"Well, good luck in finding a replacement. I was freakin' awesome!"

"Yeah," he agreed, dead serious, "you were. Listen, I feel really terrible about this. If you need a recommendation or anything—"

"Can I keep my press pass?"

Eric grunted. "All right. But I could get canned for this. So if you get caught using it, you're on your own."

I gave him a quick nod. "Understood. And thanks."

In truth, I wasn't all that upset about losing my job at WINN. I had some money saved, and if I got desperate, I could always go back to waiting tables at Paul's club. Not the ideal solution since I drove away most of his regulars through sheer incompetence, but it was nice to have a backup plan. Plus, the break would give me time to look into Mario's death, starting with the mystery man, Donte.

An hour later, I found a great, new work space—a corner office, with a big picture window (and free WiFi!) when Nick called.

"Hello?" I whispered.

"Where are you, Darlin'?"

"The Barnes and Noble Café. I sort've got fired today."

"Are you okay?"

"Actually, I'm relieved. It was a dumb job, and it just kept getting dumber. I missed you this morning," I added.

I had woken up alone in Nick's bed, not exactly a rousing endorsement of my feminine wiles, I thought, but then I saw the note he'd left on the pillow.

"Had an early morning meeting and didn't want to wake you. There's fresh coffee and croissants in the kitchen. If you go out, call Alphonso and take the gun. And since I know you won't do either, just be careful."

"Have you spoken to DiCarlo?" he asked.

"No, why?"

"I heard a rumor that the Junk Town Gang is looking for one of their members. Seems this person fucked up big time, and they're not happy about it."

"You wouldn't happen to know the nature of this fuck-up, would you?"

"Like I said, it's just a rumor, but one that shouldn't be ignored."

In the background, I could hear someone knock on

Nick's office door. "Listen, Angel, I've got to run," he said as a distinctly female voice called his name.

"Oh, is that Tanya? Tell her I said hi." Tanya was Nick's stunningly beautiful assistant who, for some reason, I used to hate. But then Nick mentioned that she was a lesbian and now I really like her.

"It's not Tanya."

"Oh." I waited for him to go on, but apparently Nick thought that was all the explanation necessary.

"I'll be home around six, and then we're going to have that talk."

It was probably just the barista's special blend that had my stomach all in knots.

*****

Occam's Razor ascribes to the idea that the simplest answer is often correct. As I didn't even have a last name for the relative Mario referred to as Donte, I decided to go with Lewis. Two hours and four espressos later, after exhausting all the professional websites top notch investigators use to track down missing people, I found the man I was looking for through the wonders of Facebook. It's amazing what people will share about themselves on the social network.

I knew it was the right Donte because he'd posted a video of himself and Mario performing a stunt suitable for the season premiere of *Jackass*. It also listed his date of birth (August 24th), his musical preference (Gangsta Rap), and his place of employment (North Philadelphia Ambulance Company). Funny, I didn't picture him working for a company whose purpose was to save lives.

I thought briefly about telling Vince what I'd discovered. But then the quadruple shot of caffeinated heaven I'd consumed had wrapped itself around my brain, strangling the common sense right out of it. Without thinking I picked up the phone and punched in the ambulance company's phone number.

A woman answered. She sounded old and cranky and

bored.

"NPAC. This is Nadine. How can I direct your call?"

Hmm, I hadn't thought of that. Note to self: Plan ahead. "Um, hello. My name is—Linda—Lovelace, and I'm with First Philadelphia Savings and Loan. I'm calling to verify the employment of a Mr. Donte Lewis with your company."

"Lewis don't work here no more."

"Oh, but it says right here on his Facebook page—I mean his application—"

"Nah. We haven't seen the guy in a week. He never showed up for his shift. Didn't call or nothin'. Didn't even come by to collect his pay check. I'd think twice about lending money to that loser."

"Thanks for the tip. Um, do you have an address for Lewis?"

"Isn't it on his application?"

"Oh, yes, of course. Listen, I'm worried that something might have happened to Mr. Lewis, Nadine, and it's very important that we get a hold of him. Is there someone there who might still be in touch with him?"

There was a brief pause before she answered. "You could try talking to Jimmy Cooke. They worked together. Give me your number and, I'll have him give you a call."

"Thank you."

"Any time, Ms. Lovelace." I could hear her snorting with laughter as she hung up the phone.

*****

I was parked at a booth at the Dunkin' Donuts three blocks from the ambulance company, waiting for Jimmy Cooke. I'd bought myself a powdered jelly doughnut and picked out a chocolate one for Jimmy. After I ate mine, I realized that Jimmy might feel awkward if he didn't like it, so I ate that one too.

"Linda?"

I looked over at the door and saw a guy in a Phillies' cap waddle toward me. He was five foot eight inches of pure beer belly.

I stood, brushing powered sugar off my face, and extended my hand in greeting. "Thanks for meeting me."

"You're not what I expected," Jimmy told me, sliding into the booth opposite me. He sounded more than mildly disappointed.

"Yeah, I get that all the time."

"Have you ever considered changing your name? I mean, it's kinda misleading."

"I'll take it under advisement. So, you'd said on the phone that you have some information about Donte Lewis. Were you good friends with him?"

"Christ, I couldn't stand the guy. But I want to know why you're so interested in finding him."

"I told you—"

Jimmy cut me off with a shrewd look. "You don't work for a bank, and your name's not really Linda Lovelace. Am I right?"

I nodded. "Look, I can't explain it right now, but if you help me out, there's—hang on—" I rooted around in my bag for my wallet and dumped every cent I had out on the table. "There's $17.23 in it for you."

Jimmy laughed and shoved the money back across the table. "Keep it. What do you want to know?"

"Did Lewis ever mention a side business he might be involved in? I mean besides working for the ambulance company."

"Lewis is one of those guys who's always got something going. He owns some dogs—y'know, pits, and I overheard him talking on the phone one day about setting them up in some fights. I told him what I thought about people who did shit like that, and he got real unfriendly after that."

"Do you have any idea why he hasn't shown up for work?"

Jimmy shrugged. "About a week and a half ago, some drugs turned up missing from one of the trucks. Lewis was the only one around at the time, and everybody thought he'd taken them. But there was no proof so nothing ever came of it."

"Well, why didn't they call the cops?"

"The company's had some legal problems recently, and the owner didn't want any more bad publicity."

"Do you know what was taken?"

"Yeah, and that's the thing. It wasn't like it was a drug you could get high off of or anything. It's called Succinylcholine. It's a paralytic, used for intubation. They carry it in their RSI kits. I don't know what the hell he'd use it for. Anyway, I'm just glad the asshole's gone."

After Jimmy took off, I fired up my laptop and typed in Succinylcholine. "What possible advantage could Donte Lewis have in stealing a drug like this?" I thought to myself. And ten minutes later, I had my answer.

CHAPTER SIX

I called Bobby on the way out of the café.

"Yo, Bran."

What? No "Sweetheart?"

"Where are you?" I shouted over the din of clinking glasses and clattering plates. I'd hoped it was somewhere good. Those espressos made me hungry, and, what with being newly unemployed, maybe Bobby would take pity on me and buy me lunch."

"I'm at Tortelli's."

"Oh, I love that place. Listen, I need to talk to you. It's important. Stay put and I'll be there in a few minutes."

"Uh, Bran, this isn't a good—"

"See you soon," I said and disconnected.

Tortelli's is a popular Sicillian restaurant located on Passyunk Avenue. They've got a terrific oyster bar and a great cover band on Friday nights that plays music from the fifties. It's always packed, so I was lucky to find parking only four blocks away.

One of the perks of a caffeine high is you feel like you can do anything. On the downside, it's just an illusion. I jogged the quarter mile, oblivious to the heat and humidity. By the time I got to the restaurant I was puffing so hard I thought I had a collapsed lung.

Before I went in search of Bobby, I made a pit stop at the bathroom. I opened the door and found a toddler pulling mini pads out of a broken vending machine while his mother yelled at him from inside the stall not to touch anything. He had opened each packet and was now affixing them to the tile wall in kind of a cool pattern.

As I bent down to pick up the stray papers he'd left on the floor, he came up behind me and wrapped his chubby arms around my neck and gave me a big hug. Kids. Ya gotta love 'em.

Maybe it was my imagination but it felt like people were staring as I worked my way through the lunch crowd. One guy nudged his friend and snickered. They must've recognized me from the last segment I had taped for the station. I'd come in fourth in an air guitar contest. I would've won but my string broke, which I thought added a touch of realism to my performance, but the judges thought otherwise.

I found DiCarlo in a booth in the back, examining the dessert cart. I squeezed past it and was about to take the seat opposite him when I felt the presence of someone sidling up next to me.

"Excuse me."

I turned to see who was speaking and accidentally stuck my hand in the Chocolate mousse. My impulse was to lick it off, but I changed my mind when I saw who had snuck up on me.

Shit! Why didn't Bobby tell me he was on a date!

Officer Blondie stared at me in kind of an "I'm not really staring at you" way. Well, of course she'd be curious. Bobby must have filled her in on how he's still in love with me.

"I'm sorry. I was just trying to get my bag," she said, reaching into the booth. "I didn't mean to startle you."

"You didn't," I lied.

DiCarlo stood, handing me a paper napkin. "Brandy,

this is Lauren. Lauren, Brandy."

Hmm, he's looking at me funny too. What is with everyone?

Before Lauren and I could finish exchanging the usual pleasantries Bobby interrupted. "Brandy, you've, uh, got something in your hair."

"What do you mean?" I raised my non-moussed hand and felt around. *Oh crap. What is that?* I began to pull. "Ow."

"Would you like me to help you?" Lauren offered.

"No, I'm good, thanks. Ow. Yes, actually, would you please?"

Lauren gave a quick tug and disengaged whatever it was, along with about three hundred of my favorite strands of hair. Discreetly she slipped it to me.

Oh, for the love of God! I've been parading around the restaurant with a sanitary pad glued to my hair. No wonder people are staring. I look like a crazy person!

"Listen," I said, treating the situation as if it were the most natural thing in the world to wear feminine hygiene products on my head, "I didn't mean to interrupt. I'll catch up with you later, Bobby."

"No, please. Sit down," Lauren insisted. "I've got to get back to work. Thanks for the lunch, Bobby. Next time it's on me. Brandy, it was nice meeting you." Her smile was quick and genuine and I like her despite my natural inclination not to.

"Nice meeting you too," I called after her and settled into the spot Lauren had vacated. I waited until she was safely out the door.

"I can see why you like her," I told Bobby, reaching for a forkful of linguine off his plate.

Bobby shook his head and pushed his plate toward me. "Could you please not make a big deal out of this, Bran? She's just a friend."

"Uh huh."

Bobby took a slow, deep breath. "Look, I just came off of a 48 hour shift staking out a guy who we're pretty sure chopped up his girlfriend and fed her to his dog. I'm tired, Sweetheart, and I'm not having this conversation right now, especially with you."

So, that explained why DiCarlo hadn't called me after the "Shoot-out at the B.A. Corral" but that last part hurt.

"Why not me?" I huffed. "Don't you think I'm capable of being happy for you?"

Bobby leaned across the table and wiped the gravy off my chin. "I don't know."

"Well, that's a shitty thing to say."

"I'm sorry. I didn't mean it the way it sounded. It's just that—look, Bran, I've accepted that you've moved on in your life, and I'm trying to do the same. But you and I have a lot of history, and it's not always easy, y'know?"

I did know, only too well. "Okay, so maybe I'm not the best person to discuss your love life with."

Our eyes met and, for a brief moment, we traveled back in time to when Bobby was mine. The yearning was so strong I half expected Barbara Streisand to pop up from behind the next booth and start belting out *The Way We Were*. And then the moment passed.

DiCarlo's mouth turned upwards into a slow grin. "So, you want to tell me what was so urgent that you had to interrupt my first official date in three years?"

"Second," I corrected him, and then I filled him in. "Bobby, just think about it. Donte was worried that his cousin was going to screw up a business deal. He was there the night Mario got the shit beat out of him, and Donte himself threatened to kill him.

"Donte had access to Succinylcholine, a drug that not only temporarily paralyzes the muscles, but can't be detected in an autopsy *unless they're specifically looking for it*. The drug goes missing a few days before Lewis croaks and Donte's the only suspect. The results of the original autopsy were inconclusive. And if that's not enough, the guard outside Lewis' door gets called away at the precise moment Lewis decides to kick the bucket. Look, I know this is all circumstantial evidence, but could you at least concede it's a possibility that Mario Lewis was murdered?"

DiCarlo didn't answer right away. He took a long slug of beer, not stopping until he drained the bottle. Then he carefully placed the bottle on the table and signaled the server for the check.

"Well?" I prompted when I couldn't stand it anymore.

"You make a good case."

"Yes!" I shouted, pumping my fist in the air.

"Okay, Brandy, don't go nuts here. Even if I agree with you, this isn't my investigation. And it's going to be a hard sell to get the D.A.'s office to agree to another autopsy."

"But you'll talk to Vince?"

"I'll talk to Vince."

*****

After leaving Tortelli's (minus the "hair bow") I was still hungry, so I swung by Paul's club. The place is closed from 3-6 p.m. in order to get ready for the dinner and late night crowds, but I knew he'd be there, regardless. My brother is a little on the obsessive side. Some people say it runs in the family but, personally, I don't see it.

I pulled in next to his 1972 Alpha Romeo, (a gift from me back in the days when I was a contributing member of society) and went in through the side entrance. Paul sat in the back booth eating a roast beef sandwich and going over the receipts.

"Hey, Paulie." I sat down opposite him and helped myself to the side of slaw. Paul held up an index finger. "Hey, Sis. Hang on a minute," he said and went back to his accounting.

"Um, okay." To tell the truth I'd expected a lot better reception, given the fact that I could've been killed the night before. But Paul never even called to see how I was doing.

After a bit he closed his laptop. "So, how're you doing?"

"Fine."

"Great." A grin began to spread across his face. "So, Mom tells me you've got plans for the entire month of August and you won't be able to go to Cousin Marlene's daughter's wedding."

And something snapped. "Paul, I can't believe this. Our childhood home was practically blown to bits by a gunman's bullets and you're mad because I sleazed out of Cousin Marlene's kid's wedding?"

Paul choked on his roast beef. "What?" Wh-wh-what?"

"You didn't know?" What was I thinking? Of course he didn't know. He would have called me. Jeez, doesn't anyone watch the news anymore?

"I'm sorry, Paulie. I thought you knew," I said, and filled him in as best I could.

Paul swung around to my side of the booth and wrapped his arms around me. "Th-thank God you're okay. Jesus, Brandy, how could you believe I knew and just didn't care?"

"I don't know. I guess I figured that violence has become such a part of the norm for me that even you've become immune to worrying about me."

"Yeah, like that could happen. I guess I've been a little too wrapped up in the club, lately," he added. "How can I make it up to you?"

"Well, there's this puppy—"

"How else can I make it up to you?"

"Well, someone has to go to Cousin Marlene's daughter's wedding—"

"I'll take the puppy."

*****

On the way back to Nick's I cruised by my house. The yellow crime scene tape had been taken down, but the boarded up windows served as a reminder of everything that had gone wrong lately, and it depressed the hell out of me. On the up side, I guess I still had at least one friend in the neighborhood. On the front step beneath the words, "Bitch-ho" someone had spray painted a huge arrow pointing directly at Mrs. Gentile's house. Karmically speaking I shouldn't have thought it was funny. I thought it was hilarious.

It was a little after four when I got to Nick's. Adrian and the puppy greeted me at the door trailing brown crumbs and bits of orange peel. Although they only stood three and a half feet between them, somehow they'd managed to reach the croissants I'd accidentally left out on the kitchen counter and had helped themselves to a Continental Breakfast. The puppy yawned revealing a chunk of orange pulp that was lodged between her teeth.

"I hold you responsible for this mess," I told Adrian. "You're the oldest."

He ignored my admonishments and waddled off, returning a few moments later with an expensive-looking Italian loafer with the toe chewed out of it.

"Bad dog!" I threw the loafer into the back of Nick's bedroom closet and took Adrian and his cohort in culinary crime for a walk.

When I got back, I still had over an hour until Nick was expected home. I debated whether to pass the time obsessing over who the woman in his office was or worrying about where the next attempt on my life would come from. Both good choices, but in the end I opted for a nap.

Here it comes again, the dream that haunts me every night. It follows me to Nick's place, my safe haven. Mario Lewis holding a gun against my temple, eyes spinning like twin roulette wheels, his drug-induced laughter echoing inside my head. Officer down, tortured wails, blood everywhere flowing like lava, why won't it stop? Something is different this time. But what? This time the blood is mine.

I feel a weight around my arms; someone pulls me to an upright position. I scream and struggle against him and feel soft lips and a soothing voice in my ear. "You're okay, Angel. It's just a nightmare." My heart rate slows as I breathe in the subtle, yet irresistible essence that is Nick. I stop struggling and open my eyes.

I blinked and looked around. Nick's gun rested on the coffee table. The front door was open, a bag of Chinese take-out strewn across the entryway. Nick picked up his gun and checked the safety and returned it to the table.

A neighbor poked his head in the door. He was in his late fifties, with a large, muscular build and a South Philly accent that was so pronounced it couldn't possibly be for real. The guy looked beyond Nick to me.

"I heard some yelling. Everything all right?" Only it came out as "err'thing a'ite?"

I flushed with embarrassment. "Yes. Thank you. Everything's fine. Just a bad dream, that's all."

"A'ite." If he saw Santiago's gun it didn't faze him. "My name's Ed," he told me. "I'm just down the hall if you need me." He pointed a warning finger at Nick who, thankfully, looked more amused than annoyed and retreated from the doorway.

"Seems you have a protector," Nick observed.

"Oh my god, how loud was I?" I stretched and rubbed the sleep from my eyes.

"You may have broken the sound barrier. Must've been one hell of a dream."

"I've had better."

"Mario Lewis?" I nodded, happy not to have to spell it out.

Nick picked up the groceries he had abandoned on his way in and set them on the counter. He put plates down and opened two Xinjiang Black Beers. Paul had told me they're difficult to find in America. I was impressed but not surprised.

Over steamed rice and Moo Shu Vegetable I filled Nick in on what I'd learned about Mario Lewis' death. "DiCarlo thinks he may be able to convince the D.A.'s office to redo Lewis' autopsy. But what if Donte gets wind of it and takes off? The cops aren't going to waste man power doing surveillance on the guy before it's even proven that his cousin was murdered."

"I can arrange some private surveillance until the results come in."

Nick believed in me, no questions asked. "Thank you," I said, choking up. Guess a noodle went down the wrong pipe.

Santiago finished his meal and took his beer over to the couch. I started to clean up the dishes, but he asked me to sit down with him instead. "If I recall, we have some things to talk over."

His tone was so serious I broke out in a sweat. "Talking is overrated, Nick. Except for the fact that people are trying to kill me, everything's cool. Let's talk about you for a change. So, what's with the army fatigues? Have you gone "military?" Y'know, you've never really explained just what it is you do during those mysterious trips you take. That would be a good topic of conversation…feel free to jump in at any time."

Nick leaned over and kissed me. "We can have that conversation another time, Darlin'. A few weeks ago you thought you might be pregnant, and your reaction to finding out that you weren't was—surprising. We need to talk about it."

"Oh, that," I said, as the Moo Shu Vegetable formed a basketball-sized lump in my stomach. "It's no big deal. I'm sure it was just the stress of the situation."

Nick offered me a half smile. "I think there was a bit more to it than that."

I couldn't imagine what. No joke. I really couldn't.

"Brandy," he said, lifting my chin so that I had to return his gaze, "I believe that a very small, but powerful part of you wished the pregnancy test had come out positive."

"What? No! Why would you think that? I don't even like babies, well, except for my Goddaughter, but that's because she's the cutest baby in the entire history of the world. No." I shook my head emphatically. "I am relieved."

"So," he pressed, "in the darkest recesses of your mind, you never wished it might be true."

"Absolutely not." I took a huge gulp of my beer.

Nick watched me with enormous patience. He seemed to be waiting for something, and I squirmed in the silence.

"Okay," I finally relented, "maybe for like—a nano second I might've wondered what it would be like if—y'know—well, haven't you ever thought about it?"

Nick looked at me steadily. "No, Angel, I haven't."

"Yeah. Me neither. So, you wanna watch the Phillies' game?" I got up and made a big show of searching for the remote. "Found it," I shouted a little too loud and turned on the television.

Nick took the remote from me and clicked off the TV. "I don't think we're quite finished with this conversation."

"What's to finish? We're on the same page. No babies."

"Brandy," Nick said, taking my hand in his, "I believe the reason you reacted so strongly to the news that you weren't pregnant is because a part of you wanted it to be true. A baby is symbolic. It implies a future together. But that's not something I can guarantee."

"I'm not asking for a guarantee." I was lying and we both knew it. "Look, let's just forget it, okay?"

"It's not that simple, Angel."

"Yes, it is," I said, panic rising in my belly, "...unless you've changed your mind about me...oh my God, that's it, isn't it?" *Just like Mr. Sheffield.*

"This isn't just a matter of how we feel about each other," he said, quietly. "The reality is our relationship makes you a target. There are a lot of people out there—"

"Oh, puh-leeze."

I jumped to my feet, one hand on my hip, the other waggling my index finger in his face, channeling Queen Latifah before she went all mainstream. "Spare me the Turner Classic movie spiel. 'I'm no good for ya, kid. You're better off with me.' You said you love me. Are you trying to take it back? Because there are no take backs.

You said it and I get to keep it."

"I do love you."

"Then, there's no problem. Look, you want to slow things down? Fine. I'm not asking for an engagement ring or your Letterman's jacket. I don't want to change you and I sure as hell don't want you to change me. All I want is for you to give us a fair shake. And then if you want to walk, I won't stop you."

Nick studied me for a beat and then deftly pulled me down onto his lap. "Has anyone ever told you that you're a piece of work?"

"Let's just say you're not the first."

We let the discussion drop for the time being, and I settled back in his arms and tried to ignore the creeping anxiety that curdled my stomach. But my mind would not let go of the very real possibility that I could lose Nick before we'd ever even gotten started.

I turned the game back on. It was the bottom of the ninth and the Phils were trailing six-nothing.

"Get a hit," I prayed. It was a long shot.

CHAPTER SEVEN

"What's the puppy's name?"

"It doesn't have a name. If I name it, I'll have to keep it."

Janine lifted Rocky's cat carrier off her futon and onto the floor, gathered her shoulder length auburn hair into a pony tail and flopped down on the bed that doubled as her couch/dining room table.

"Makes perfect sense. I feel the same way about the guys I've gone out with lately," she said, shoving a slice of mushroom pizza into her mouth.

I'd arrived at the door of Janine's walk-up studio apartment with Rocky, Adrian, and Little No-name in tow. She asked me if I was okay and did I want to talk about it. I answered "yes" and "no" respectively and she hugged me and moved on.

It would take another two days until the glass company could replace my windows and I didn't want to outstay my welcome at Nick's. Not that he was giving me the boot or anything. In fact, he'd begged me to stay.

"Don't go, my angel. Never leave my side."

Okay, what he'd actually said was, "You're welcome here for as long as you want," which was a generous offer but, for all my Big Girl sensible spiel about taking things one day at a time, my feelings were hurt by the lukewarm invitation. I guess it's my fault for saying, "No, no, no. I couldn't possibly impose," when what I meant was, "Please, insist!" But that's the trouble with Nick. He treats me like an adult and takes me at my word.

"Thanks for letting me crash here tonight, Neenie. Fran offered me her extra bedroom, but she's got enough going on already with Eddie and the baby."

Janine stretched across the bed and snatched her pillow from Adrian who had been happily gnawing at it like it was prime rib. "What are you thanking me for? This is fun. We haven't hung out together in ages."

That's Janine, God bless her. Only she could take a life and death situation as an opportunity to catch up on girl talk.

"Hey, so how's Mike?" she inquired. "When you saw him did he happen to mention me?"

Mike met Janine a little while back and he really liked her. We all heaved a collective sigh of relief when she expressed an interest in going out with him.

"Uh, your name didn't come up. But don't take it personally. We were a little busy."

"Oh. Well, how about you call Bobby and ask him if Mike's going to ask me out."

"Good idea, Janine, and then I'll ask him what he got on his history test and who he's taking to the big dance on Friday night!"

"Just call him, okay? It'll get your mind off your problems."

In truth, I was happy to have an excuse to call. I'd been trying to wait it out until DiCarlo called me with Vince's decision about the new autopsy, because I didn't want to appear pushy. Plus, I'd already called twice today and he'd threatened to stop taking my calls if I didn't knock it off. I pulled out my phone and hit speed dial.

Bobby waited until the fifth ring to answer. "Yes?" He

sounded a tad exasperated. I chose not to take it personally, even though it probably was personal.

"You busy?"

"Up to my ass. But that's okay. Actually, I was just going to call you."

"Did you hear from Vince? What did he say?"

"It's a go."

"Whoo hoo!"

"Yeah, and that's not all. I just got word they've arrested someone in connection with the shooting at your place."

"Oh, Bobby, that's great news." Maybe now my life would get back to some semblance of normal. "Who is he?"

"Name's Anthony Gibbons. He's a fringe member of the Junk Town Gang. It's gonna be a long haul. He's not talking. Listen, Brandy," DiCarlo added, as if he'd read my mind, "just because they've got someone in custody doesn't mean you're off the hook. Until Lewis' death has officially been deemed a homicide, you're still number one on their dance card. And even then, they may not be so forgiving."

"But why? Once it's proven—and don't say it, Bobby, I know I'm right, that Lewis was murdered, won't they want to go after the person who really killed him?"

"Sweetheart, when you took Lewis down you humiliated the entire gang. And that viral video didn't help. They have to avenge their honor or lose their street cred." His voice tensed. "I'd like you to at least consider getting out of town for a while.

Or, I could find out who killed Lewis and maybe that will be enough to get them to back off.

Janine pinched me and gave me the rolling hand sign for "hurry up and get to the point."

"So, Bobby, speaking of Mike Mahoe," which was the worst transition ever, since we hadn't mentioned Mike's name once in the entire conversation, "Janine was wondering if he was going to ask her out."

I could almost feel the vein in Bobby's temple pounding against the phone.

"Have you heard anything I said?"

"I did, Bobby. Every word. Look, this isn't about me being brave, or stubborn or stupid. And I promise I'll think about your suggestion, but—just for tonight—I want to pretend everything's all right." My voice broke. "I need this."

He waited a beat, then, "Tell Janine Mike's gonna call her."

*****

"So, Garrett, John tells me that you hail from Minnesota and that since you moved to Philadelphia, you've been working on anti-smoking bans in all public areas. How did you find your way to our fair city?"

I was seated opposite John and Garrett at the super trendy, *Café L'Orange,* in Roxborough, where everyone pretends to like opera and truffle soup. We ended up there because Garrett had been "dying to try their veal scaloppini," and I went along with it just to show him it's not *always about me,* but really, what kind of a person orders veal? I guess Garrett's obsession with political correctness doesn't extend to his palette.

I dabbed at the corners of my mouth and was about to fire off another round of questions when I felt a sharp pain in my shin. I looked over at John and winced.

"Brandy, isn't that Mrs. Krababappel over near the door?" he said, standing up.

"Who?"

"You know, our fourth grade teacher, Mrs. Krabababpel. We really have to say hello. Excuse us for a minute, will you, Garrett?"

John practically dragged me to my feet and hauled me outside.

"What are you doing? You've been asking Garrett questions since the minute we got here."

"It's called showing an interest, John. The world doesn't revolve around me you know."

"Since when? And what's with the British accent? You sound like you're interviewing him for the BBC."

"It's called using proper diction, John."

"Yeah? Well, knock it off. It's weird. Just be yourself, okay?"

"All right, fine," I sulked. "But let's be honest here. We both know that being myself didn't exactly wow him, so I thought I'd try a different approach."

John's Adam's apple did a little wiggle dance, a sure sign that I'd hit a nerve. "How did you—I mean—Garrett just needs time to get to know you. Trust me, he's going love you."

"Yeah? Well, what if he doesn't?"

"He will. C'mon, Bran, Garrett's the first guy I've met in God knows how long who actually has something to offer. He's got a real job, his own apartment, he's worldly. He knows about wine and art and…and…the capitals of all the European countries. Remember Pete? I dated him for two months last year. He lived in his mother's basement and he smelled like bug spray."

"Oh, yeah. Whatever happened to him?"

John did a major eye roll. "I'm trying to make a point here."

Before I could think of a snarky response his cell phone rang. It was Garrett calling to let him know his Trout Almandine was getting cold.

"See?" I said. "Garrett never once mentioned that my meal was getting cold. He hates me."

"You ordered Vichyssoise."

"Yeah, and I only did it to impress him. What I really wanted was a BLT. Look, you might think it's silly, but Garrett's important to you, so I really want him to like me."

"I like you," Johnny said, throwing his arm around me. "In fact, I love you."

We walked back to the table and the Vichyssoise was sitting there waiting for me; little lumps of cold potato swimming in a pool of heavy cream.

John signaled our server over to the table. "She changed her mind. She'd like a BLT."

*****

Five sleepless nights (on the floor of Janine's studio apartment) later, I was back home. The windows and doors had been replaced and the steps scrubbed clean. All that remained was a pervasive feeling of doom and a bill for the reconstructive surgery on my house that, with my recent work history, would take decades to pay off. I celebrated with a Bud Light and some pistachios.

In the middle of shelling about three pounds of nuts (pistachios are cool, because they're a snack *and* an activity—a snacktivity, if you will) my phone rang. I checked caller I.D., happy for the sound of anyone's voice as long as the conversation didn't start with "I'm gonna kill you, bitch."

It was Alphonso. "What'chu up to, Sweetcakes?"

"Cleaning my gun."

"Right," he snickered. "Although, now you mention it, it's probably not a bad idea."

My stomach clenched. "Why? What's wrong?"

"I heard some interesting news about the guy who shot up your house."

"Anthony Gibbons?"

"That's the one. Word on the street is the cops didn't have enough evidence to hold him, so they were lookin' to release him today."

I put down the pistachio nuts, having suddenly lost my appetite. Gibbons was free to finish what he'd started.

"Well, that's just dandy."

"You're not listening, Alexander. The operative word here is was. He hung himself at the Roundhouse this morning."

"Get out!" Relief flowed through my veins,

overshadowing all sense of decency.

Only, if he was getting out, why would he kill himself?

I put the question to Alphonso.

"This was the real deal, if that's what you're getting at."

"Yeah. And Mario Lewis died of a gunshot wound to his thigh."

"I'm telling you, this is legit. I've got a friend with some local gang connections. He was picked up on a B&E charge last week and was there when Gibbons was brought in."

"So?"

"So, according to this guy, Gibbons was trying to make a name for himself by going after you. He thought it would impress the higher ups. Only trouble is the gang didn't authorize the killing."

"Um, not that I'm disappointed, but why not?"

"I don't know. Could just be good business sense. With all the illegal shit they've got goin' on, the last thing they need is public scrutiny."

Adrian hopped up on the kitchen table and snagged the bag of pistachio shells, dumping them all over the floor. Satisfied with a job well done, he wondered off to eat the couch. I picked the shells up and tossed them in the trash.

"Alphonso, I know I've been sort've slow on the uptake lately, but I still don't get why Gibbons would kill himself."

"Gibbons showcased the gang in a really bad light. He didn't just act without permission; he went and fucked it up. That's a huge public embarrassment. You don't cross your gang family and live to tell about it. I guess he figured he was going to end up dead either way, so he might as well choose the least painful method."

"Well, that's a little drastic."

"Brandy, the JTG specializes in torching their victims. Dead or alive, it don't make a difference. In fact, they prefer alive. Makes more of a statement, y'know what I mean?"

In spades. Fighting the mental image of burning flesh that Alphonso had conjured up for me, I said, "So, now that Gibbons is out of the picture, can we just forget the whole thing and go back to business as usual?"

Alphonso chuckled softly through the phone and almost parroted Bobby's warning. "I wish I knew, Sweetcakes. It's all fucked up how this pride and revenge thing works. The gang may have wanted Gibbons dead, but they could blame you for forcing the circumstances that made it happen."

Unhh! The clenching in my stomach turned into a full-fledged panic attack. I got hot all over, my forehead breaking out in an unholy sweat, frizzing up the bangs that had taken me twenty minutes to straighten with a flat iron. I tried to talk, but nothing came out.

"You still there?" Alphonso asked. "Listen, I feel like hanging out and watching a movie tonight. Something heartwarming, with maybe that Julia Roberts chic in it. I'm coming over."

"You don't have to do this, Alphonso. I'll let Nick know you offered."

"This has nothing to do with Nick," Alphonso said, dropping his customary street swag. "We're way past that. We're friends. Friends watch each other's backs."

*****

Alphonso fell asleep on the couch ten minutes into *Pretty Woman*, his head resting on my Mr. Peanut Pillow, (a classic, which I won off e-bay in a huge bidding war…okay, not exactly a war, since I was the only bidder, but I *still won*). He woke up just as Richard Gere proclaimed his love for the hooker-with-a-heart-of-gold.

He sat up and peered at me as if he were inspecting bruised fruit. "You crying?"

"Don't be ridiculous," I snapped, wiping my eyes. "I've got allergies."

"Uh huh."

"*I do.*" I fake sneezed. *Good touch, Brandy. High five!*

Alphonso stretched his legs and rubbed the sleep out of his eyes, a gesture I found endearingly child-like, considering the man was 6'2" with a semi-automatic hanging out of the back of his pants. His phone beeped and he checked for a text message and smiled.

"You gonna be okay?" he asked, rising, "because I got some business to take care of. But I could stay…if you need me to," he added and glanced longingly at the phone.

I shook my head. "I'll be fine. So, what's her name?"

"Who?"

"Your *business*."

Alphonso's grin got wider. "Nicole."

"Have fun," I told him and walked him to the door.

"You're sure now?" He hesitated at the threshold.

"I'm sure. Alphonso?"

"Yeah?"

"Thanks for tonight."

*****

"Have you been avoiding me, Darlin'?" Nick stood at my door at 5:00 a.m. the next morning, looking sexy beyond words in disheveled formal wear and black, horn rimmed glasses. He was holding a box the size of a toaster oven.

I glanced down at my bare legs, the rest of me hidden beneath Hello Kitty shortie pajamas, which I'd like to say was a relic from my youth, but, in actuality, was a recent purchase. I looked back up at him and blushed.

We'd been playing phone tag for days, which may have been by design on my part. Ever since our talk, my insecurities had grown exponentially, to the point where I was convinced Nick was going to leave me. I happened on a solution to this while in the throes of insomnia in the middle of the night, when all your epiphanies seem like *the best idea ever!* I figured if we didn't see or speak to each other, he wouldn't discover my considerable flaws, thus giving him no reason to break up with me.

"Avoiding you? Of course I'm not avoiding you," I

have found that the best defense is a strongly-worded denial, spoken in huffy tones.

"That's good, because I've missed you," he said, completely disarming me.

I opened the screen door and let him in.

"What's in the box?" I asked. I'd hoped it was something to eat. Something delicious, like doughnuts.

"I'll show you in a bit." He shifted the box to one arm and pulled me to him with the other. My arms automatically wrapped around his neck, my ingenious plan to play it cool forgotten in the pleasure of his touch.

He smelled faintly of expensive cigars and aged bourbon. The dark circles under his eyes told me he'd pulled an all-nighter, and yet, he exuded a sexual energy that was so palpable it made me weak.

"You look nice," I said, the blood vessels in my breasts constricting. "I'm feeling a little underdressed."

Nick tossed the box on the coffee table and turned his attention back to me. His hands, warm and sure, slid down my spine, coming to rest just under my butt. "Funny," he said, inching his hands up the leg of my jammies. "I was thinking the exact opposite." And then he did something about it.

Thirty minutes later I sat up on the couch, wearing only the white, button down dress shirt Nick had discarded along the way. Nick, naked, and considerably less tense, gave me a lazy smile and leaned in to kiss me.

"So, do you make a habit of dressing for breakfast?" I asked, eying the tuxedo jacket on the floor, "or was this a special event?"

"Alana's law firm hosted a charity auction last night. It lasted longer than expected."

"You were with Alana?" I tried to sound breezy and not the least bit threatened that he'd spent the wee hours of the morning in the company of one of his former bedmates (a beautiful, smart, sophisticated, viper of a former bedmate. And I wasn't completely sure of the "former" status.)

Nick shrugged. "She was there. I was there. That was about the extent of it. I called to see if you wanted to come," he added, "but you didn't pick up."

And if I had answered, would I have agreed to go? I don't even own formal wear—unless you count the Princess Diana wedding costume I begged my mother to buy me, on sale, the day after Halloween, when I was ten.

I did a mental Alana hate fest, only I knew she wasn't the problem. What I was really threatened by was the ease with which she traveled in Nick's world. Jeez, I hate self-reflection. I always come out looking so bad.

I decided a change of subject was in order. "There wouldn't by any chance be doughnuts in that box, would there?"

"I'm afraid not. But it is for you," Nick said, handing me the package. "I had to bid on them because they reminded me of you."

Nick spent the evening with Alana, but he was thinking of me. In your face, sophisticated viper lady!

I ripped open the carton. Inside was a pair of worn, regulation boxing gloves.

"I remind you of a blood sport?"

"They're not just any gloves, Angel. They're the ones Sylvester Stallone wore in *Rocky*, in the scene where he went the distance."

"Oh my God, are you serious?"

Hands shaking, I lifted the gloves out of the box and held them against my cheek. Rocky was my hero. My *go-to* guy whenever I felt like giving up. This was so much more than an expensive gift. It was a life line.

"I love them, Nick. Thank you."

"You're very welcome, Angel."

I started to put them on when something stopped me. Outside, a dog barked in the distance. A trash truck lumbered down the street, grinding to a halt in front of my house. A neighbor shouted goodbye to his wife, a car door slammed, and a V-8 engine pulled away from the curb. But, inside, all I could hear was the pounding of my heart and the thoughts in my head.

Goddamnit to Hell, Santiago. First, you tell me you can't commit to a future with me, and then you go and do something so fucking endearing I can't commit to a future without you.

I am so screwed.

I set the gloves back in the box before I started blubbering all over them, and headed for the kitchen. "I'll be back in a minute," I mumbled. "I'm just going to make some coffee."

"You okay?" he called after me.

"Absolutely."

I threw some water in the espresso maker and sat at the kitchen table, fuming.

I knew it was dumb. *Nick loves me. Why can't that be enough?*

I put the question to Adrian, who had followed me into the kitchen. Adrian didn't answer me directly. Instead, he parked himself next to his food bowl, his front paws folded in front of him as if in prayer. *Please, Lord, make her feed me.*

I picked up his dog bowl and scooped some kibble into it. Adrian cocked his head in expectation.

"You're right, as usual," I told him. "So Nick says he can't commit. But that doesn't mean anything. People change their minds all the time. I'm making a big deal out of nothing. I should just enjoy what we have now and stop obsessing about the future. Thank you for this little talk." I set down the bowl, poured the coffee and went back into the living room.

Nick was already dressed and on the phone. He was speaking mostly in Spanish but I caught Lewis' name before he hung up. He turned to me, shirtless, under his tuxedo jacket.

"That was the guy I hired to watch Lewis. According to Kenzo, Lewis left his house about an hour ago and drove over to that stretch of abandoned warehouses a few miles north of the naval yard. There were cars and vans parked all along the perimeter of one of the buildings. Lewis parked and went inside."

"Was he alone?"

He nodded. "Except for a couple of dogs with him. Kenzo tried to get a closer look, but there was a group of Samoan bikers with an impressive looking arsenal hanging around outside, and they didn't seem in the mood to be messed with."

Nick picked up his .38 from the top of the TV set and casually gave the cylinder a spin. Satisfied that it was fully loaded he opened his jacket and slipped it into his shoulder holster. "I'm going to go meet Kenzo down there and check it out."

Oy. While I had absolute faith in Nick's ability to beat the living crap out of anyone, the odds didn't seem in his favor.

"Nick, why do you have to go? If there's really a dog fight going on, can't we just call the police?"

"We're not certain of anything, at this point, and it's not wise to tip your hand unless you're sure. I promise you I'll call the police if it becomes necessary. I'll be fine, Angel. I don't want you sitting here worrying."

"I have no intention of sitting here worrying," I said, heading upstairs to get dressed, "because I'm coming with you."

CHAPTER EIGHT

The area adjacent to the Philadelphia Naval Yard was a once thriving commercial district comprised of brick two-story warehouses and manufacturing plants that fell on hard economic times when business moved south. Flanked by I-95 on one side and the Delaware River on the other, these abandoned buildings made the perfect venue for various and sundry criminal activities.

We took the La Sabre since Nick's car, a 1964 XKE Jaguar, would have stood out in any crowd, no matter how isolated the area. While he didn't openly object to my coming along, I sensed a minuscule drop of unease, which I chose to ignore, because if I acknowledged it I would feel bad that I was doing something against his wishes, but that's what's so great about Nick. He accepts me the way I am. Rationalization intact, I sat back in the passenger's seat and watched the city whiz by.

Kenzo, a short, skinny, guy with a long face and enormous eyes, was waiting for us the next building over. He was sitting in his car, smoking. Now, he threw the cigarette onto the ground, gave a quick nod to Santiago, and ignored me completely.

"He's still in there, as far as I can tell," he reported.

"Do you need me to hang around?"

"I'd appreciate it," Nick said.

I eyed Kenzo. He didn't look like he'd be much good in a fight. I probably outweighed him by about ten pounds. "I'll bet I could take him," I thought. That notion was dispelled a quick second later when he whipped out a pair of speed chucks, absently spinning them with precise and deadly force.

"So, what's the plan?" I asked.

Nick scanned the building. There was a fire escape ladder leading up to the roof. "We need to see what's going on in that warehouse," he said. "Kenzo, you stay here in case we get company. I'll be right back."

Kenzo was still twirling the speed chucks. Maybe it was my imagination but he seemed to be actively glaring at me.

"I'll come with you," I said.

Again, a nano second's hesitation, then, "Come on."

Nick went first and climbed the ladder with ease. I trailed after him like an asthmatic eighty-year old scaling Mount Everest. He reached the roof and turned to pull me up the rest of the way. "Great view of the city," I said, to cover my intense fear of heights. "What now?"

"Now, we cross over to the other building and check things out through the skylight."

The gap between the buildings was about five feet. No problem for a pole vaulter, but for me, it might as well have been the Grand Canyon.

"Cross over? As in leaping tall buildings in a single bound?"

"Actually, I thought we'd use this." Nick grabbed a six-foot plank, probably left by some other reprobate during a similar escapade. He placed it over the narrow gap between the buildings and set out across it.

"You can stay here if you want," he said, glancing back at me.

I looked down and swallowed hard. *What am I trying to prove? I'll fall and kill myself. It will be so embarrassing.*

"Wouldn't miss this for the world," I said, and forced my feet onto the board.

Nick reached behind him and took hold of my hand. "You're doing fine, Darlin'. Just another few steps."

As I landed on the next roof over, I thanked God and resumed breathing.

Nick motioned for me to follow him, and as we approached the skylight I could hear the raucous sounds of a crowd gone wild. We stopped inches from the filthy glass window and crouched down. Nick's face was tense. "I've seen dog fights before, Angel. These people are devoid of conscience. It might be best if you don't look."

Nick was trying to shield me from the most despicable realities of life, and I loved him for it. But remaining blissfully ignorant was how we allowed these things to happen in the first place. I leaned over and looked.

About a hundred people ringed a makeshift pit in the middle of the room. The pit measured between fourteen and twenty feet square with plywood sides and a dirt floor. Judging by the ragged condition of the two dogs inside the ring, they had been going at it for a while.

The crowd was predominantly adult males, with a few scattered women and young children thrown into the mix. Whenever a particularly vicious attack occurred they reacted collectively with an exuberance bordering on satanic frenzy.

In a sudden burst of energy, the larger of the two animals sank its teeth into the other dog's throat and ripped it wide open. Blood gushed from a gaping hole. The injured dog collapsed in the middle of the pit, and the fight was over. Only, just when I thought it couldn't possibly get any worse, it did.

A guy standing on the sidelines stepped into the pit. He was large and muscular, with a swastika tattooed on his bald head. He didn't look happy.

"The dog that collapsed is probably his," Nick surmised. "His dog shamed him by losing the match, so he has to do something to win back audience favor. Turn around, Brandy," he warned.

Before Nick's words could fully register in my brain, the owner hoisted his injured dog upside down by its hind quarters and paraded it around the pit. The crowd came alive in anticipation of a good "show." Sickened by the scene unfolding before me, I tried to turn away, sure that he was going to rip the dog's legs off. Only, just then, Nazi-Boy made a quick turn and swung the dog hard, heaving him straight over the tops of the heads of the crowd.

Some of the younger men tried to reach up and bop it back into the pit before it hit the ground, like a beach ball at a Phillies' game, but they weren't strong enough.

The audience roared as the dog crash landed on the pavement floor. Satisfied by the massive cheering that ensued, the owner left the pit, spitting on the mangled remains of his dog before walking out of the warehouse.

A blinding rage swept over me. I scrambled to my feet and ran over to the edge of the roof, tracking Baldy as he strode toward a row of cars parked along the highway. Nick came up behind me and pulled me away from the ledge.

"He's getting away," I screamed, and lunged for the makeshift bridge. My only thought was to get this guy and do to him what he'd done to countless innocent dogs.

Nick held tight to my hand. "He's not going to get far, Angel. I promise you that."

We made our way in silence back across the wooden plank and down the fire escape. Kenzo was waiting at the bottom of the stairs.

"Keep an eye on our friend over there, would you?" Nick said. "But don't make contact with him unless it's necessary."

Kenzo nodded and took off, the speed chucks dangling at his side.

Nick turned to me and handed me his phone. "Go

back to the car, Darlin', and in a couple of minutes call the police. Tip them off about the dog fight, but don't identify yourself. It should take them about twelve minutes to get here."

"What are you going to do?"

"Just wait for me in the car. I've got some business to attend to." He was calm beyond reason, which meant someone was going to die.

Oh shit. "Nick, no. The cops will be here soon. They'll take care of him."

"Not to my satisfaction, Angel," he said, removing his gun from the holster.

"Well, not to mine, either." I ran to keep pace with him. "But if you kill this ass hole you'll go to jail…and…and…I won't have a date for my cousin Marlene's daughter's wedding, and, well, you don't know my family. I'll never live that down. *Nick, please!*"

We had reached the row of cars. The guy was four vehicles, down, standing with his back to us, talking on his cell phone in a loud, angry voice, oblivious to the danger he was in.

Nick moved quickly and was on him before he could take his next undeserved breath. He leaned into the guy, pressing his knee hard against his kidney, one arm snaked around his neck. With his other arm, he brought the gun up to the guy's face, and shoved the barrel into his mouth. I cringed at the sound of teeth breaking like a dog crunching on a chicken bone.

Oh God, oh God, Oh God. Please don't kill him, Nick. Please don't kill him.

A dark stain appeared at the crotch of Nazi-Boy's pants and worked its way down his leg. It left a puddle in the dirt.

"You're real tough, aren't you?" Nick crooned. "You like torturing animals? Does it make you feel like a man?" He shoved his knee deep into the guy's back, eliciting a guttural cry.

"How about I give you a lesson in empathy? Give you an idea of how those animals you starve and bait and torture feel."

The son of a bitch deserved all that and more and, God help me, I wanted him dead. But not like this. Not by Nick's hand.

On shaky legs I positioned myself in front of them. The guy stood stock still and wild-eyed, looking absurdly comical with a bloody mouthful of .38. Nick had zoned out, having gone deep into his past. This did not bode well for Nazi-Boy's future.

"Nick," I said, summoning the practical side of me. "If you kill him, he won't hurt. Hurt him bad, but let him live to remember."

And so he did.

*****

Nick and I didn't talk much on the way home. I sat with my head resting against the car window, eyes closed, as two questions played like a loop in my mind. *If I hadn't been there, would Nick have killed that guy? And, if there were no possibility of him getting caught, would I have wanted him to?* I didn't have an answer to either one, and that frightened me most of all.

"I'm going to be tied up for the next few days," he informed me as he pulled up in front of my house. "I've got an errand to do for Sal."

Father Sal is an old friend of Nick's, and a priest in the Badlands, one of the city's most impoverished and dangerous areas. At times Sal has to resort to extreme measures (read: illegal) to help his parishioners, and that's where Nick comes in.

"Should I be worried?" I asked.

"Can I stop you?"

"Good point."

He unbuckled the seat belt and handed me the keys. I started to open the door but he reached over and pulled it shut, watching me with his beautiful, liquid brown eyes.

His expression was, as always, hard to read, but I was getting good at picking up on infinitesimal signs. The man was in pain.

"I'm sorry," he said, and hugged me to him.

I knew better than to ask why. And, anyway, I already knew the answer.

*****

"...and then the cops showed up and busted the place, only Donte must've slipped out earlier because he wasn't listed in the police report." I took a healthy bite of 'cheesesteak wit' and licked the liquid grease that ran down my arm. I was sharing a bench with Uncle Frankie at Pat's Steaks. At midnight the line was still wrapped around the block; a testament to the best cheese steak on Earth. We had to scramble to get a seat.

"Hey, did you know it's a felony to even attend a dog fight in Pennsylvania?" I asked.

"Yeah. But good luck enforcing it. This shit is all pervasive. Still, you did good, Midget Brat."

Of all my relatives, the person I've always been most comfortable confiding in is Uncle Frankie. He's protective without being smothering, and he doesn't try to improve me. Still, I figured it wasn't worth mentioning the more graphic details of my adventure with Nick, like, for instance, the guy we'd left for dead. Anyway, I'm sure he'll be fine after the hip replacement surgery. Plus, lots of people function perfectly well with just one kidney.

Uncle Frankie dug into his cup of fries and popped the last one into his mouth. Then he eyed mine, still half full. I didn't have much of an appetite, so I slid them over to him.

"You sure?"

I nodded. "Uncle Frankie, can I ask you something?"

"Absolutely." He squinched up his eyebrows. "You okay?"

"Yeah. Fine. It's just that...well, do you think people can change?"

"What do you mean?"

"I mean do you think we're capable of profound turnarounds from our basic nature, or are we destined to play out the hand life gave us?"

"Wow," he said, through a mouthful of French fries. "You sure get philosophical late at night."

"Never mind," I shrugged. "I don't know what the hell I'm talking about anyway. I'm just tired."

Frankie considered this for a minute. "I think it's like that old joke, 'How many psychiatrists does it take to change a light bulb? One, but it's really got to want to change.' I think if the desire is there, it's do-able." He waited a beat, and when I didn't say anything he added, "Are we talking about Santiago?"

"No. I was just, y'know, wondering."

Uncle Frankie cut me a sympathetic, knowing look and finished off the rest of my fries.

*****

Being unemployed is not without its perks. It gave me a chance to catch up on my laundry and to check out some really great daytime TV. That took about twenty minutes of my day. Then I called the police station a couple of times to see if the new autopsy results had come in.

"Not since you called fifteen minutes ago," DiCarlo told me.

"Oh, well, keep me posted."

"You're at the top of my list."

I called John next. He didn't pick up so I called a couple of six more times.

He answered after eight rings. "What's wrong?"

"Nothing. Why?"

"You called me six times." He seemed a kind of annoyed.

"Seven. How come you didn't pick up?"

"I'm in the middle of a photo shoot."

"So who are you shooting? Maybe I could come down and help you."

"I don't think so. I've gotta go," he said, and hung up.

I'll bet he wouldn't have hung up Garrett.

I walked into the living room. The puppy had made up a new game called "Give the Cat a Heart Attack." I wasn't real sure of the rules, but they seemed to include lying in wait for Rocky to come down the stairs and then chasing her back up again. I decided to cut the cat a break and take the dogs for a walk.

On the way back, I ran across my neighbor, Heather, and her pug, Mr. Wiggles. Mr. Wiggles and I have an adversarial relationship. Several months ago, he peed on my shoe. On purpose. Heather says it's a sign of affection, but I have my doubts.

"Ooh," said Heather, bending to scratch the puppy behind her ear. "You have a new dog. She's sweet."

"Yeah, thanks. You want her?"

Heather laughed like I couldn't possibly be serious.

"No, really, Heather, you want her, she's yours. Look, Mr. Wiggles really seems to like her!" In truth, Mr. Wiggles was actively ignoring her, the pint-sized, pedigreed snob.

Heather looked skyward. Dark clouds were gathering and the air buzzed with negative ions. We were in for a whopper of a summer storm.

"She needs a rain coat," Heather decided. "I'll make her one with room to grow."

"Listen, you're sure you don't want another dog?"

"Ha ha. Good one, Bran. Well, see ya later."

I sighed. "See ya, Heather."

It was lunch time so I decided to go visit Paul at the club. His best server was on vacation, and I figured he could use my help...or I could use the tips. One or the other.

Paul was behind the bar taking "to go" orders. "Hey, Sis. I was just about to call you." He hung up the phone and I followed him to his office.

"So, how come you're not at work? Don't you have to do the mid-day traffic report? By the way, you make a way better Godfrey than the other guy did. You really make traffic come alive."

"I got fired."

"Oh. So, uh, do you need some m-money to tide you over?" He reached into his drawer and pulled out a wad of cash.

"Paulie, that's really sweet of you, but I didn't come here looking for a handout. I thought maybe I could work it off."

Paul winced. "Bran, couldn't you just take the handout?"

"Just give me a chance, will ya, Paul? I've really been brushing up on my people skills. Here, watch this." I gave him a big, friendly smile and pantomimed taking a plate off a serving tray and placing it on the top of his desk. "Can I get you anything else this evening? The apple pie is to die for."

"Um, you p-probably don't want to m-m-mention our food and d-dying in the same b-b-breath. It's k-kind of a turn off."

"Duly noted. So, when do I start?"

Half an hour later we were back in Paul's office. "Are you sure you don't want to take this?" he asked, waving a wad of money at me.

"I'm good, Paulie. And just for the record, I didn't tell that woman that a 25% tip is customary. I said, '25% of our customers marry.'"

"Come back tonight," Paul said, too polite to choke on his words in front of me. "We can try you out parking cars again."

"Love you, bro."

"Love you, too."

*****

I woke up the next morning with a dog on either side of me and a cat on my head. The thermostat said 90 degrees, and I was swimming in sweat, which I thought would burn off the cheesesteak calories, but I guess sweating only counts as a calorie burner if it hurts while you're doing it.

I hopped in the shower and got dressed and then went downstairs and turned on WINN. Godfrey the Traffic Dog had officially retired. He'd been replaced by something that looked like a hedgehog, but I couldn't be sure. I also couldn't figure out the tie-in with traffic, unless there were numerous hedgehog-related deaths during high-density traffic hours on I-95.

The dog fight bust had barely gotten a mention in the news. Granted, it was small potatoes compared to high profile, celebrity busts with millions of dollars on the line, but it still felt disrespectful, to say the least, to the dogs that suffered at the hands of these people.

The lack of press infuriated me, and I spent the next several hours in a rage-infused web search frenzy learning all I could about dog fighting and the moral degenerates who engaged in it. Turns out the lure of the money, the excitement of the fight, the sick thrill of torturing another living thing crosses all cultural, economic, and political boundaries.

Nick called just as I was taking a break. Since I started seriously working out at the gym (well, visiting it occasionally, anyway) I've tried to cut down on my chocolate cupcake habit. I was down to two a day, and only the icing off of three more.

I got a pang of yearning at the sound of his voice. "Are you back from your errand for Sal?" I asked.

"Safe and sound, Darlin'. I wanted to pass along a bit of news. Kenzo lost track of Lewis. He hasn't seen him since the morning of the dog fight. My guess is he heard about the new autopsy and split the state."

"Unh! If the police had just listened to me in the first place, the man would be behind bars by now."

"I think you might be forgetting about due process, but I understand your frustration."

"So, what are the chances that I'll get to see you?"

Did that sound too needy? Oy. Now I'd spend the rest of the day wishing I could take it back. Low self-esteem is exhausting.

"I've got a late training session set for tonight, but I'll be through by ten."

"I'll be over then." Love has no pride.

*****

"Brandy, where are you? Carla and I have been waiting outside Freddy's for half an hour."

Yikes. I'd told Janine and Carla I'd meet them for Happy Hour at a local bar and grill. It was our way of economizing, since Janine's been out of steady work for almost a year, and I, apparently, was unemployable. I'd spent the afternoon alternating between job hunting off Craig's List and playing on-line Scrabble. The job pickin's were slim. A parochial school in my neighborhood was looking for a P.E. coach, and the Acme needed baggers. It was a toss-up as to which occupation I was less suited for.

"Oh, Neenie, I'm sorry. You guys go on in and I'll be there as soon as I can."

"Well, hurry up. The Buffalo wings go fast, and you always complain about the fish sticks."

"Set some aside for me. I'm on my way."

Twenty minutes later I found Carla and Janine seated at a booth in the back of the bar. They were drinking Mojitos and Carla was arguing with the server. They had stockpiled the wings for me, a definite no-no in Happy Hour etiquette.

"I can't keep bringing you free appetizers until you finish the ones you have."

"These are for our friend," Carla explained to the server and half the restaurant. She's depressed, and, by God, if Buffalo wings make her happy, I will see to it that she has them."

There was no hole for me to crawl into so I waited for the server to leave before slinking into the booth.

"I'm not depressed," I said, stuffing a wing into my mouth. I washed it down with a Bud Light.

Carla and Janine exchanged a look, complete with eyeball rolls.

"I'm not depressed. Okay, so I'm out of work, but so are you, Janine…no offense."

"None taken," Janine said with a cheerful Mojito glow. "I'm just better at it than you are. Brandy, you can't sit still for a minute. This must be killing you."

"I've been keeping busy. Just yesterday I painted Adrian's toe nails (my dog really wants to explore his feminine side) and I promised Mrs. Gentile I'd paint the interior of her house in exchange for her dropping the petition against me."

That spurred another round of eyeball rolls.

"I'm right here, you guys."

Carla fixed me with a stare. "Brandy, honey," she said, invoking her right as a slightly older friend to impart parental wisdom to me, "You're probably smarter than Janine and me put together—no offense, Janine—"

"None taken."

"—and yet, you've been knocking around in a job that's beneath you for years now. It's time you figured out what really matters to you and go for it."

Carla was right about my needing to find a job I cared about, but she was dead wrong on at least one count. In her own, dipsy way, she was one of the wisest people I knew.

Janine's phone rang some time into her third Mojito. "It's Mike," she mouthed. "How do I look?"

Oh, jeez. This could be a disaster. I pulled the phone out of her hand.

"Mike, it's Brandy. Janine is um, indisposed at the moment. Can I relay a message…she'd love to…no, I don't have to ask her….Saturday night is fine…she's looking forward to it too."

I clicked off and handed the phone back to Janine. "He's taking you to that new Sushi place on Market, followed by some foreign film whose name I can't pronounce. Listen, Neenie, Mike's a really nice guy, so don't break his heart or anything, okay?"

"I wasn't planning on it. Bran, are you all right?"

"Fine. Great. Why do you ask?"

Janine and Carla exchanged another look, this time, minus the eye exercises.

"What? I'm fine, you guys. I'm just looking out for Mike is all. So if you don'twant the same things in life, you'd better tell him now, because he could fall in love with you and end up really getting hurt."

Nobody said anything for a minute. Then, Carla waved her hand in the air, signaling the server. "Another round of Buffalo wings for our friend, here. And keep 'em comin'."

CHAPTER NINE

The sun was just disappearing over the Schuylkill as I set out for Nick's studio. I wasn't supposed to be there until 10:00 p.m., but I took a detour to Paulie's to drop off Adrian and Little No Name. My brother is a soft touch, and I figured some bonding time might score the puppy a new home. Plus, I didn't want to have to worry about them being left alone if I got invited to my own sleepover.

"Now, d-don't get any ideas that I'm going to keep her," Paul warned, in between bouts of wheezing. "I'm n-not a dog person."

"I won't," I lied. "Thanks for babysitting. I'll be back tomorrow to pick them up. Oh, and you might want to take them over to the park in the morning. Puppies are total chick magnets. Be good for Uncle Paul, you guys."

Once the dogs were safely ensconced at Paul's I still had some time to kill. And, since I was only about forty minutes away, (practically around the corner) I thought I'd drive by Donte Lewis' place—because that's the spontaneous kind of gal I am! I just wanted to see where he lived, is all. I promised myself I wouldn't even get out of the car, and I knew that I wouldn't because I always keep my promises.

North Philadelphia touts some of the oldest Victorian houses in the city, as well as beautiful murals that depict a rich cultural history. Unfortunately, none of that was evident on the street where Donte Lewis resided. His block was ugly, stark and mean. One side of the street had been taken over by government-subsidized apartments built in the hideously boxy style of the mid-sixties. On the other were ramshackle row homes, circa 1940. Their owners had obviously given up the fight against natural erosion and gang graffiti.

Donte lived in a side by side duplex located at the end of the block. An unlit alley snaked around behind it like the River Styx. His was the only house with any semblance of livability. The other half of his duplex was a boarded up abomination with trash strewn all over the porch, and a dead patch of lawn out front.

The next unit over looked like an abandoned fortress with metal bars covering glassless windows. The stucco siding was riddled with bullet holes.

There were no lights on at Donte's. I parked across the street from the duplex, cut the engine, and sat there, thinking.

"Okay, you've seen it," said Sensible Me. "Now move along. On your way."

"Yeah, but Lewis is gone," tempted Compulsive Me. "It's safe to get out and look around a little."

"Excuse me," Sensible Me butt in. "Not to be a Debbie Downer, but these things rarely turn out well for you. If memory serves me right, you usually get caught in the act of snooping."

"Perfect timing," reasoned Compulsive Me. "The odds of not getting caught are in your favor now. And who knows, you might find evidence to tie him to his cousin's murder. C'mon. You know you want to."

I honestly did not want to. But there is something wrong with me. I just had to go take a look. I grabbed my cell phone, mace, and brass knuckles and climbed out of the car.

The heat of the day lingered on the pavement as I made a mad dash across the street. It was doubtful that anyone would have noticed me, anyway. There wasn't a soul in sight.

I walked up the sidewalk and headed toward the alley. A six-foot high cinder block wall ran along the perimeter of the property, with a rusted iron gate that led into a small back yard. In the dark I could barely make out the broken padlock that hung from the latch.

The gate had been left partially open, so I squeezed on through into the yard. Tiptoeing up to the back door of the apartment, I tried to peer in but it was too dark to see anything. I thought about jiggling the door handle, when common sense made an overdue appearance and reminded me that Breaking & Entering is still considered a crime in Philadelphia, no matter how many times I've gotten away with it. Besides which I'd started to feel seriously creeped out, so I let go of the knob and turned to leave. Just a hair too late.

My body snapped to attention at the sound of a car rolling down the alley. It stopped just on the other side of the cement wall, the engine idling.

"Keep going, keep going, keep going," I silently chanted.

Damn it. Whoever was behind the wheel cut the engine. The car door opened and quickly closed, and a shadow appeared at the gate.

"Oh, crap, it must be Donte!" screamed both Sensible and Compulsive Me in perfect two-part harmony. They'd finally found something to agree on.

I scanned the barren back yard, but there was no place to hide. *How many times have I gotten myself into these situations, and when the hell would I learn not to?* Both good questions, but they would have to wait. My mind went numb and autopilot took over.

Turning back to the door, I was all set to hip check my way in, when I noticed someone had already done the work for me. The lock had been jimmied. "That's weird," I thought, only I didn't have time for an in-depth analysis, as whoever had been in the car was now squeezing through the gate.

I pushed my way into the apartment, figuring I'd leave by the front door, like in some delightful, screwball comedy where the main characters keep *just* missing each other and hilarity ensues.

The door led into a small storage room. It had a weird smell, like bad BBQ. As warm as it was outside, it was surprisingly cold in the apartment. It struck me as odd that Donte would leave the air conditioning on, but I guess if he was about to be indicted for murder, he wasn't all that concerned about running up his electric bill.

I hauled ass out of the storage room and into the living room, dodging furniture in the dark. My heart was three steps ahead of the rest of me, as I reached the front door and lunged for the lock. *Christ on a stick*. It was a key-operated dead bolt with no key in sight.

The back door scraped open and the mystery man entered the apartment. His rubber soled shoes squeaked as he moved across the linoleum floor.

Shit. Shit. Shit!

With ever-growing panic, I retreated from the front door and escaped into the kitchen, scanning the room in search of a weapon. A vegetable peeler sat on the counter in front of me. *If I ever get out of here alive, I could really use one of these things.* I scooped it up, wielding it like a shiv.

There were steps just off the kitchen that led to the basement. With any luck at all there would be a basement door. The BBQ smell got stronger as I fumbled my way down the cellar stairs. It filled my lungs with a sickeningly sweet, musky, yet, slightly metallic stench, and I almost gagged as I felt my way across the pitch black room.

Overhead, footsteps hesitated at the entrance to the

basement and, to my horror, began descending the stairs. Frantic for a place to hide, I inched away from the bottom of the staircase. Without warning, a beam of light illuminated the room. I sucked in a breath and fell backwards, and crashed on top of something soft…and hard… and…oh, Jesus…crispy.

My stomach roiled, and I screamed so loud it could have woken the dead guy I'd landed on. At least I thought it was a guy. The skin was torched, and it flaked all over me as I struggled to right myself.

Someone strode across the room and offered me a hand. I took it, allowing the person to whom it belonged to help me up.

"Are you all right?" Kenzo asked; something he must've learned in a Social Skills class. Etiquette did not come naturally to this guy.

"No, I'm not okay! I just gave a lap dance to a dead guy. A *cooked* dead guy. And what the hell are you doing here? You scared the crap out of me."

My eyes slid downward to the guy on the floor. What was left of him looked familiar. Bile worked its way up my esophagus. My skin got all clammy, and I was pretty sure I'd wet my pants. I put my hand to my nose in a fruitless attempt to block the smell of burnt flesh.

"I've got to get out of here."

Unfazed, Kenzo took out his phone and punched in a number.

"Are you calling the cops?"

Mr. Personality ignored me and grunted into the phone. "You were right…yeah, she's right here. Oh, yeah, and she found a corpse." He handed the phone to me.

"Hello?" I screeched, bordering on hysteria.

"Hello, Angel."

"H-h-how did you know I was here?"

"I had a feeling when I told you Donte had probably left the state that you might take it as an invitation to browse. So I asked Kenzo to swing by Lewis' place, in case

I was wrong about him leaving the area."

"Turns out I wasn't the only one browsing, and you should see what Lewis did to this guy. He burned him, Nick. He burned him bad."

Santiago went quiet; the two of us sharing the unspoken thought that it could have been me.

*****

Ten minutes later I stood alone on the street corner and waited for the police to arrive. Kenzo had taken off the minute I punched in 911, mumbling something about outstanding warrants and deportation.

"Hang tight, darlin'," Nick had instructed me. "I'm on my way."

"It's really not necessary, Nick. The cops are rounding the corner as we speak," I lied. "Besides, this could take a while. Oh, they're here. I'll call you when I get home."

Before he had a chance to protest I hung up. Because the truth was I just couldn't face him.

I'd fucked up. Acted on impulse with no regard to my own safety or the ramifications of my actions. How many times had my high school principal, Mrs. Marlowe, lectured me with those exact words?

I thought I was getting better about this. Damn it, I was getting better. But sometimes opportunities presented themselves and I just couldn't seem to turn them down.

The worst part was Nick had predicted that I wouldn't be able to control myself. So, he quietly took care of it, without even a hint of judgment. It was one of the things I loved most about him—his unconditional acceptance of me. Only, at that moment, I felt like about four years old.

After what seemed like an eternity, a fleet of cop cars careened down the street and descended on the crime scene, followed by an ambulance and two fire trucks. Bringing up the rear was a van carrying a local news crew. The logo painted on the side said W.I.N.N.

I didn't recognize any of the cops, which was odd since, over the past year I'd had ample opportunity to meet most of them. And, just my luck, the one that took my statement was a stickler for details.

"So, let me get this straight," Officer Picky said, five minutes into it. "You were taking a walk, alone, at night…in this neighborhood?"

"Is it against the law?"

"No."

"All right, then."

"But entering someone's house without their express permission is against the law. How did that happen?"

Hmm…how did that happen? When confronted with a question for which no good can come of a truthful answer, it is best to have an alternate response ready to go. What's even better is having a somewhat plausible one. I had neither, so I decided to wing it.

"Okay, so like I was saying, I was walking by and I thought I smelled smoke."

"I don't smell smoke."

"Are you going to let me tell this?"

Officer Picky did a magnificent head shake. "Please. Do."

"I smelled smoke, so, naturally, I had to go check to see if anyone was asleep in the house."

"Naturally. So you jimmied the lock and let yourself in."

"I didn't jimmy the lock. It was already broken."

"Ma'am, just admit you broke in."

"I will not!" I stuffed my hands inside the pockets of my jeans and turned them inside out. "I have no tools. What do you think I did? Pick the lock with my teeth? Besides, I'm totally inept. Anyone will tell you that."

He barked out a sound I can only describe as harrumph.

"Just go on," he grunted.

I was really warming to my story when I got a shout-out from the news van.

"Yo, Alexander!"

The voice belonged to Ben Hyatt, the station's hot shot reporter. Ben's reputation was fierce. Word had it he'd kill his own mother just to make sure he'd be first on the scene when the news broke.

Hyatt sprinted over to me with Olympian speed. "What are you doing covering this story? I heard you got canned."

Ignoring Ben, I turned to the cop. "Could we be done now? I've told you all I know, and I'm willing to come down to the station tomorrow. But right now, I just want to go home."

The cop nodded. "Don't leave town," he added and left me alone to deal with Hyatt.

"Oh, this is priceless," Ben said, catching on. "You're the woman who called in about finding the body. Hey, you're not thinking of breaking this story yourself, are you?" He sidled up next to me, real chummy. "You give me an exclusive and I'll pay you double what the station would offer."

I pretended to consider this.

"So? Do we have a deal?"

"Let me put it this way, Ben. Bite me."

*****

The thought of going home to an empty house terrified me, and it was too late to pick the dogs up from Paul's. Besides, he'd find out about my adventure soon enough. No use wrecking his night.

The idea of going to sleep was even less appealing. I knew what was in store the minute I'd close my eyes, and I wasn't all that anxious to revisit a char-broiled corpse in my dreams. Plus, by morning the house would be swarming with reporters all wanting to interview the freak that kept finding dead people.

The only place I could think of to go at this time of night was The South Street gym. Open 24/7, it was a haven for hard-core jocks and insomniacs. During my adolescence, I'd spent a good many nights holed up in my uncle's office lamenting the fact that "nobody understands me." Frankie had a microwave, an unlimited supply of popcorn, and a comfy couch. What more could a girl ask for.

Greg Piscitello, one of the night managers, let me into Frankie's office. Greg's known me since I was fourteen, and I consider him an uncle of sorts.

"Rough night, honey?"

"Not too bad." I shrugged. "Just needed an air-conditioned place to crash."

Greg offered up a sympathetic smile. It said, *'I don't believe you but I'll respect your privacy.'*

"Let me know if you need anything."

"Thanks, Greg. I will."

*****

"Mom, was I dropped on my head as a baby?"

"Brandy, don't be ridiculous. Why would I drop you on your head?"

I stood in my kitchen making breakfast, which was a real challenge considering about all I had in the cupboard was a box of year-old Rye Crisp. Shifting the phone to my other ear, I stuck a stale end slice of bread into the toaster.

"I don't mean on purpose or anything. Just—y'know—by accident."

It was the only logical explanation. Head trauma, suffered at an early age. Clearly not my fault.

"Brandy, you're not making any sense. It's because you've got too much time on your hands," she decided. "I didn't want to mention it, but your brother tells me you got fired."

I'm going to kill Paul.

"I wasn't fired. The company needed to downsize. It happens all the time. Besides, I've got plenty of other offers."

Big mistake calling my parents. I just figured they'd be upset when they heard I'd been involved in yet another catastrophe, so I'd reassure them I was fine. Turned out, I needn't have worried. Since they retired to Boca Rattan, my parents have lived blissfully unaware of their only daughter's daily drama. Which gave them ample time to sweat the small stuff.

My dad saved me from having to list my phantom job opportunities by weighing in on the subject. "Does she need any money?"

"Your father wants to know if you need any money."

"Tell him I'm fine, but thanks."

"She's fine. She's not fine," my mom added in what she believed to be a whisper. Then again, in Boca, where the median age is seventy, I suppose it was.

*****

"Remind me again why we're doing this." John stood, one leg poised on the first of seventy-two stone steps leading to the east entrance of the Philadelphia Art Museum. He was sweaty and flushed, and that was just from the walk from the parking lot.

"We're doing this because I have to get in better shape."

"And I'm here because?"

"Because we never get to hang out anymore, and you've missed me terribly."

"I'm missing you less and less by the minute," John grumbled. He hiked up his pants exposing designer workout shoes. I recognized the brand as a favorite of sheiks and other multi-billionaires.

"Jeez, John. Those shoes cost more than my mortgage."

"And well worth every penny. The leather comes from real Himalayan yak."

"Ha, ha. Good one!"

"What do you mean?"

Oh, crap. He was serious.

I pretended I didn't hear him and scanned the broad expanse of stairs. The last time I ran "The Rocky Steps" I was seven. Wow. I'd forgotten there were so damn many of them. The top looked to be about a mile away.

"Um, shouldn't we stretch first or something?"

"Nah." John unhooked his hip flask from his belt loop, put it to his lips and chugged. Mountain Spring water with added vitamins and minerals dribbled down his chin. "We don't want to sap our strength."

"We're not crossing the Sahara, y'know."

"Suit yourself," John shrugged. "At least one of us will be well hydrated."

We started up the stairs. After about ten steps a group of elderly Japanese tourists came up behind us. One of them had a walker. John and I paused to catch our breath—I mean to tie our shoes—and they sprinted past us, humming *Eye of the Tiger*.

"Show off's," John said. "The trick is to pace yourself."

"Oh, totally." I wondered how much longer I'd have to keep up the pretense that I was going to make it to the top. My legs were beginning to cramp.

We hobbled up to the first plateau and surveyed the vista. Eakins Oval and The Benjamin Franklin Parkway were spread out before us.

"So, do you want to go get something to eat?" I asked.

"Yeah, okay."

We headed back down the steps. When I got to the bottom step I looked up. The old lady with the walker had reached the top of the stairs and was now pumping her fists in the air, Rocky style.

We could've beat her if we wanted to, right?"

John nodded. "Absolutely."

Personally, I had my doubts.

*****

Twenty minutes later we sat opposite each other at the Merchantville Diner, in Jersey, scarfing down chicken parmesan and the world's best homemade cheesecake. I had to get out of my neighborhood to enjoy a meal in peace. Ever since the other night, people have crawled out of the woodwork, in the guise of *concerned friends*, to ask about my gruesome discovery.

"It's getting so's I can't answer my phone anymore. Last night I got a condolence call from Nancy Rappaport." I scraped up the last crumb of cheesecake and popped it into my mouth. If John hadn't been sitting there, I would have licked the plate.

"Who's Nancy Rappaport?"

"That's what I said. Turns out we'd gone to summer camp together when we were nine. Sheesh. Some people have no boundaries. Hey, I'm still hungry. You gonna eat your pie?" I reached over and stabbed a forkful.

John shoved the plate toward me. "Go to town, Sunshine. You've had a rough week."

"Have I told you I love you?"

"Not nearly enough."

"Oh, speaking of dessert, how did Garrett like the brownies I made him?"

In an attempt to win Garrett's affections, I'd spent the better part of an afternoon concocting a confectionary masterpiece for him. I figured I could use the *brownie points*. (Sometimes I crack myself up.)

"Um, he wasn't actually able to eat them, because he's on a gluten-free diet."

"Oh, no. I should have checked first. What does he have? A wheat allergy or something? That can be life threatening."

"Nah, it's nothing like that. He's just into eating super healthy is all."

Funny, he seemed a lot more likable when I thought I'd almost killed him.

"Well, he appreciated the effort," John continued, in an obvious attempt to mollify me. Only I wasn't in the mood to be mollified.

"You're just saying that."

"No. He said so."

"Yeah? So, what'd he say?"

John coughed and mumbled something into his hand.

"Take your hand away from your mouth. I can't

understand you."

"He said, 'nice try.'"

"Nice try? You can't dress that up as a compliment, John. He was obviously being sarcastic."

"Maybe I'm not telling it right. Look, Bran, don't worry about Garrett, okay? Before you know it, you guys are going to be the best of friends."

"Right."

I dropped it for the time being and called to the server. "Could I get a double espresso, please?"

"Sure thing, hon."

John made a face. "Do you really want to drink that so late in the day? You know it's going to keep you up."

"That's sort've the idea," I confessed. "Ever since that night at Lewis' house, I haven't been all that anxious to go to sleep. Hey, you want to come over tonight? I'll let you go through my closet and make fun of my wardrobe."

John gave me the once-over. "Believe me, it's tempting. But I've already got plans with Garrett to check out a new, experimental jazz club in Manayunk."

I waited for the obligatory, "You could come along if you want," but it was not forthcoming.

I reached for the espresso and downed it in two gulps. "Well, we're still on for the Woody Allen retrospective on Friday, aren't we? Garrett could come along if he wants," I added. I'd figured I'd lead by example.

John squirmed in his seat. "Ooh. I forgot about Friday. Garrett scheduled me for a jorei massage at the Spirit Life Center. Look, I'd cancel but he had to pay in advance, and it costs an arm and a leg."

I felt the blood rise to my brain. My mouth opened and I struggled to shut it again before something rude popped out. I looked like a disgruntled guppy.

"Y'know, I can't believe you're crapping out on me. I was totally looking forward to this."

The server returned with our check, and John grabbed it off the table. I was so mad I didn't even pretend to fight for it.

"Look, Bran. I'm sorry. I know I screwed up. Don't be mad, okay?"

To be totally honest, my reaction had more to do with jealously than missing an in-depth analysis of *What's Up, Tiger Lily*. But it went deeper than that.

"I'm not mad," I finally decided. "And I know you think this is about Garrett not liking me—which—okay, it is. But—well—c'mon, John. You hate experimental jazz. You said it sounds like they're perpetually tuning up. And the Spirit Life Center? Seriously? We make fun of those people. They give you the willies, remember?"

"So, what's your point?"

I hesitated. "My point is I feel like you're re-inventing yourself—and for all the wrong reasons."

"I'm just trying to broaden my horizons. Is that a crime?"

God. Why am I doing this? Never mind that John's turning into someone I barely recognize just to please old-stick-up-the-ass Garrett. He's happy. Just shut up.

"Look, I'm sorry. I guess I'm just overly sensitive these days. Forget I said anything."

John put some money down on the table and handed me the bag of leftovers. "Don't worry about it," he said. "I shouldn't have flaked out on you for Friday. So, how can I make it up to you?"

I thought about this for a minute. "Well, as long as Garrett isn't going to eat those brownies, do you think you can ask for them back?" After all, no sense in them going to waste.

*****

John dropped me off at my house. As I walked up to the porch, I caught a glimpse of Mrs. Gentile peeking out her front window through faded, floral curtains. They were the color of overcooked spinach.

Oh, man. I still haven't gotten around to painting her living room. Maybe if I pretend not to see her, I can just slip inside...

Her head disappeared from the window. In a flash she flung open her front door and stepped outside.

"Oh. Hi, Mrs. Gentile. I was just about to knock. I wanted to see about getting started on your living room."

My neighbor scowled as if I'd just left a giant turd on her porch, and rattled off something in Italian which I didn't understand. I'm guessing it wasn't very nice. After she ran out of ways to curse me in her native language, she switched to English for the finale. "You and your hooligan friends are a disgrace to the neighborhood."

Hooligans? I hadn't heard that word since my elementary school's third grade production of Oliver!

"I'm sorry, Mrs. Gentile, but I don't know what you're talking about. I just got home. I haven't had time to be a disgrace to anyone."

She leaned her wilted body over the railing and pointed a gnarled finger in my face. "Don't get smart with me, Missy. A car full of young men stopped right in front of your house. They knew you, all right. They were calling your name. They sat right there in the middle of the street, with the engine running and Satan's music blaring. It was blasphemous, I tell you."

A giant lump of fear settled in my belly. "Um, this is very important, Mrs. Gentile, and I'm not kidding. So I'd appreciate it if you'd think hard about your answer. Were any of the, um, young men carrying a blow torch?"

"How should I know?" she bristled. "What do you think I am? The neighborhood busy body?" She turned and stomped back inside.

I was just about to leap over the rail and follow her into her house when my phone rang. It was Vince Giancola.

"Vince, I'm really glad you called. I need to talk to you." I shoved the key into the lock and opened my front door.

"Let me go first," Vince said. "I have some good news and some bad news." Take your pick."

CHAPTER TEN

I'd had enough bad news to last a life time. "Tell me the good news."

I wanted to sit down, but Adrian and little No-Name hogged the couch. Rocky was sandwiched between them, purring contentedly while the puppy licked her head. Nobody moved for me, so I flopped down on the floor and kicked off my shoes.

Vince took a deep drag off one of the cigarettes he swears he doesn't smoke and coughed. "Okay," he said finally. "I know how much you love to be right, so here goes. I got the results of the second autopsy."

"And?"

"You're really going to make me say it?"

My heart beat quickened in anticipation. "Yep."

"Fine. You were right. Traces of Succinylcholine were found in Mario Lewis' body. It's now officially a murder investigation."

"I knew it!"

"Do you want to gloat or do you want to hear the rest?"

"Both. I'm entitled."

"Yeah," he agreed softly. "You are."

"Thanks. So, where do we go from here?"

"The police found some coke residue at the scene, and they've locked into a theory that the murder was somehow related to a drug deal gone wrong. They've got a BOLO out on Donte Lewis in connection with the corpse he left sitting around in his basement. That is, unless you're planning to bring him in for us—and I'm only half joking."

"Let me get back to you on that. So, what's the bad news?"

"One of our informants told us the Junk Town Gang is getting ready to make a move. Brandy, I'd take this seriously if I were you."

"Yeah. About that."

Vince listened without interruption while I filled him in on Mrs. Gentile's gang sighting. When I was finished, he let out a smoky breath.

"Well, I don't think you won over any hearts when you busted up that dogfight the other night. You ended up costing a lot of really bad people a shit load of money."

"No one can prove I was there…I mean I wasn't there, so of course there would be no proof."

"Don't con me, Alexander. Everybody knows you were there. It had your M.O. all over it. Dispatch said a female called it in, but we couldn't get a read on the cell phone number. And the guy that had his liver handed to him in the parking lot—well, whoever took him apart was no amateur. By the way, you can tell your boyfriend I said, 'well done.' Off the record, of course."

I get nervous talking to law enforcement officials about Nick, no matter how good a friend they are. So, I thought it best to change the subject.

"Have the cops been able to I.D. the guy in the basement yet?" That half a face still haunted me.

"Unfortunately, no. They were able to get some prints, but they don't match anything in our database."

"Okay," I mused aloud. "So the cops are looking for

Donte. But what about the other guys? Roger King said three people showed up the night Mario got beat up. They'd all threatened to kill him. And one of them had a blow torch."

Vince snorted. "The night Mario got beat up? What the hell are you talking about? I swear to God, Brandy, if you're holding out on me—"

Crap. I'd promised Roger I wouldn't drag him into it. Now what?

"I'm not keeping anything from you, Vince. At least not intentionally. Look, I swear I'll stop by your office tomorrow and tell you everything I know. But right now, I've got to go."

"Nine a.m. Sharp."

"Ten, and I'll bring bagels."

I could almost hear him grind his teeth down to nubs. "Fine," he growled. "And for Christ's sake, watch your back."

*****

It's astounding how much you can accomplish by eliminating sleep from your daily routine. First, I updated my resume to include jobs I thought I'd be good at but have never actually performed—like audience warm-up comedian for Jay Leno, or air traffic controller. Next, I alphabetized my spices, which took about two seconds, seeing's all I had were salt and pepper. After that, I spent about an hour teaching Adrian how to Rumba, like that dog on the internet everyone thinks is so cute. I figured it could be a real money maker.

Turned out, Adrian didn't have much interest in learning a new skill. I'd brought my laptop into the living room so that he could study the video, but he kept slinking off to sleep behind the couch.

The house seemed unnaturally quiet; every noise magnified ten fold in the dead of night. Vince had said he'd try to beef up patrol in my neighborhood, but the city is so strapped for cash I didn't hold out much hope of that happening.

I felt lonely, and scared, and a little bit sick from eating an entire box of chocolate pudding. I wanted someone to cuddle with and tell me everything was going to be all right…someone with strong arms and high cheek bones…and a scent that was intoxicating. Someone who would whisper dirty things in my ear to take my mind off the fact that bad people wanted to kill me. Someone who would love me, and protect me, and never let me go. In short, I wanted Nick.

Unfortunately, Nick was away on overnight business, the details of which were left to my imagination. To his credit he'd asked if I felt okay about him leaving. I'd told him, "Oh, of course. No problem," because I didn't want to sound like some needy weirdo. (I feel he should learn these things gradually, as it's still early in the relationship.)

So I did the next best thing and called Janine. Okay, she was like the third or fourth best thing, the second being a date with Indiana Jones. But Janine had the advantage of being real… and amenable to phone calls in the wee hours of the morning.

She picked up immediately. "Yo, Bran. What's wrong?"

Someone sneezed in the background. It was a distinctly masculine sneeze.

"Oh, Neenie, you've got company. I'm sorry. Oh! Is it Mike? Wow, I guess you guys really hit it off. Call me later and tell me all about it…he can't hear me, right?"

"Slow down. You sound like you're on crack. How much caffeine have you had?"

"Not much. Listen, I'll let you get back to your, ah, date."

"Hah! I should be so lucky. I'm filling in at the diner."

Janine used to wait tables at the 24 Hour Diner on Broad Street. By her own admission, she was awful. But whenever they're desperate they call her to fill in for the graveyard shift.

"So, what's up?" she asked.

"Not much. Just felt like saying hi."

Janine paused. "Hmm."

"Hmm what?"

"Nothing. Have you eaten dinner?"

"It's three a.m. Of course I've eaten dinner."

"Standing over the sink eating the skin off a ready-made chicken does not constitute dinner."

"I don't do that!"

"You do so. I've seen you...and more than once. Come on down. I could use the company. Only creeps come out this late at night."

"Excuse me?" That, from the sneezer.

"I'm talkin' here. This doesn't concern you. Keep eating." To me she said, "I'll see you when you get here."

*****

The prevailing feature of the 24 Hour Diner was *old.* Not retro-cool- refurbished old. Just plain old. Ancient tobacco smoke clung to grease stained walls. Formica tabletops bore the scars of former teens, with "love 4ever" etched onto their surface. A phone booth, the kind that Clark Kent used to morph into Super Man, stood vacant in a corner.

Janine sat opposite me in a booth in the back of the diner. She wore a bright pink uniform which clashed with her auburn hair. The outfit was very snug and made her breasts look enormous.

"Don't you have to wait on people or something?" I asked.

Janine's eyes swept the restaurant. "Nah. They're good. Anyway, they know where to find me if they need something. "I'm right here if you need anything," she called out. "See? They're fine."

I picked up my fork and stared hungrily at the plate in front of me. It was piled high with turkey, and mashed potatoes, succotash, dressing, and a dollop of jellied cranberry sauce. It gave me a sense of well-being just looking at it. No wonder they call it comfort food.

The potatoes were creamy white with the hole in the middle that stored the extra gravy. I speared some turkey with my fork and dipped it into the potatoes. Sheer heaven.

"So anyway," I said in between bites. "I was walking out to my car and a police cruiser stopped in front of the house. Guess who the cop was. Nancy Beringer," I blurted out before she could open her mouth.

Janine is terrible at guessing games. She always comes up with answers that can't possibly be right. Like, if the question is, "What is America's most popular ice cream flavor?" she'll say pistachio, thinking it's a trick question or something. You never want her on your team on game night.

Janine's eyes narrowed. "How come the cops are keeping tabs on your house? I thought they arrested the jerk that shot it up."

"They did. And I really thought that would be the end of it."

I forked up some succotash, careful to avoid the lima beans, and gestured to Janine to help herself.

"Y'know, once a little time had gone by and nothing else happened, I figured I was off the hook. But then somebody started a rumor that I shut down a local dog fighting ring, and it pissed off the gang all over again."

"Rumor. Right. So, is that why you're here instead of home in bed?"

I nodded, embarrassed by the confession. "I don't know which sucks worse, anymore. My nightmares or my real life."

"You know I'm here for you, hon. Just tell me what you need."

I put down my fork and pushed the plate away, having suddenly lost my appetite. "I don't know, Janine. I've been screwing up so badly lately."

Janine leaned in to hear me as my voice sank to a whisper. "Bobby once said he thought I had a death wish...I don't...do I?"

Neenie made a face. "You don't believe that any more than I do...or any more than Bobby does for that matter. Bran, if you hadn't helped Dave Wolinski when he got shot he would have died. I wouldn't exactly call that screwing up. And what about the puppy you saved from an abusive owner? Not to mention all the poor dogs that were forced into fighting. Sweetie, you had to do something. I mean what kind of a person would you be if you let those assholes get away with it?"

"You're right. What kind of a person would I be? And that night at Donte Lewis' house? That was just a case of unfortunate timing."

"No, that was just stupid. Look, I get off in a few hours. Why don't you sack out here? When I'm done with my shift we can go back to my place."

The turkey had a relaxing effect on me. Plus, Janine really had helped me to view my life through a different perspective—one where I didn't come off feeling like an impulsive loser, but rather a credit to humanity.

"Okay. I'm just going to stretch out here for a while," I told her. "But I'm way too keyed up to fall asleep." I put my feet up on the booth and laid my head down. And in the next instant I was out like a proverbial light.

*****

Having slept for three hours in the fetal position on a rock hard booth at the diner, I was not exactly ready to face the day. It would save me a trip to the D.A.'s office and the price of a dozen bagels if Roger agreed to talk to Vince.

"Roger, it's Brandy Alexander. Is Candice there? Can you talk?"

Roger King's rich baritone erupted in laughter. "Candice is right here, but it's okay. I told her all about that night a few days after I met with you. I figured if she found out I'd kept something from her, she'd give it to me worse than anything those gang bangers could come up with. Ow, stop hitting me, woman! So, Brandy, what can I do for you?"

I filled Roger in on the autopsy results and ended with my conversation with Vince. "It might really help with the investigation if you'd talk to him, Roger. But the last thing I want is to put you in danger."

"Candice has been trying to get me to do the same thing," he admitted. "I'll give your friend in the D.A.'s office a call. Maybe when they find Lewis' cousin we'll be able to put all this behind us."

I truly hoped it would be that simple.

"I'll tell you this much," he continued. "It's been a hell of a lot quieter around here since Mario's been gone."

"How's his family doing?" Now that my bruises had healed I felt slightly more kindly toward his girlfriend. I suspected Sherese might not be the most balanced person in the world on a good day. But grief over the loss of her significant other, no matter how much of a worm he was, had to be hell.

"Every so often Candice goes to check on the kids. She brings them casseroles that the little girl can reheat without too much trouble. Lord knows their mother ain't fit for nothin'. Ow. There she goes hitting me again. Candice, you know it's true."

"It may be true," his wife said, taking over the phone, "but it's not very charitable. She's younger than our Kendra. She's got no education, no family—'cept her children—and the state keeps threatening to take them away. Maybe they'd be better off, but that's not for me to decide."

Thinking about Sherese's young children made my stomach hurt. "There has to be something I can do to help them," I thought. And the battle between my alter egos was on.

"Do not get involved," warned Sensible Me.

135

"But in a civilized society, that's what we do. We help each other," countered Impulsive (and apparently, more compassionate) Me.

Note to self: Google Multiple Personality Disorder.

Anyway," Candice announced, "I've got some chocolate chip cookies baking in the oven, and I know how much you like them." She allowed herself a small chuckle. "If you find yourself in the neighborhood…"

"Thanks for the offer. I may take you up on it."

I was saying my goodbyes when someone knocked on my door.

Adrian and the puppy raced me down the stairs. I nudged them out of the way and took a quick look out the peep hole.

Paul stood on the steps wearing a Classic Rock tee-shirt and a red Phillies cap. I opened the wooden door and unlatched the screen. Next door, Mrs. Gentile slammed hers shut.

"What's with Mrs. Gentile? She called me a hooligan." Paul took off his cap and stepped inside.

"Maybe she's still mad about the time you accidentally broke her window with a Frisbee."

"Really? It's been like fifteen years. You'd think she'd be over it by now. Besides, I told her it was you."

Paul drifted toward the sofa. I'd put Hello Kitty Band-Aids over the bullet holes, because I didn't have the money to get the couch fixed. I thought they added a touch of whimsy.

"Why do you have Band-Aids all over your couch?" He sat down and inspected them.

"They're not Band-Aids. They're art. It's all the rage. So, how come you're here? I mean I'm glad to see you, but you never leave the club. Are you feeling okay?"

"I'm fine. I was thinking about going for a jog, and it would be nice to have some company."

"Oh. Well, I guess I could use the exercise…but I'm not much of a jogger. Could we meander instead?"

"Um, Bran, I meant, could I borrow the puppy. You can come along too, if you want. But I know you're busy with…" he looked desperately around the room. "…stuff."

"Paul, I've been out of work for weeks. The last thing I am is busy. But if you don't want my company—"And then it dawned on me. "Ohhh. You want to take the puppy so you can pick up girls." I grinned. "You devil."

Paul turned a deep shade of pink. "Well, you're the one who suggested it in the first place."

"Because it works. Who can resist a puppy? Paulie, it's fool-proof. And you're right, I can't tag along. Girls will think you're unavailable."

"Okay, could we please change the subject now? It's embarrassing enough. Oh, hey. I was down at Lorenzo's Music on Locust and I ran into John and Garrett. They were going into a hair salon."

"Oh, I know the one you mean. It's supposed to be real cutting edge," I said, and waited for my incredibly clever comment to sink in. Paul just groaned. My brother needs to work on his sense of humor. That was hilarious.

"Anyway, speaking of Garrett, what do you think of him?" I tried to sound light-hearted, to covey that I thought he was just swell, and that I was asking merely for conversational purposes.

"He seems like a nice guy." Paul stood up. "I should probably get going. Where's the leash?"

"Hey. Where are you going in such a hurry? We hardly ever spend time together. So, where were we? Oh, yeah. You were saying that Garrett seems just okay."

Paul began to sweat. "I said he seems nice. L-look, I don't want to have this discussion. Now, if you'll g-get me the leash—"

"What discussion? I was just asking for your honest opinion. John is one of your oldest friends. I would think you'd show more of an interest."

Paul sat down, defeated. "Ok-k-ay. You're not going to

stop pushing, so w-we m-might as well get this over w-with." He took a deep, cleansing breath. "You're my sister, and I love you, but—for some people, well, l-l-let's just say you're an acquired taste."

"An acquired taste? You make me sound like aged gorgonzola—which Garrett probably loves, the pretentious twit. God, Paulie. I want to like him. I really do. But it would really, really help if he liked me back. Hey, I know. John says he's an opera buff. Maybe season tickets to the Academy of Music…"

Paul stood again. "I'm sure you'll think of just the right gift to buy Garrett's affections. But in the mean time my throat is beginning to close up from all the dog fur on the rug. Don't you ever vacuum?"

"Who has time? I'm too busy trying to buy Garrett's affections."

Paul winced. "I'm sorry. I didn't mean it."

"Yes, you did. And the worst part is you're right. No," I corrected myself. "The worst part is it hasn't worked."

"Y'know what?" Paul grabbed my arm and yanked me off the couch. "I've changed my mind. I want you to come along. I haven't had much luck lately. Maybe you can find someone nice for me."

"Really? Because I don't want to intrude. Let me go get my jogging shoes."

I was half way up the stairs when my conscience kicked in. Stupid conscience.

I turned around and went back downstairs. "Actually, I think I'll pass on this excursion. I'm busy with…stuff." I handed Paul the leash. "Go get 'em, cowboy."

*****

The next day started off promising. Nick called. *Yay, yippee, yahoo! Great, great, great!* It's not that I'm insecure…exactly. But our relationship was still new and completely undefined. I didn't know what was reasonable to expect.

Did Nick consider himself my boyfriend? Did I call

him too much? Did he call me enough? Were we exclusive? God, I hoped so. I mean it wasn't much of a stretch for me, given my lackluster love life, pre-Santiago. But was I now Nick's one and only? Would it be rude to ask? We had a lot to sort out, but for now I was content that he'd called. It meant he still liked me.

"How was your trip to…" I let the sentence hang in the air in hopes that he'd fill in the blank. He didn't.

"It was fine, Angel" His voice held a smile, and it warmed me.

I've canceled my classes at the studio today. I thought you might want to take a ride out to Ambler to see Popeye."

How did he know? The dog had been weighing heavily on my mind, but I didn't want to face that heartbreak alone.

"That would be great."

"I'll pick you up in an hour."

Let's see…walk the dogs, shower, wax, pluck…oy. "An hour and a half okay?"

"See you then."

*****

We took Nick's truck. It was a nice change of pace from the La Sabre, whose senior moments now included a broken gas gauge and an oil leak. I leaned my head back in the seat, content to steal glances at the man beside me. Nick drove with one hand on the wheel, the other resting on my thigh. I shifted in my seat, ever so slightly, and his hand fell between my legs and stayed there. I wondered if he knew I'd done it on purpose. By the smile on his face, I'd say he did.

"So, what's new, Darlin'?" he asked, as his fingers made skillful use of their new location.

"Um, not much." His touch intensified and I let slip an audible moan. "I've missed this—I mean—you. I've missed you."

Nick's smile deepened. I knew I should tell him about

the autopsy results and the latest threat on my life, only—when I thought about it, what was the rush?

Just as things started to get really interesting, a SEPTA bus bolted out in front of us and then slowed to a stop. Nick lifted his hand from between my legs and swung wide to get out of its way. After that, he left both hands on the wheel. I was really disappointed. Stupid bus.

Except for the fact that one of us was carrying concealed, and the other was a V.I.P. on the J.T.G. top ten hit list we were just like any other couple, out enjoying the Montgomery County country-side on a beautiful summer day.

I wanted to indulge myself for a bit in this idyllic fantasy, but as we drew closer to Jacob's Place, I was seized by anxiety. A question that had plagued me since the night of the dog fight loomed large in my mind. And before I could stop myself, it just popped out.

"Nick, if I hadn't been there that night down by the naval yard…would you have—"

Nick pulled over to the side of the road and turned off the engine. He unbuckled his seat belt and angled himself so that his head rested against the window. He closed his eyes, briefly, and when he opened them again, he looked into mine. And I knew that whatever he said to me, it wouldn't be a lie.

His voice sounded husky, as if he'd just woken up from a deep sleep. "You want to know if I would've killed that guy."

I nodded.

"I would like to be able to say no, Angel, but the truth is, I just don't know."

I sat there in silence, taking it all in. Then, that old, Alexander, look-on-the-bright-side spirit kicked in. "Eh. It could be worse. Let's just take that as a no."

*****

Judy Harrison filled us in on Popeye's progress (or lack, thereof) as she led the way to the kennels.

"Popeye began eating on his own, but he's so distrustful of humans he won't let any of the staff members near him. He becomes very agitated when anyone goes inside his cage, and he actually attacked one of our employees. It's gotten so bad that no one wants to work with him."

His appearance hadn't changed much since the last time I'd seen him. But the apathy had been replaced by aggressive agitation. He began pacing back and forth in his kennel as we approached.

I watched him for a few minutes and then turned away, remembering what Judy had said the first time I'd met her. *Sometimes the damage runs so deep it's a lost cause.* The thought filled me with sadness. I'd go back to her office and make a donation I couldn't afford and be on my way.

Judy must've noticed the look of dejection on my face and she took pity on me. "Hey, one of our dogs just had puppies. Let's go take a look." She linked arms with me and pulled me toward one of the newer buildings. I glanced back at Nick as he lingered near Popeye's cage.

"You coming?" I asked.

"In a minute."

We were about to enter the building when Mrs. Harrison looked back in utter shock. Nick had opened Popeye's locked kennel door and entered the cage.

"Hey," she protested, and began running back toward the kennels.

Nick cautioned her away with a swift shake of his head. Judy stood and watched, as if hypnotized.

Without hesitation Nick strode over to a bench and sat down, and turned his back on the snarling dog. He sat motionless for several minutes, while Popeye, back hairs bristling up and down his spine, circled him, sniffed the air, and finally, lay down at Nick's feet.

They sat that way for about twenty minutes. I was equal parts scared to death that Nick would be eaten alive, and impressed as hell with what I'd just witnessed.

Careful not to make eye contact, Nick slowly let his arm drop to his side. Popeye raised his head, his one good eye watching Nick. After a moment, he sniffed his hand and then licked it. And then, Popeye rolled over on his back in submission.

"No one is going to believe this," Judy Harrison whispered, trembling. "This is nothing short of a miracle."

That was Nick. An enigma wrapped in a miracle.

*****

On our way back from Jacob's Place, we swung by Nick's martial arts studio. It's not in the swankiest part of town, but, somehow, his storefront has managed to remain free of the usual signs of urban street life. Nick pulled up to the curb and hopped out.

"I'll only be a minute. Do you want to come in or wait for me here?"

I wasn't totally in love with the idea of waiting in the car, but my phone rang just as I reached for the door handle. It was Janine.

"Guess I'll wait in the car." I watched him as he disappeared into the studio.

"What's up, Neenie?" Absently, I began rooting through Nick's c.d.'s. I picked up one by an artist I'd never heard of, with a name I couldn't pronounce. The words on the cover looked Russian.

"I was just thinking. I still owe you a birthday present. What do you want? And don't say *nothing, or peace on Earth,* or other shit I can't really give you."

"Janine, my birthday was three months ago."

"I know. But I have something to tell you, and I don't want you to be mad. I thought if I got you a nice gift, it would soften the blow."

"Just tell me," I sighed. "But if it's about who accidentally threw my ipod down the garbage disposal, I already know it was you."

"How did you know? I replaced it that same afternoon."

"Yeah. With one you bought off that illegal street vendor down at 17th and Market. By the way, he sells ipuds, not ipods."

"Oh. Well, that wasn't it anyway, so I may as well tell you. Mike and I are going out again."

"That's great! Why would I be mad?"

"Because Mike thought it might be fun to make it a foursome, this time, and—"

"Wow. Janine. I don't know about this. I mean, maybe down the line Nick and I could go out with you guys, but it seems a bit premature right now."

Janine's relief was palpable. "Okay, well, just thought I'd ask. Hey! Since we thought of you first, and you did turn us down, I guess you won't mind if we ask Bobby and that cop he's going out with. Right?" She ended, hopefully.

"You guys are going out with Bobby and Lauren?"

"Just say the word, Bran, and we'll cancel."

"Janine, don't be ridiculous. I'm not one bit upset. Why would I be? I was just surprised is all. I've met her. She's nice. Listen, I've gotta go. I'll call you later. We'll do lunch."

We'll do lunch? Why am I talking like a Hollywood agent from like 1993?

Nick got back into the car before I had time to process what Janine had told me. Which meant I blurted out the first thing that came to my head. "Nick, I think we should arrange a double date."

Nick pulled his seat belt over his shoulder and started the engine, checked the rear view mirror and eased into traffic. "A double date? As in dinner and bridge with the couple down the block?"

Okay, when he put it that way it sounded really lame. "Not exactly. I mean—" What did I mean? Unhh. I felt left out. Pure and simple.

"I should get to know your friends. And I want you to know mine. We could go to brunch, or meet for coffee…"

Shut up. Shut up. This is way too soon. I'm scaring him. I can see it in his eyes. "Y'know what? Ha, ha. I was only kidding. I hate bridge. And my friends are boring. Let's just—"

"It's a good idea, Angel. We'll do something in your world, and then we'll do something in mine."

What? Is he crazy? This a terrible idea. His friends run the gamut from rich, influential, society folk, to people you get in touch with on the sly when you want someone whacked. And I don't know which group intimidates me more.

"Um, well, we can talk about it later." *Because right now I have to think about how to get myself out of this.*

The thing is I was scared. What if the whole experiment in 'worlds-mixing' blew up in my face? DiCarlo certainly wasn't a fan of Nick's. Uncle Frankie had reserved judgment, but whenever I brought up his name, there was a definite upsurge of tension in the air. Carla— well, she was a fan. But I don't think that would score any points with Uncle Frankie, seeing as I'd met Nick through Carla. Carla knew him in her pre-Frankie days, and they may have been more than passing acquaintances. I really didn't want to know.

Nick popped in a Tom Waits c.d. and we suspended conversation for the length of Heartattack and Vine. We rounded the corner of my block just as Tom warbled the last notes of "Ruby's Arms."

DiCarlo's car was parked out in front of my house. He was leaning against his Mustang, arms folded, legs crossed. It was anybody's guess how long he'd been there. All I knew for sure was he didn't look happy.

CHAPTER ELEVEN

In point of fact he looked downright pissed off.

"Well, this is fortuitous," Nick said, mildly. "No time like the present to start the bonding process." I couldn't tell if he was just yanking my chain, but I figured it was best to weather this particular storm alone.

"Maybe not such a good idea, Nick." I couldn't imagine what Bobby would possibly be mad about. I hadn't done anything, in…what? *Days!* "How about I see what's up with DiCarlo, and I'll call you later."

In response Nick pulled alongside Bobby's car and popped the gear into neutral. DiCarlo looked up as Nick pulled me to him. His mouth brushed the nape of my neck, sending chills down my spine "If you're sure, Darlin'."

"I, um…" I caught the tail end of a devilish grin as he closed in on me and kissed me for all it was worth.

Now, I'm not normally one for PDA, but in this case, I made an exception. Nick was staking a claim, which I found oddly endearing. Maybe he felt the tiniest bit threatened by Bobby. Or maybe I'm just so darn irresistible he simply couldn't help himself. Okay, that probably wasn't it. I finally chalked it up to the alpha male tug-of -war between the two of them that had been going on since they'd first laid eyes on each other. Still, it was one hell of a kiss.

When Nick finally let me go, he was still smiling. "Tell DiCarlo to brush up on his bridge game."

As I opened the door to get out, Nick touched two fingers to his forehead in salute to Bobby and drove off.

Bobby launched himself off the car and met me at the curb. "Was that display for my benefit?"

"Yes. Yes, it was. In fact, Nick only kisses me when you're around, so stick close." *God, I hate it when he's right.*

I shielded my eyes from the sun and looked up at him. The left side of his cheek was swollen and bruised, with the beginnings of a spectacular shiner settling just under his eye. His dark hair curled at the ends and hung limply over his collar. His jeans were ripped at the knee, and blood oozed from a nasty scrape.

"Bobby, what happened?"

"Had a run-in with a perp. He was all hopped up on meth." Bobby laughed, but not because it was funny. "The asshole was still holding the knife. It was covered in the blood of the woman he'd just stabbed. He swore she accidentally ran into it. Twelve times."

I dug around in my bag for my first aid kit, but all it held was a fuzzy band aid and an unwrapped cough drop.

"C'mon in the house and I'll take care of your knee for you."

He shook his head. "Nah. I've got to get going. I just came by because you weren't answering your phone. Jesus, Brandy, people try to get a hold of you, they get worried. Y'know?"

"Why are you getting so bent out of shape? I must've turned if off after talking to Janine. Has something happened? Is Paulie all right?"

"It's not about Paul, okay? It's about you." Bobby paced the sidewalk for a bit and then leaned back against his car again. He shoved his hands into his back pockets, causing the material in front to stretch tight across his crotch. Not that I noticed…much.

"I met Vince for a beer last night, and he told me the rumor about the Junk Town Gang getting ready to make its move. He also said you knew about it."

"Well, that Vince is a regular Chatty Cathy, isn't he?"

"Knock off the jokes, Sweetheart. This is serious."

"You think I don't know that? It's on my mind every minute of every day. But what am I supposed to do? Stop living just so they don't have the pleasure of killing me themselves?"

My voice went all soprano, so I took it down a notch. "Bobby, I'm scared shitless. Is that what you want me to say? Fine. But I am not going into hiding. I could be there the rest of my life."

"Well, where the hell's Santiago off to? Why aren't you staying with him?"

"Who says I'm not?"

"Janine. I spoke with her, too."

"Are you freakin' kidding me? Who else did you talk to?" I whipped out my phone and tried to scroll down my contact list. I'd planned to wave it in his face, as I yelled sarcastically, "Did you miss anyone?" Only, I forgot my phone was turned off.

I shoved it back in my bag.

"So, why aren't you staying at Nick's? Not that you'd be much better off," he grumbled under his breath, just loud enough for me to hear it.

"Maybe he has faith in my ability to take care of myself," I shouted.

"Then he's an idiot."

Whoa. Dead silence, followed by the sound of Robert Anthony DiCarlo trying to suck the words back into his mouth. "Fuck. I'm sorry. I keep forgetting you're not my business anymore."

A punch in the gut probably would've hurt less. I started to walk away, but he latched onto my arm and spun me around. "Shit, Brandy. You know I didn't mean that, either. At least not the way it sounded."

I shook his arm off and sat down on the front step. I knew he didn't mean it. Not really. And anyway, that wasn't the problem. "Nick isn't here because I didn't tell him."

Bobby joined me on the step. "Why not?"

"Because *I'm* an idiot."

DiCarlo put his arm around my shoulder. "It's too soon in the relationship and you don't want to get overly dependent on him. You're afraid of scaring him away. How am I doing so far?"

"You're batting a thousand, kid." I stood up. "Let's go inside before Mrs. Gentile falls out of her upstairs window. Hi, Mrs.Gentile." I waved up at my neighbor, and she waved back, using just her middle finger. I considered ratting her out to Father Vincenzo, but he'd never believe me.

Bobby followed me up the walk and waited while I rummaged through my bag for my keys. On the other side of the door, Rocky meowed in anticipation. She was desperate to get to DiCarlo.

My cat is in love with Bobby DiCarlo, and she doesn't care who knows it. As soon as he walked through the door, she was all over him like a cheap, furry, little suit.

"How's my girl?" DiCarlo bent down to pet her.

"Your girl chewed a hole through my computer cord. I'm not too thrilled with her at the moment." I headed upstairs. "Just going to get some antiseptic for your knee. Be right back."

When I came back down, I found Bobby sitting at the dining room table. He was holding a sketch pad in his hand. "What's this," he asked. He pointed to a childlike rendering of what appeared to be an alien with spaghetti all over his face.

"Oh, that," I said and tried to grab it from him. "It's nothing."

He held the pad aloft and began to turn the pages. "Did you draw these?"

"I've got a lot of time on my hands. I decided to take an art class. Could you close that, please? I'm not ready to show my work."

I knelt down by his leg and rooted through the first aid kit for antiseptic. He wouldn't put down the damn sketch pad, so I chose the one that stings.

"Hold still." I swabbed his knee.

"Jesus Christ," he hollered and jumped up. "What are you putting on there? Gasoline?"

"Oh, stop being such a baby. And will you please put that thing down?"

I covered his wound with a bandage and stood up.

Bobby gazed at the pictures for a moment longer. "Shit," he said, getting it. "You're trying to draw that burn victim, aren't you?"

"Well, so what?" I countered. The best defense is a well played offense. Unfortunately, I had neither.

The little vein in Bobby's temple began its ritualistic dance. "Leave it alone, Bran. You're in enough trouble without borrowing any more." He walked back into the living room.

"Bobby, I know this guy. At least, I think I do. The cops haven't been able to identify him. How can this possibly get me into trouble?"

"If there's a way, you'll find it."

His back was to me. I wanted to plant my foot on his well-formed ass and push him down. Instead, I flung open my screen door.

"Great to see you, DiCarlo. Sorry you can't stay longer."

A flash of anger crossed his beautiful face. "You know what? Do whatever the hell you want. You will anyway." He stepped outside and I started to slam the door behind him, except that I hadn't gotten the last word in. I followed him outside and down the walkway.

"You think you know everything, don't you?" I yelled.

Only he had stopped listening. Bobby's eyes were trained on a tricked out, dark colored sedan parked across the street. His brow furrowed as the car slowly pulled away from the curb.

The car windows were tinted, as if it belonged to royalty or the Godfather, and the license plate was spattered with mud. Instinctively, I memorized the numbers and letters that were still visible.

"Do you have new neighbors?"

I scrunched my eyes to get a better look, and as I did so, I noticed the passenger side window start to go down. Bobby, almost imperceptibly maneuvered himself between me and the car.

In an instant, a gleaming piece of metal appeared at the car window. Simultaneously, I felt Bobby's full weight, and he slammed me to the ground as a hail of bullets passed over us.

I knew Bobby was alive because I felt his heart thumping against my back. I opened my eyes and looked for blood and found plenty. I truly hoped it was mine.

"Are you okay? Oh my God, Bobby. You saved my life."

DiCarlo rolled off me and stood up. He scanned the street, but the car was long gone. He looked down at me and grimaced.

"Try not to panic, Sweetheart, but you're bleeding. I'm not sure where it's coming from."

"I do." My arm felt like someone had set it on fire.

Gingerly, he rolled me over. "Okay, here's the problem," he said, and picked a chunk of Mrs. Gentile's terracotta planter out of my shoulder. She was going to be so mad.

"This'll need stitches. And probably a tetanus shot. There's another piece still embedded in your arm."

"Can you get it out? It really hurts."

Bobby shook his head. "I'm afraid if I do, I won't be

able to stem the bleeding. Where are your house keys?"

"On top of the TV."

Five minutes later I was strapped into DiCarlo's mustang, on our way to the E.R. He'd packed my shoulder with clean strips of laundry he'd found hanging off Mrs. Gentile's wash line. I shouldn't have gotten such a kick out of that, and I knew I'd pay for it later, but at the moment, it made me laugh. Probably just delirium setting in.

The pain was making me dizzy. "Are we there yet?" I whined.

"Are we there yet?" he repeated. "You sound like my three-year old."

I knew Bobby was trying to start a fight in order to keep my mind off things, but it wasn't working. It hurt like a mutha. Every bump in the road was like a direct shot in the arm.

After what felt like an eternity, we turned into the entrance of the E.R. I sat up in the seat and, suddenly, my head felt like it was going to explode. "Bobby," I shouted.

"Hang tight, Sweetheart. We're almost there."

"No. I mean—this is it. This is where I know the dead guy from!"

"What?" He parked his car in a no parking lane and popped a mag mount beacon on the roof. Then, he climbed out of the car and ran around to the passenger side to let me out.

I clung to his arm with my one good hand, as blood seeped out of my right shoulder. "The dead guy—y'know, Crispy Critter. He was a guard at the hospital."

"Are you sure?"

"Positive. I spoke to him."

"What's his name?"

I tried to picture his name tag, but drew a blank.

"Bobby, I need to sit down." I was starting to get the chills.

"We're so close, Sweetheart. Just a few more steps."

"O—"

151

I woke up on a gurney in a cubicle. A young, male nurse stood over me waving smelling salts under my nose. It made me nauseous, so I pushed his hand away and sat up.

"Take it easy. You lost a fair amount of blood." He eased me back down and made notes on my chart. "The doctor will be with you in a minute. In the mean time I'm going to clean your wound."

I looked around for Bobby, but he was nowhere in sight.

"Excuse, me. Where's that guy I came in with?"

The nurse cut away at the sleeve of my tee shirt. Damn. It was one of my favorites. Classic Firesign Theater.

"Your friend's in the hall. I'll get him for you when I'm through."

Bobby peeked in from the other side of the curtain. "How're you feeling, Sweetheart?"

"Fine. Great." I felt a sudden, sticking pain in my shoulder. "Ow. What was that?"

"Something to numb your arm," the nurse said. "This should take effect in a few minutes." He finished cleaning the wound and signaled for Bobby to enter.

"Keep her company, will you?"

Bobby looked like he could have used a gurney himself. I'd forgotten that as tough as he was, the sight of blood made him woozy.

"Bobby. I'm fine. Really. You don't have to stick around. A couple of stitches and some antibiotics and I'll be good to go."

"I brought you here, I'm taking you home. Well, where I'm taking you is up for debate. You're not going back there."

DiCarlo's phone rang, interrupting my protest before I could get rolling. He looked at the readout and walked toward the curtain. "Be right back," he said, and disappeared outside.

Funny thing about curtains. They're not much good at

keeping out sound. I didn't even have to strain to listen in on his conversation.

"Yo," he said. "Yeah… I ran into a little problem…no, we're still on. It's just going to take a little longer is all. I'll pick up some pizza and wine on my way home… Yeah, me too."

I fished my phone out of my pocket and stuck it against my ear, just as Bobby walked back through the curtain.

"Oh, that would be great, Nick." I positively gushed with girlish enthusiasm. "Half an hour? Perfect."

The nurse did a double take, probably checking to see if my brain had seeped out of the wound in my shoulder. I ignored him and kept talking.

"Steak and baked potato sound wonderful. I'll see you soon." I pretend-disconnected and smiled at the phone as if we'd just had sex.

"Well, I guess you won't be needing a ride after all." DiCarlo shoved his phone into his back pocket. I couldn't tell if he was relieved or annoyed. Maybe a touch of both.

"Bobby," I said, and started to well up. (I'm sure it was the anesthetics. Everyone knows lidocaine makes you cry.) "Look, um…"

Robert Anthony DiCarlo, my first love, peered at me with such intensity, I nearly lost it.

"What I'm trying to say is—" *Unh!* "Look," I blurted out in a rush, "you could have been killed today, because of me. And you ended up saving my life. I—I don't know what I'd do if anything ever happened to you."

Bobby crossed the room and held me close. Half of me was comforted by his warmth. The other half was, literally, too numb feel it.

"Nothing's going to happen to me, okay?"

I nodded, unconvinced. "Okay." I wiped my tears with the back of my hand. "You can go now."

Bobby kissed me and let me go. "So, I'll see you soon then."

I nodded again. "See ya."

He reached the curtain and then spun on his heel and came back the other way.

"Nothing," he repeated, and kissed me again. And then he left.

I felt a pair of eyes on me. I'd forgotten the nurse was still in the room.

"What are you lookin' at?"

*****

When I was sure Bobby was gone for good I called Nick.

"Hello, Darlin'."

I could just make out the murmur of some deep, masculine voices in the background.

"You busy?"

"Just finishing up. How was your visit with DiCarlo? Were you able to smooth any ruffled feathers?"

"Yeah, everything's cool...listen, there's been a little accident."

Instantly, Nick's tone changed from playful teasing to high alert.

"Are you okay? Where are you?"

"At the E.R. Look, I'm fine. Really. I was just calling to see if you could pick me up. But if you're in the middle of something, I can grab a cab."

"I'll be there in twenty minutes."

He was there in ten.

"That was fast." I slapped on my "brave" face—the one my mother used to say fools no one—but it was the best I could do under the circumstances.

If Nick noticed, he didn't let on. "I know how impatient you are. If I got here any later, you might have tried to jog home."

I laughed, mostly because it was true.

He ran his eyes over my bandaged shoulder. "You were in one piece when I left you, this afternoon, Darlin'. What happened?"

154

"Funny story." We walked back to the car, and I told him how I'd acquired my latest injury. When I got to the part where Bobby saved me from the gunman's bullets, Nick's jaw tightened. A fractional change in expression, but it was enough to set off my internal alarm.

I tried to make light of what happened by cracking a joke. Only it's hard to spin getting shot at into an amusing dinner party anecdote. I abandoned the effort and changed the subject.

"When I called it sounded like you were busy. Anything interesting going on?"

"I was on the street talking to some of my contacts. There was a rumor going around about a possible JTG hit." He turned to face me, his look somber. "Turned out to be more than a rumor. I shouldn't have left you alone."

"Nick, you couldn't possibly have known. And anyway, I wasn't alone. It was just bad timing."

We had reached the car. Nick held open the passenger door and waited while I maneuvered myself into the seat. Then, he leaned over and buckled me in. I could have done it myself, but I let him.

The lidocaine had just about worn off, and the pain meds hadn't had a chance to kick in yet. I shifted in my seat and tried to ignore the uncomfortable pull of stitches in my shoulder.

Nick was unusually quiet on the ride back. He stared straight ahead, both hands gripping the wheel. The silence was unnerving. It was probably only about four minutes, but it seemed like an hour. I wondered what he was thinking. Note to self: Take mind reading lessons.

Finally, he broke the silence. "I'm glad DiCarlo was there for you, Angel."

I leaned over and kissed his cheek. His skin felt smooth and warm on my lips.

The corners of Nick's mouth relaxed and he dropped one hand off the wheel and onto my knee. I put my hand on top of his, our fingers intertwined.

The last vestiges of day time began to slip away. A new moon hung in the sky like a giant croissant, reminding me that I hadn't eaten dinner. "I'm hungry," I announced.

He swung the car around and we headed east on Spring Garden. I watched, longingly, as we passed about four Dunkin Donuts and a McDonald's. When we got to 3rd Street, he hung a u-ie and drove back the other way. A block later he pulled up in front of a tricked out diner and parked. We were in the Northern Liberties section of town, just north of Center City. I read the neon sign on the roof. *Silk City*.

The place was ultra cool and jam-packed with college students, young professionals, and artsy types. There was a bar and dance club to the left and a restaurant on the right.

I followed Nick to the dining area, where, miraculously, a booth opened up. (Well, maybe not so miraculously. It probably had more to do with the host's rather obvious attraction to Nick than an ability to turn water into wine.)

Nick sat across from me, his back to the wall. "I've been thinking about what happened tonight, Angel, and something doesn't add up."

I took a look at the menu. Ooh. Truffle fries. I promised myself I'd eat super healthy in the near future and ordered a giant plateful. "What doesn't add up?"

"It seemed like everyone I talked to heard the rumor about the hit, but no one had any specifics. This isn't how it usually works."

"Well, maybe they just weren't into ratting out a fellow gang banger."

"They will if the price is right. It just doesn't fit the pattern that nobody would claim bragging rights." He shook his head, thinking.

"I got a partial on the license plate, but I should have paid more attention to details."

"You were a little busy trying to stay alive. Give me what you've got on the plate and I'll see what I can do."

After dinner Nick swung by my place to pick up the dogs and Rocky and waited while I threw some things in a bag. It was getting to be quite the routine. When I was all packed he drove me over to his apartment.

I followed him into the bedroom and he deposited my bags on the floor. Suddenly, all the tension I'd felt earlier flooded back. *What if he doesn't want me there, only he doesn't know how to tell me?* I sat on his bed, smoothing out the sheets with my hand.

"Nick, I really appreciate you letting me stay here for a while, but I have other options. So, if you need your space, just let me know."

He stood over me, the look in his eyes saying it all. "I don't need my space, Angel." And to prove it, he invaded mine.

Afterwards, he rolled over on his side and propped himself up on one arm. I spooned into him, relaxed by the combination of superb love making and prescription pain killers. It was sheer bliss—for about a minute. And then my phone rang. It was my mother. Crap.

I had to pick up. She'd left fourteen messages. "Hey, Mom. What's up?" I could feel Nick's breath, hot on my back. He pressed his lips against me, and I felt them form a smile.

"Doris Gentile called. She said you broke her planter."

*****

"He kissed you?" Franny stood wide-eyed at the counter of Caperelli's Guns & Ammo, a local gun shop located at 10th and Wharton. My goddaughter, Chrissy, snuggled in close to Fran's chest, asleep in her baby carrier, while her mother checked out an array of unloaded pistols and revolvers, "especially designed with ladies in mind."

"It's not what you think, Fran. There was nothing romantic about it. It was just a spontaneous, *Hey-I'm -glad-we're-alive-let's-kiss-on-it kiss.*"

"Uh huh."

"Shut-uh-up. We could've been killed, for God's sake."

"Hey, you and Bobby have a unique way of celebrating life. That's all I'm sayin'."

That was not all Fran was saying. And the worst part was she had a point. Something stirred inside me when DiCarlo kissed me. It didn't begin to be on the same level as me and Nick, but there was just enough there to leave me wondering if we'd ever completely reconcile our past.

"Could we drop this now?"

"Already dropped. Okay, this is the one you want." Fran handed me a Smith & Wesson 638 Bodyguard, a small, .38 caliber revolver.

"It's not loaded, right?" I frowned, holding it loosely between my thumb and forefinger.

"Of course it isn't loaded. And why are you handling it like it's a flaming bag of dog poop? Hold it like you mean it." She wrapped her hand around mine and adjusted my grip. My hand started to shake so hard I nearly dropped the damn thing.

"Brandy, what is wrong with you? You go to the firing range all the time."

"I know. But this is different. I was hitting paper targets. If I actually go through with this, I will forever have crossed a line. The sole purpose for me owning a gun would be the intent to do bodily harm to someone before they did it to me."

"Yeah, well, that seems like a good plan, hon."

"I guess."

Franny pried the gun out of my hand and laid it on the counter. "Look, if you're not absolutely sure, then you shouldn't be doing this. If you carry a weapon, you need to know without a shadow of a doubt that you will use it. A moment's hesitation could cost you your life."

I thought about the parade of people that have attempted to kill me over the past year. An ax murderer, a knife-wielding crack addict, an incestuous obstetrician, and a freckle-faced pimp that looked like Howdy Doody. Not to mention Mario and his gang of merry men. It was getting old.

I picked up the Smith & Wesson and turned to the clerk. "How much?"

*****

On the way back from Caperelli's we stopped off at a children's store to get some things for Chrissy. "It's important that we stimulate her intellectually," Fran told me. "I don't want her to get bored."

"Fran, she's a month old. Her idea of a good time is eating her feet. Ooh, look, a slinky!"

I picked out a stuffed pink hippo for my goddaughter and a pair of booties in the shape of cupcakes. Then, I wandered over to the older kids' section. A black and white hobby horse was stationed at the end of an aisle. A little boy, about two years old was strapped into the plastic saddle, and he was rocking back and forth. A woman stood next to him, her cart filled to the brim with toddler toys.

My thoughts wandered back to Sherese's little boy, riding the back of the filthy couch that was parked in front of their house. On impulse, I walked over and checked the price on the hobby horse. It was way too extravagant a purchase for someone recently unemployed. I picked up the box and tossed it into my cart.

One Easy Bake Oven, one Baby Einstein, three board games and six classic children's books later my cart was filled to overflowing as well. I got to the checkout counter and whipped out my credit card. I'd worry about how I'd pay it off later. It would give me something to do when I was living out of my car.

"What's all this?" Fran came up behind me and began unloading her cart.

"I got a few things for Marios' kids. They have nothing, Fran. And don't say it. I know it won't change their lives. It's just something I wanted to do, okay?"

"Did I say anything? Here." She lifted a large box of diapers off a rack behind her and plunked them down with the rest of her purchases. "You said she had a two-year old, right? These should fit."

I cut her a grateful smile. "Thanks."

She shrugged it off, embarrassed. Fran is mush, pure and simple. But if you tried to acknowledge it in any way, she'd kill you where you stand.

Vince called as we were loading her car up with our packages.

"I checked out your lead on the burn victim," he told me. "You were right, per usual. He was a part time guard at the hospital. You ever get tired of being right?"

"I'll get back to you on that. What was his name?"

"Calvin Doyle."

It was all falling into place. They must've met at the hospital when Donte was working for the ambulance company. They got to talking, discovered their mutual love of blood sports and turned to dog fighting for fun and profit. But something must've gone horribly wrong after the last dog fight, and Donte decided to terminate the partnership. Permanently.

I shared my theory with Vince as I shoved the rest of my purchases into the trunk and slammed it shut.

"Beats me, kiddo. But the sooner we locate Lewis the sooner we can put all this to rest. Speaking of which, finding the motherfucker that shot at you and DiCarlo is our number one priority."

I hoped so. Because I hated to see what would happen if Nick found him first.

*****

Fran dropped me off in front of Nick's building. "Do you need help carrying everything up?"

"Nah. My car is parked across the street. I can just transfer it into the trunk."

"Oh. Okay." She seemed disappointed.

"Uh, Fran, would you like to come upstairs for a while? I'm sure Nick wouldn't mind." Actually, I had no idea if he'd mind. But she seemed to really want to.

She shot me a wistful look, a rarity for Fran. "Could I? We won't stay long. It would just be nice to sit on a couch that doesn't smell like baby vomit."

I used the key Nick gave me to unlock his front door. It was cool and dark in the apartment, with a hint of spice in the air. Nutmeg.

Adrian and the puppy were sacked out near the bay window. Adrian swished his tail in a half-hearted wag and closed his eyes.

"Wow." Fran said, taking in the high beam ceilings and wall to wall book shelves. "This is...nice."

A door opened down the hall and Nick emerged from his bedroom. He was freshly showered, his hair hanging in damp clusters around his shoulders. Faded blue jeans clung to his muscled legs. He was wearing a dark blue work shirt, unbuttoned all the way, exposing the most recent scar on his chest.

Fran's mouth formed a perfect, silent O, followed by an equally quiet, but just as emphatic "My God."

Nick buttoned his shirt and walked over to me and kissed me hello. I could taste mint tooth paste on his breath. He turned to Fran and smiled. "It's nice to see you again, Franny." Nick's eyes settled on my goddaughter. "Hello, Christina Brandy. You are beautiful."

Surprise registered on Fran's face, and I could see Nick's stock skyrocket. He'd remembered her baby's name. And he called her beautiful.

"I took the dogs for a run," he informed me, "and everyone's been fed. I've got some business in West Philly, and then I'm meeting Sal at Mic's House of Billiards. "You're both welcome to join us."

I appreciated the invitation, but I was determined not to cramp his style. And anyway, I had some plans of my own.

Nick finished getting dressed and walked with Franny to the elevator. He was holding baby Chrissy in his arms. In that moment, he never looked sexier.

I closed the apartment door and picked up my phone to make a call.

"Hey," I said. "It's Brandy. I was hoping you'd keep me company tonight."

CHAPTER TWELVE

"Depends on what you got in mind, Sweetcakes."

I could hear the laughter in Alphonso's voice and thought back to a year ago, when he was commissioned by Nick to baby sit me. We'd come a long way since that first meeting. Alphonso is my companion of choice when I need brawn and brains to watch my back. Plus, he's got a really cool Hummer. And while I do feel a bit guilty about the sheer excess of it all, it's a nice change of pace from the granny mobile I usually drive around in.

"Relax, Jackson. It's nothing illegal or life threatening."

"Man, where's the fun in that?"

"Okay, it could be a *little* life threatening," I confessed, remembering the day Mario's girlfriend introduced her fist to my face. "Does that sweeten the pot at all?"

"I'm gonna need some details."

Two hours later, under cover of darkness, Alphonso pulled his Hummer up to the curb directly in front of Mario Lewis' house. The scant light of the moon did nothing to enhance the atmosphere there. I glanced across the street to the Kings' home. Their neatly manicured lawn and cheerful painted exterior reminded me that hope was not completely forsaken in this part of town.

Alphonso cut the engine and hopped out of the car. I hesitated briefly and then followed suit. Sherese's old couch still occupied its place on the sidewalk, joined now by a disgustingly gross looking double mattress. Both were rain soaked victims of the last big storm. The air reeked of mildew.

"I can handle this," Alphonso offered. "Why don't you stay in the car?"

"It'll be faster if we both go."

The house was dark. According to Roger, Sherese spent most of her time lying around in the living room in a drug-induced haze. We'd do what we'd come to do and leave. What could go wrong?

Alphonso bent over the trunk and began unloading its contents. I could see the top of his Glock tucked discreetly into the waistband of his pants. It was an abrupt reminder of exactly what could go wrong.

He grabbed the largest box and set it down on the curb and piled the rest of the toys on top. Lifting them chest high he started walking up the path. His biceps bulged under the weight. I took a moment to admire them, and then I grabbed the box of diapers with my one good arm and dragged it across the lawn.

We arranged the boxes on the front porch, carefully tucking them behind the posts, so that they wouldn't be visible from the street. The house remained shrouded in silence. No crying babies, no television blaring from inside. There wasn't a soul in sight. Which made the sound of a shrill female voice, within spitting distance of our heads, that much more startling.

"You trespassing, mutha fuckers. You move and I'll bash your fucking heads in."

Crap. A quick glance told me Sherese had materialized from the side gate. It had been closed up tight when we'd arrived. Now, it swung open just wide enough for her to slip on though. She moved unsteadily toward us wielding a metal baseball bat.

I dropped the diapers to the ground and flattened my back against the house, in order to get out of Alphonso's way, in case he felt inclined to save me. Apparently, he didn't see any urgency in the situation. He just stood back, arms crossed, and let me take the lead. So I did.

"Hi, Sherese. I don't know if you remember me. My name is Brandy. We met awhile back." My tone was casual, social, even. We could have been two neighborhood acquaintances who happened to run into each other at the grocery store, having chatted previously at a party.

Alphonso cast me a withered frown that said, "What the hell are you bringing that up for?" But I'd already gotten her attention.

She squinched up her eyes and struggled for the second time in as many weeks to place me.

"It wasn't under the best of circumstances," I admitted, having inexplicably chosen that moment to become scrupulously honest.

The reminder did the trick, and suddenly the bat was headed my way. Alphonso casually reached out and ripped it out of her grip, only inches from my face. He tossed it onto the porch and grinned.

"Took you long enough," I muttered.

Sherese lunged for her weapon, but Alphonso was quicker. He caught her by the waist and yanked her off the step. In return, she spit and clawed at his face, just missing his eye. A thin trickle of blood ran down his cheek.

"God damn it." He grabbed her wrists and pinned them behind her back.

"Sherese," I broke in. "We're not here to hurt you, so knock it off. I just wanted to bring your kids some toys. That's all."

She stopped squirming and craned her neck beyond Alphonso's massive arms to the stack of boxes on the porch.

"Why'd you bring this shit?" She thrust her chin out,

defiant, yet curious. "I can take care of my kids just fine. We don't need your charity."

"We could all use a little charity, every once in a while. Look," I said, my voice softening, "I know you blame me for Mario's death. And I know his being gone must cause you a lot of pain."

Her face contorted into a heartbreaking expression of grief and vulnerability. "You don't know nothin'," she screamed, and yet there was no heat to her words now.

Alphonso let her go, and she slumped down on the steps. She wrapped her arms around her bare knees, and I watched in silence as tears rolled down her cheeks. "You don't know nothin'," she repeated, more to herself than for my benefit. And suddenly it hit me. Sherese was grieving, all right. Only not for Mario.

Alphonso and I exchanged awkward glances. "Well," he said, taking charge. "We've got to be going."

"Sherese," I offered. "Would you like some help taking these things into the house?" I wish I could say I was driven by compassion, but the truth was I had to pee.

Ignoring me, she lifted her head and wiped the snot from her nose with the corner of her sleeve. Then she hoisted herself up by the crumbling wood railing and walked into the house. Alphonso shrugged and gathered up the presents. I took the diapers and followed him in.

There was a table lamp near the door, and I switched it on, illuminating the small interior. Fast food wrappers littered the living room rug. A pile of unwashed clothes sat in a corner, smelling of sour milk. A beat up, old fan hung precariously from the window. Someone had jammed a crayon into the ancient, rusted blades.

Sherese pointed in the direction of the bathroom and flopped down on the couch. A half-eaten bologna sandwich and a scoopful of Kraft Macaroni and Cheese sat on a plate on the coffee table in front of her. The cheese had long since congealed, turning it a crusty brown.

She lit a cigarette and leaned back, staring into space.

Alphonso stood at the doorway and pulled his phone from his pocket. He raised his eyebrows at me and mouthed something. It looked like "Hurry up."

I walked toward the bathroom and nearly tripped over the toddler. He was asleep on the floor in the hallway, sprawled on his back. A tiny bit of baby drool seeped out of the corner of his mouth. I peeked around the corner and spied his sister, curled up on a an unmade mattress in a small, airless bedroom. They deserved better. Then again, so did their mom.

When I got back to the living room, Alphonso was on his hands and knees. He'd taken a Swiss Army knife from his pocket and was now putting together the hobby horse. I had a thought that made me smile, but if I verbalized it, he'd probably kill me. *Alphonso would make a great dad.*

There was nowhere to sit but the sofa, so I pushed aside a fat, paper bound manual to make room for myself. I glanced at the cover. It was a GED prep book. Was Sherese studying for her high school diploma?

I was about to ask her, when her eyes filled up again. She brushed the tears away with the back of her hand. "He didn't deserve to die. Not like that," she stated, flatly.

"I'm sorry about Mario," I said, just to be polite. The truth is I wasn't one bit sorry. Mario was a festering sore on the universe, and Sherese and the kids were better off without him.

Sherese's head shot up. "You think I'm crying over that asshole?" She snorted, as if she simply couldn't believe how naive I was. "That man was too dumb to live. He made my life miserable. If Donte hadn't of killed him I would've."

"Then who—" I let the question hang in the air, as something else caught my attention. The GED book had fallen open onto the floor. I bent down to pick it up and saw two words written on the inside flap. Calvin Doyle.

Holy cow. Sherese and Calvin Doyle? Man, I so did not see that coming.

Sherese took the book from me and rubbed her finger lightly over his name. She spoke without anger. Only a deep sadness. "Cal thought I was smart. Smart enough to get my high school diploma. Maybe even go to college. Sometimes he'd come around when Mario wasn't here and we'd just talk. He was nice to me and the kids."

Alphonso finished putting together the hobby horse and stood back to look at his handiwork. The newness of it looked incongruous in the dingy apartment. "Okay, that's all done. Well..."

He gave me the eye and cocked his head toward the front door, but I wasn't ready to leave. Not when things were just getting interesting. I shook my head in response. He sighed and pulled his phone out of his pocket again. "I'll be outside."

The screen door closed behind him, and I turned back to Sherese. Maybe I shouldn't have pried, but she really seemed to want to talk. Either that or I was just being nosy. "Did you meet Cal through Donte?"

Sherese nodded. "Donte. What a worthless piece of shit. He met Cal when he worked for the ambulance company. One day they came over to talk to Mario. They had some business they wanted to do. That was before Mario started using so heavy. But even then, he was never too bright. Donte could talk him into doing any fool thing. You know what I'm talkin' about?"

Having checked out the photos on Donte's Facebook page, I knew exactly what she was talkin' about. "Was Cal the one in charge of the dog fighting business?" Maybe I'd feel better about the way he'd died if I could blame him for something truly despicable.

Sherese stubbed out her cigarette in the middle of the corroded Mac n' Cheese. "Hell, no. Cal wasn't into that shit. He was always gettin' on Donte and Mario to stop. He didn't think it was right what they did to them dogs and didn't want nothin' to do with it. He even give my kids a puppy. It was a real sweet little thing. Had a heart on its butt. My daughter called him Lovey. Dumbass name if you ask me, but she insisted."

I looked around. "Where's Lovey now?"

Sherese lit another cigarette. "Dead, probably. One night Donte and Cal got mad at Mario for getting' high all the time and fucking up their business. They beat him senseless and then took the dogs away. Mario got so desperate for drug money he took the puppy and set him in the trunk of his car, figuring he'd make a few bucks by trunking. That's what he was doin' the day you shot him."

I was so caught up in Sherese's story it took me a full minute to connect the dots. Popeye was her family pet. It served no purpose to mention his fate. Instead I asked, "Sherese, you said Cal wasn't involved in dog fighting. But now you say he was mad that Mario was fucking up their business."

"They was in another business together. And before you ask me, I don't know nothin' bout it. All I do know is it was some big damn secret that was supposed to make them rich. Cal promised to take me on a cruise when the money started coming in."

She paused for a moment. Then, "Cal and Donte hated that Mario was high all the time. I heard them talking one night when they thought I was asleep in the bedroom. Cal said he was sorry he'd ever got started with Mario. And if the boss found out, they'd all be dead."

And now they all were. Or pretty near. "Sherese," I said, as an idea worked its way through my brain, "The police believe Donte killed Cal. Do you?"

"I don't know. But I wouldn't put it past him." She stared down at the food encrusted dishes, lost in thought.

After a full minute of silence I figured I'd outstayed my welcome. "Well, I guess I should be going, now." I started for the door, but she called me back. Her voice, devoid of rancor, was surprisingly soft and girlish.

"About them toys you got my kids? It was nice and all. But you didn't have to do that."

"But I wanted to."

Sherese shook her head. "I mean you don't have nothin' to feel guilty about. I know you had to shoot Mario. He would've killed you, otherwise."

I had no idea how much I'd needed her absolution until she offered it. "Thank you for saying that."

She lifted herself off the couch and walked me to the door. Her eyes cut away from me as if she were embarrassed. "What's your name again?"

"Brandy."

"Brandy. I know Cal did some bad things, but he was good to me."

I don't know why, but I felt really bad having her say my name. It was like we were friends and, somehow, I was letting her down.

"Sherese, if Donte killed Cal, the cops will get him. And if he didn't, they won't stop until they find out who did."

"See?" she said, chin upturned. "That's the difference between you and me. You believe it."

I didn't want to tell her how wrong she was.

*****

I found Alphonso slumped down in the Hummer, half asleep. He opened his eyes when I knocked on the window and he rolled it down just enough for me to poke my nose in.

"You planning to let me in?"

"No."

"Please? Hey, I could drive if you're too tired."

"How're you going to drive this thing? You can't even see over the dashboard." He popped the lock. "Get in," he grumbled.

I ran around to the passenger's side and hauled myself up. "Look, I'm sorry I took so long. But I couldn't leave her. Not with her being so upset and all."

Alphonso shook his head. "You're such a pushover. The woman tried to bash your skull in, and you can't do enough for her."

"Look who's talking, Mr… Pony …Put-er-together-er." Okay, totally lame, but it had been a big day.

*****

I woke up the next morning, naked and entwined in Nicholas Santiago's arms. Funny, I hadn't gone to sleep that way.

It was after midnight when Alphonso had dropped me off. Nick wasn't home yet, and I was feeling restless. Adrian and the puppy were sacked out on the couch in Nick's office. I did a cursory snoop through his mail, figuring if he didn't want me sifting through his personal belongings, he would hide them better.

My logic wasn't completely unfounded. In a moment of weakness, I'd warned him about my overactive curiosity.

"Don't worry about it, Darlin'. I trust you."

"But I just got through telling you why you shouldn't."

He'd responded with a beatific smile. "I know you, Brandy Alexander. And I trust you to behave exactly the way you do. If you're privy to something I'd rather you didn't know about, that's my fault, not yours."

In my mind, that's practically permission.

"Good morning," Nick whispered in my ear. "When I came home last night you were dead to the world."

"I couldn't sleep, so I popped an Excedrin P.M."

"Living dangerously, eh?"

"You could say that." I raised the covers and peeked underneath. Nick was wide awake in every sense of the word. "I don't seem to be wearing anything. Did you have your way with me last night?"

"If I had, drug or no drug, you would have remembered." His hand reached out to caress me as he gently nudged his knee between my legs. "Speaking of which…"

I repositioned myself to accommodate him. "Does this

171

count as exercise?" I asked. "Because it would save me a trip to the gym."

In response, he got up on his knees, grabbed my legs and threw them over his shoulders. His smile was borderline wicked. "Consider me your personal trainer."

Half an hour later I scratched the gym off my *to do* list.

Nick rolled over onto his back and leaned his head against the backboard. I tucked in under his arm, my head resting on his chest.

"So," he said, and his heartbeat quickened marginally. "I heard you had a little adventure last night."

"How did you—oh. Alphonso. When did he call you?"

"From the car. He said you and Sherese had a real heart-to-heart."

"I was going to tell you."

"It's not a requirement, Angel."

"No. I want to. I went over there because I felt bad for her and the kids. But after talking to Sherese—I don't know. I have a weird feeling about this, Nick. I think there's more to Calvin Doyle's murder than what I've assumed to be true."

"Do you have anything concrete to go on?"

"Not much. She mentioned the guys had been working for someone else. And they didn't want him to know Mario was causing trouble." I shrugged. "Maybe I'm just stirring things up because I'm bored, or I'm trying to avoid thinking about gang bangers coming after me."

"Trust your instincts, Brandy. They're among your strongest assets. Talk to me."

I told him how Sherese had met Calvin and that they were close. "I don't exactly know what that entailed, but he was nice to her in ways nobody else ever was."

"Until you came along."

I ignored that and continued. "We were right about Donte meeting Cal at work. But, according to Sherese, Cal wasn't a part of the dog fighting ring. That was strictly a cousins thing. Well, them and the charmer who threatened

Roger King."

"But Doyle was there the night Mario got beat up. Wasn't he the one who'd threatened to shoot him?"

"Yeah," I conceded. "Only, from what I gather, he was just there to protect his other interests."

"Meaning Sherese?"

"Sherese and whatever other business dealings he had going with Mario and Donte. One thing was clear. He was scared. Said if the boss found out, they'd all be dead. Which begs the question, who's the boss?"

Nick leaned across me and reached for the hand rolled cigarettes he kept in the drawer of his bed stand. He put one to his lips and looked around for a match.

"I thought you'd quit."

It was supposed to come out like a mild observation… y'know, no big deal, just wondering. Instead, it sounded the way I meant it. *Oh my god, you're two puffs away from lung cancer!*

"Being good is overrated. Everyone needs a vice, Darlin'."

"Oh yeah?" I challenged. "So, what's mine?"

"Me."

I considered this. "Well…" I took the unlit cigarette from his mouth and tossed it back into the drawer. Pushing him onto his back, I straddled him. "In that case, I'm about to be very, very bad."

By the time we left the bed it was almost noon. "What are your plans for today?" Nick asked. He was dressed in his workout clothes; a pair of loose fitting sweats and a snug tee shirt. In his hands he held two demitasse cups of espresso. He gave me one and took a sip from the other.

I thought about making something up. Something nice and safe like job hunting, or going curtain shopping with Franny. But this was Nick, not Bobby. "I want to find out more about Calvin Doyle…who he hung out with…stuff like that. All roads may lead back to Donte Lewis, but I'm not convinced of that just yet. I'm going to start by talking to that guard, Edie Wyncote. She worked with Doyle at the hospital."

A look flickered across his face; brief, but all too familiar.

"Or maybe I'll go curtain shopping with Franny."

Nick finished his espresso and placed his cup in the sink. I walked him to the foyer and waited while he gathered his keys, his sunglasses and his gun. When he was ready to go he put his arms around my waist and hugged me to him. "Be careful curtain shopping," he murmured into my hair. "Call if you need me."

*****

When I got to the hospital security desk, I saw two unfamiliar faces in place of Edie and Calvin Doyle.

"Hi. I'm looking for Edie Wyncote. Is she working today?"

"Edie's on a break," one of them told me. "She usually brings her lunch and eats outside in the garden on the third floor."

I found her sitting with a group of co-workers, huddled under the shade of an aluminum striped awning. She looked up in recognition as I walked toward her. "Hey, hi. You're back."

"Hi, Edie." "Listen, I was wondering if I could talk to you a minute." I cut my eyes toward her lunch mates and added, "It's sort've personal."

She shot me a quizzical look. "Sure."

Edie got up and gathered the remains of her lunch and tossed it into the trash bin. I followed her to the other side of the garden where she settled on a wooden bench. I took a seat next to her.

"I'm here to talk to you about the guard I saw you with the other day. Calvin Doyle."

"What about him?" Her tone was mildly curious.

The question caught me off guard. I'd thought the police would have interviewed the hospital staff by now. Clearly, she didn't know what had happened to him, and I didn't want to be the one to tell her. Unh! This just served as another illustration of why I should plan ahead.

"How well do you know Calvin?" I asked.

"Not real well. He just works at the hospital part time, and sometimes we share a shift." Edie frowned. "Look. I'm not comfortable talking about Calvin behind his back. Is he in some sort of trouble?"

Not anymore he's not. "Um, Edie. I have something to tell you."

I tried to gloss over the details, alluding to the notion that I was working with the police and wasn't at liberty to divulge more than a cursory, "He's dead and we're looking into it."

"I can't believe it," Edie whispered. "He was a nice guy." That seemed to be the general consensus, unless you asked Mario, whose ass Cal had wanted to cap…and did. "Do the police have any idea who killed him or why it happened?"

I spread my hands out in front of me, a gesture meant to convey I wish I could tell you, but I have to follow orders. "Edie, you said Cal only worked at the hospital part time. Did he have another job?"

"Not that I know of. He didn't talk much about his private life."

I thought for a moment. "How about hobbies? Or friends? Did he ever mention anyone he hung out with or anything like that?"

She shook her head. "I'm sorry. Nothing comes to mind." She glanced over at the table under the awning where her friends had been seated. The table was empty. "My break is up," she announced, rising. "I've got to get back to work."

I stood too. Scrounging around in my pocket book, I found an old Acme receipt. I tore it in half and took down Edie's number. Then, I scribbled my name and number on the other half and handed it to her. "Edie, if you do happen to think of anything, could you give me a call?"

"Sure thing." She studied the slip of paper a moment. "Listen, I don't know if this is the kind of stuff you mean but, sometimes when Cal's shift was over, someone would come around in a van to pick him up."

"Did Cal ever mention who it was?"

"No. But I remember the van, because there were words written on the side of it. You know, like advertising for a business."

"Can you recall what it said?"

"Wait." She closed her eyes as if trying to conjure up an image. A minute later her eyes popped open. "The sign said K-9 Security Services."

"K-9 Security Services," I repeated, committing it to memory. "Are you sure?"

"Yeah, I'm sure. Hey. Do me a favor. Let me know what you find out."

"I will. And, thanks."

CHAPTER THIRTEEN

I was just leaving the hospital when John called me. "Hey, Sunshine. I'm trying out a new recipe I saw on the Food Network today. You want to come over for dinner?"

A real, home cooked meal sounded like heaven. Nick had scheduled some late training sessions, which left me to fend for myself. My idea of fending is a bowl of corn flakes and a stack of peanut butter crackers. "That'd be great. Will Garrett be there?"

John was immediately on guard. His voice pitched low. "Why?"

"No reason." Actually, I had come up with a new strategy to win Garrett's favor. I figured I'd appeal to his love of culture and dazzle him with my extensive knowledge of fine art and literature.

"I didn't invite him. It's just you and me."

Crap. I memorized those Trivial Pursuit cards for nothing.

"Maybe we should make it for another time. I'll bring Nick over, you ask Garrett, and we could do a game night."

"You hate games. And besides, you have the attention span of a flea. The last time we played Monopoly you quit before we even finished setting up the board." John began to cackle.

"What's so funny?"

"I was just picturing the four of us together. You and Garrett would be trying not to strangle each other, while Santiago and I bonded over the fondue pot and a rousing game of Yahtzee."

I really love John, but sometimes I want to smack him. "Fine, John. Make your little jokes."

"Bran, why are you pushing this?"

"Because I want Nick to know my friends. And how is Garrett ever going to learn to like me if we don't spend any time together?"

"Will you stop obsessing about Garrett? It is what it is."

"It is what it is? What does that even mean, John? Of course it is what it is. What else would it be? What I want to know is how to change what it is."

"You're giving me a headache. I'll see you at seven."

I took a circuitous route back to Nick's apartment, via my neighborhood. It's not that I didn't love staying with him. Hell, I'd camp out in a tent on top of Mt. Saint Helen's as long as we could share a sleeping bag. But this was my home, and I missed it.

As I turned onto my block, a sudden, intense, flash of anger surfaced and formed a burning lump in my esophagus. At first, I'd thought my lunch was taking a walk down memory lane. (I'd indulged in a couple of spicy shrimp tacos at a food truck in Powelton Village. Maybe not the best idea, but who can resist Taco Tuesday!)

However, indigestion didn't account for the clammy hands and palpitating heart. God damn gang bangers. I hated being at anyone's mercy. What I hated even more was being afraid. Would I ever feel safe in this world? I pulled over to the curb in front of my house and sat there feeling very sorry for myself. And the next thing I knew, the tears were falling again. *Note to self: You cry too damn*

much. Look into hormone therapy.
*****

According to their website, (which featured pictures of big, scary looking dogs with bared teeth and names like Zeus and Diablo) K-9 Security Services offered "a variety of services for all of your commercial and residential protection needs." What it didn't advertise is someone that worked there knew Calvin Doyle. Maybe they could shed some light on who killed him.

I called the police station to give them the inside scoop on my investigation. That resulted in a brief, but spirited conversation with a cop I mentally dubbed Officer Crankypants, who, apparently, did not share my enthusiasm for working as a team. Duly noted. I printed out the address and stuffed it in my pocket.

I'd taken the dogs on a long walk and was running late for John's. No time now for a shower, so I cheated and doubled up on deodorant. It left a white streak on my shirt, which would bother John no end. I laughed just thinking about it.

Along the way I stopped to get some Ben & Jerry's, in case John was on another health food kick and mistook fruit for a real dessert. When he opened the door to his apartment, I handed him the ice cream and then did a double take—the cartoon kind where the guy's head swivels all the way around in surprise and a big bubble appears above him with the word YIKES written inside in capital letters.

"Oh, hey!" I said, with way too much enthusiasm. "You got your hair…done! Um, is that a perm?"

"Garrett says they're making a comeback. So, what do you think?"

"It's uh…it's…nice."

John looked skeptical. "We tell each other the truth, remember? Here, I'll start. You've got deodorant on your shirt. Okay, your turn. And be honest."

I sighed. "Honestly? It looks like you're trying out for

the lead in Annie!"

"Damn it, I knew this was a bad idea."

"Then, why—"

"Garrett thought it might be fun for me to experiment with my style." I'm not sure, but I thought I detected a note of sarcasm in his voice. He walked into the kitchen carrying the cartons of ice cream. I followed behind him, thinking.

"Don't worry," I said. "We can fix this. I mean, how many times have we watched *Legally Blonde?* Remember the way Elle solved the crime with cosmetological reasoning? You just need to wash it out is all."

John shook his head. The curls flounced around like they were spring loaded. "No good. I already tried, but I waited too long."

"So cut it all off. Bald is sexy."

That got a laugh out of him. He paused. "Listen, Bran, thanks for not giving me a hard time about this."

I shrugged. "It's only hair, John."

"You know I'm not talking about the hair, right?"

"Yeah, I know."

Over Mario Batali's recipe for Fettucine Bolognese I filled John in on Calvin Doyle. He listened with growing agitation, his eyes wide, his fork poised in the air. When I was finished, he waited a nano second before laying into me.

"All right, I tried not to say anything, because of you being so nice about my hair. But I've got to be honest with you. I think you're an adrenalin junkie."

"Well, what the hell is that supposed to mean?"

"You know, addicted to dangerous situations. If you need excitement, why can't you just have sex in public places like normal people?"

"God, John. I know what it means. But do you honestly believe I enjoyed being shot at? Or that I went looking to get trapped in a cellar with Barbeque Man? I'm not getting some kind of sick thrill out of any of this. And just to set the record straight, once and for all, I *don't* have a death wish, and I'm not going off the deep end. Look, you weren't there at Sherese's. Calvin Doyle wasn't much, but he's all she had. The least anyone can do is to help her find out the truth about who killed him. Now, could we please just shut up about it and move on?"

John raised his hands, palms up—a gesture—I believe, that was meant to convey, *you win, but only because I'm so damn fed up with you.* This was confirmed in his next breath.

"I don't know why I bother. You've been this way since you were four. First day I met you, you fell out of your grandmother's tree, trying to rescue a cat—which turned out to be a plastic bag."

"Fine, so I didn't rescue a cat. But I scored one for the environment. That bag could've ended up in the ocean where a whale would mistake it for plankton and choke to death on it. I will not apologize for being eco-friendly."

"Now you're just being purposely obtuse."

"Is it working?" My phone rang. "Hello?" I said into the phone.

"Hey, Darlin'. Where are you?"

"I'm having dinner at John's. Are you still at the studio?"

"Afraid so, and I only have a few minutes. But I've got some news. Based on the partial plate and description you provided, the police were able to track down the owner of the car that was involved in the shooting. It's registered to Donte Lewis."

"Donte?" I did a quick timeline of events. "That doesn't make sense, Nick. Why would Donte disappear after the dog fight and then show up a week after Doyle's cooked body is discovered in his home, cruise down my block, in his own car, in broad daylight and attempt to kill me? And why would he leave Cal sitting in his basement anyway? That's just plain stupid, even for Donte… unless…"

"Unless someone was setting him up?"

"Exactly."

"You may be on to something, there, Angel. Listen, I don't mean to rush you off the phone, but I've got to get back to work. By the way, this is inside information. So act surprised when DiCarlo tells you."

"How did you—"

"Hear about it? Can't say, Darlin' I wouldn't want to lose all my mystery."

Like that could happen.

I disconnected from Nick and sat staring at the phone.

"What's going on, Sunshine?"

"Not sure yet." I cradled the phone in my hand for a beat, thinking. Then I punched in Mike Mahoe's number.

"Yo, Brandy." Ever since I fixed him up with Janine, Mike has been decidedly happier to hear from me. "What's goin' on?"

"Mike, I have a favor to ask you, and please don't feel obligated to help me just because I arranged for you to go out with Janine."

There was a long pause. "You still there?"

"Yeah," he said, sounding less happy. "What do you need?"

"A little information." I did not buy into the idea that Donte had set Cal on fire and then left him in his basement. It just didn't jive with what I knew about the man. But it fit Torch's M.O. perfectly. What if Cal hadn't died at the scene? What if his body was taken to Donte's after the killing occurred? That would lend more credence to the idea that Donte was being set up.

"I need to know if Calvin Doyle was killed in Donte Lewis' house or if his body was transported there afterwards."

"Why? Why do you need to know this? Ah, shit. Doesn't do any good to argue," he said, more to himself than to me. Fine. I'll get back to you."

"Thanks, Mike. I wouldn't ask you if it wasn't really important." But he'd already hung up."

*****

John threw me out at ten. "Some of us have jobs, Sunshine. I've got to be up at 4:30 for an early morning photo shoot."

"But it's still early. C'mon John, don't be such a wuss."

"Do you really think resorting to name calling is going to get you what you want?" He cast a wary eye in my direction. "Unless, this is about you not wanting to be alone, in which case, I'm still going to bed, but you can crash here on the couch."

It was a tempting offer. I didn't know when Nick would get home, and, no matter how safe I felt at his place, the fear button in my brain was on permanent press. I didn't relish the idea of going back to an empty apartment. So, of course I told John, "Don't be ridiculous. I love my alone time."

"Uh huh," he said, and rolled his eyes.

John insisted I take home the leftovers, labeling the containers with *use by* dates and instructions to freeze them if I didn't eat it within the next few days. Knowing John, he would call to make sure they'd been properly refrigerated.

"You sure you're going to be all right?" he asked as he walked me to the door. His pixie face, framed in unnatural curls, was earnest, and a wave of gratitude washed over me.

"Absolutely. And call Carla. She'll work wonders with the hair."

After a mini debate with myself (the advantage of which is either way I can't lose) about whether I'd come across as horribly intrusive and needy, or spontaneous and fun, I called Nick from the car.

"Hey, Darlin'. What's up?" He sounded distracted. *Crap. Intrusive and needy.*

"Oh, hi. It's nothing. I just thought I'd stop by and uh, give you some leftovers, but it sounds like I caught you in the middle of something. I'll catch up with you later at the apartment."

"That's very thoughtful of you," Nick replied, as if he believed every word of bullshit I'd just uttered. "We're on a short break, and then I've got thirty more minutes of this session. Another client is scheduled after that. But if you can give me about half an hour I can let you in, and you can hang out in my office while I do my last training."

"If you're sure…"

"You'd be doing me a favor, Angel. I haven't had a chance to eat yet, and I'm working up an appetite."

Typical of Nick, letting me save face. God, I loved this man.

*****

I got to Nick's studio with twenty minutes to spare and pulled in behind a new, red, Audi Spider. "Wow, somebody has the big bucks," I sniffed. "Still, it doesn't have the leg room of my La Sabre."

I sat in the car while he finished up with his client. The neighborhood wasn't the best, but there seemed to be an invisible "No kill zone" surrounding his place that the *boyz in the hood* took seriously. I kept my windows rolled up, the doors locked, and my cell phone handy, anyway.

While I waited I pulled out the leftovers container and popped the lid. John probably hadn't counted on me getting hungry on the way home in the car, so he hadn't included any utensils. Not a problem. I picked at the contents with my thumb and forefinger.

After a short while the studio door opened. Nick held it ajar and a woman exited the building. With a distinct lack of precision, I popped some dangling fettuccini strands into my mouth and scooted forward in my seat for a better look.

She headed toward the Audi with Nick close at her heels. Her incredibly toned body was encased in a black unitard, giving her a sexy, feline look. Her long, dark hair was pinned up in a bun. When she reached the car she undid the clasp. Her luxurious tresses tumbled free like she was the star of a shampoo commercial or a porno film. And to cap it all off she was a dead ringer for a young Angelina Jolie.

My stomach churned, and I wrestled with the urge to jump out of the car and knock her on her perfectly formed ass—just for being that beautiful. But, for once, common sense prevailed. I took a deep breath and gave myself a stern talking to… something about trusting Nick and blah, blah, blah… I wasn't really listening. I was too busy watching him drape his arm around her shoulder.

Shit! I leaped out of the car and immediately tripped over the curb. Down I went, Fettuccini Bolognese flying everywhere. I think a little landed on Catwoman's unitard.

She jumped back. Nick casually undraped his arm from her shoulder and helped me to my feet.

"Hello, Darlin'. I'll be with you in a minute." He turned to the woman in the unitard and again settled his arm across her shoulder. I watched this chummy tableau with growing agitation, when Nick—suddenly and inexplicably—grabbed her by the throat.

In the split second it took for me to process what was happening, the woman thrust her arms upwards between Nick's and broke his hold. Before he could recover his advantage, she delivered a lightning fast punch that stopped just short of his larynx.

Nick reeled back and smiled. "Nice."

My heart resumed beating as they bowed to each other and stepped away.

After Nick finished congratulating his star student, I waited patiently for an introduction. Only I must have suddenly become invisible because nobody stepped up with a "Hi, how are ya?" Just as well, I supposed, seeing as when I tripped I'd ended up wearing most of the leftovers.

Nick and the woman walked around to the driver's side of the Audi and she waited while he opened the door for her. "You displayed excellent technique tonight, Azure. We'll work on increasing your reaction speed in our next session."

Azure? Oh, Puh-leeze. I'll bet her real name's Nancy, but after getting in touch with her true self through a weekend course in "How to pretend to be evolved by changing your name to something metaphysical sounding," she found her "inner Azure." Maybe I should start calling myself Magenta, or Puce.

As I was pondering this, Azure and Nick hugged and did the French kissy face thing. (I'm beginning to hate the French. Way too much kissing.)

Nick watched her drive off. I hung back on the sidewalk and fought down the slow burn that rose up from my belly. It was a tough job, so I didn't notice him until he was right there beside me.

"You're awfully quiet, Angel. What's up?"

"Not a thing," I said cooly. "Sorry about your dinner. Guess I'll see you back at the apartment." I cast my eyes downward to my shirt. There were red, wormy stains where the fettuccine had landed. I brushed the remaining strands off and turned to leave.

Nick caught me by the wrist and spun me around. "Not so fast, Darlin.' You're upset. We're going to talk about it."

"Fine," I muttered, only it really wasn't, because I had no idea in the world what to tell him. I scanned my list of acceptable excuses. I'm tired…I'm hungry…I'm…

"I'm retaining water."

Nick's mouth twitched, but at least he had the good grace not to laugh. "I'm sorry to hear that. So, is that it, or is there perhaps something else on your mind?"

Oh, where to begin? "Nope. I'm good."

He cocked his head, eyebrows arched. "Why don't we finish this conversation inside?" He spoke quietly, but his tone said that there was no room for argument.

I hated to admit it, but I was relieved to know he wouldn't stop asking until I told him the truth. Because that's what we always did in the end. We told each other the truth.

Taking me by the hand, he led me through the door, past the studio and into his office in the back of the building.

The red velvet chair beckoned me and I sat in it, tucking my feet beneath me.

Nick sat on the couch opposite me and leaned slightly forward. I could smell the pheromones wafting off his body.

"So," he said, "What's really going on?"

"You didn't introduce me." Oh, man. It sounded even stupider out loud than it did in my head.

"That was thoughtless," Nick admitted. "I'm sorry."

It would have been so easy. All I had to do was open my mouth and say, "That's all right," and I could have walked away with a shred of dignity intact. *But nooo.* "I got jealous, okay?" I continued in a rush of words, and once the truth train had left the station I couldn't shut up for love or money. "I mean she's so beautiful, and…well, competent. And then I come along, tripping over my own two feet, and I thought you might be ashamed of me—and really, who could blame you? Food falling from the sky and…and…stop laughing. That's not even the worst of it."

The worst of it was *why* I wanted him to introduce me. The fact is I needed clarification. As in, "Catwoman, I want you to meet Brandy, the love of my life and my future bride." Or even, "Unitard Lady, this is my girlfriend, Brandy, with whom I have an exclusive relationship." Really, any variation of the theme would have sufficed.

"So, what is the worst of it, Darlin'?"

I dropped my head into my hands. Nick gently pulled them away and lifted my chin until our eyes met. "Tell me."

Well, here goes nothin'. "Are you seeing anyone else? Or planning to? Because it's fine if you are…no, wait, that's a big fat lie. It's not fine at all. But we never said we'd be exclusive, and I just want you to know I'm not seeing anyone else, and I'm not planning to. But if you are I'll deal with it because I love you. But I need to know—"

"I have no interest in seeing anyone else, Angel."

"Really?"

"Why are you so surprised?"

I sighed. I would have to explain it to him. "Nick, you and I both know you could have anyone you want. I'm just…ordinary. But any woman in her right mind would want you. And most of the crazy ones, too."

Nick stared at me with such intensity it made my knees weak. He leaned in so close I could feel his breath on my lips. "Brandy Alexander, you are so far from ordinary, words fail me. If I've made you feel less than cherished, that is my deepest regret. I don't know what I can offer you beyond that, Angel, but you are my heart."

Oh. My. God. "How long until your next client arrives?"

"About Fifteen minutes."

I unfolded my legs and joined him on the couch.

*****

On the 1800 block of Kensington Avenue, a large, black and gold banner stretched across the roof of a low slung, steel-gray building, home of K-9 Security Services. The same ultra alpha dogs pictured in their on-line ad glared down at me as I maneuvered Nick's truck into a parking spot right out front.

The Le Sabre was temporarily out of commission. When I'd started it up in the morning, the engine groaned as if it were about to give birth, coughed up a dying breath and refused to turn over. Nick offered to have it towed to his mechanic and he lent me the truck.

Janine, riding shotgun, raised a shapely, perfectly tanned leg and planted her bare foot on the truck's dashboard. Her toe nails glittered with frosty pink polish. She had agreed to accompany me on a mission to glam up my wardrobe, a prospect that delighted her no end. But I had some business to take care of first.

"How long do you think you'll be?" She dug into her

pocket book and took out a half empty bottle of nail polish, opened it, and inspected a chip on her little toe.

"Not long. I just want to ask a few questions about that guy, Doyle. Turn the air on if you get too hot, and try not to spill anything, okay?" Franny had gone into labor in the back of the truck the month before. The miracle of birth aside, it was a real mess to clean up.

I hopped out and made my way to the metal door facing the street. There was an intercom on the wall. I pressed it, and a moment later, a thick, Philadelphia accent popped up on the speaker. "Can I help you?"

"Hi. I was wondering if I could speak to the owner."

"That would be Wade Stoller, only he don't *tawk* to solicitors, hon."

"I'm not a solicitor," I said, shifting my weight from one foot to the other. I hate *tawking* to disembodied voices. It's very disconcerting. "Um, this is a little hard to explain. Would you mind if I came in?"

"Hang *awn*. I'll buzz you in"

I whipped my head around to Janine and gave her two thumbs up. She raised her nail polish bottle to return the fat digit salute and the bottle slipped out of her grasp, turning her thumbs up into an instant *oops* shrug. Oy.

The buzzer went off and I entered the building. There was a reception counter to the right with framed photos on the wall behind it showing happy, secure customers and their loyal canine protectors. A woman in her mid sixties came out from behind the counter as I approached. She could have passed for a friend of my mother's, if you didn't count the multiple ear piercings, and skull and crossbone tattoos parading up and down her forearms.

A Doberman stood at attention by her side and eyed me with malevolent intent. Okay, to be fair, that was mere speculation on my part, but, just to be on the safe side, I didn't make any sudden moves.

"Wade will be right with ya, hon."

"Great. Thanks."

She left Adolph there to entertain me while she walked down a long hallway, presumably, to announce my arrival.

Just when I'd given up on anyone materializing, a man emerged from the back room. He was over six feet tall, with a slight paunch that said either he kicked back a couple of brewskis every night, or he wasn't as dedicated to his ab cruncher as he once was. Otherwise, he looked to be in good shape. His face was tanned, and he was dressed in blue jeans and a work shirt, and cowboy boots that looked like they'd seen better days. I could hear the soft jingle of spurs as he walked toward me.

Two deep indentations sliced his furrowed brow, making him appear perpetually worried. He gave me the once-over and I caught a subtle sign of recognition on his face.

I smiled. *See? I may be a minor local celebrity, but I'm still just regular folk.*

"Wade?" I extended my hand.

He recovered quickly. "That would be me. And you are—?" His grip was almost too firm, and my hand felt uncomfortably small inside his.

"Oh, sorry. My name's Brandy."

"Brandy Alexander, the reporter? I used to watch you on the early morning news show. Hey, how come I haven't seen you, lately?"

"Long story," I mumbled. "Got some irons in the fire, moving in a different direction. Gotta weigh my options. So, anyway, do you have a minute? I had something I wanted to ask you."

"You looking to get some guard dogs, you came to the right place. I'm not just blowing hot air. Our dogs are the best in the business." He lowered his voice. "We have our share of celebrity clients, and they could tell you. Except I respect their privacy."

"I will definitely keep that in mind. Um, could we sit down?" My shoulder was getting better, but it was my first day off pain killers and I was definitely feeling it.

Wade gestured to a couple of plastic chairs in the corner in what constituted the waiting area. We sat down and I spat out my carefully rehearsed tale.

"I was visiting a friend at the hospital the other day, and I ran across this guy. We started talking—you know how it is." I thought of Nick naked and made myself blush. "So anyway, he dropped something, and I ran out to give it to him, but he'd already driven away."

"I don't mean to be rude, but why would you come here looking for him?"

"Oh, well, he was picked up in a K-Nine Security van. So I thought maybe he worked here. I was in the neighborhood, so I decided to check it out. His name is Cal. I didn't catch his last name."

I waited for confirmation that he knew him, but all I heard was the soft tinkling of one of his spurs as he tapped his foot on the tiled floor."

"Ring any bells?" I asked, finally.

Wade shook his head. "Sorry. The person that told you this must've gotten us mixed up with another company. We have a strict policy against taking riders. That would be grounds for dismissal. It's an insurance thing," he explained. "I have to protect my business." He stood, signaling the end of our chat.

I stood, too. "Well, I appreciate your time. So, um, I was thinking, Wade. This place would make a wonderful piece for a report on local businesses, and it could be a real boost for you. Do you think I could look around a bit?"

"Sorry." He cut me an apologetic smile. "I don't have time to escort you around."

Just then Tattoo Lady came back into the room. "That sounds like a great idea, hon. Wade, I'll take her around. We could use the publicity." She grabbed my hand and whisked me down the hallway. Wade started to follow but she cut him off. "I thought you said you don't have time for this. And anyway, Ted's on the phone with that new client. He wants to talk to you. Pick up line three."

The woman and I continued down the hall. It led to an outside kennel. Rottweilers, Pits and Dobermans were housed in four by eight enclosures. They looked hungry. I swung wide and inched a bit closer to my tour guide.

"Don't worry, they're well trained. They won't hurt you without provocation or a command. My name is Kaye, by the way. Wade is my nephew." She gave a hearty chuckle. "Wade isn't a people person, so I'm usually the one to deal with the public."

"Have you worked here long?"

"Three years in May. Started right after my divorce. What a jerk wad. I still don't know what I saw in him."

"I met a guy the other day," I confided, "and we really seemed to hit it off. I thought he was really nice, and cute, and well…you know how hard it is to meet nice guys."

"Tell me about it," she agreed. "This guy sounds like a keeper."

"That's actually what brought me here in the first place. I saw him getting into a K-Nine Security van, and I came here looking for him. I told Wade he'd left something behind and I wanted to return it." I giggled like a nine year-old. "Guess I was too embarrassed to tell him the truth. Anyway, his name is Cal."

"No one by that name works here, hon. But we have two drivers, besides Wade, that is. Ernesto and Phil. Maybe one of them knows your guy. They're over in the parking lot hosing down the vans."

"Listen, Kaye, maybe I should talk to them myself. I mean, if you're there, they may not admit they disobeyed company policy and used the work van to give a friend a ride."

She cut me off with a puzzled frown. "Company policy? There's no company policy."

Hmm…No company policy…which means either Kaye isn't up on all the legalities of the business or her nephew is a big, fat liar.

"Oh. I must have misunderstood."

Kaye tugged my arm and we slowed to a stop. "Between you and me, they're not the classiest act in town. So if that person, Cal, is a friend of theirs, I'd be careful." She shrugged, and the tattooed skull on her left rotator's cuff bobbed its head in seeming agreement.

We resumed walking, and I spotted a smaller set of kennels. They housed a couple of Labs, a beagle and two young pit bulls. "Are they guard dogs too?"

Kaye shook her head. "Not hardly. These babies are drug sniffers. My nephew has a small, side business. He's got a couple of companies that use him on a regular basis. He trains the dogs himself. You'd think they were his kids the way he fusses over them."

We reached the parking lot. There were two white vans and one black one; each with the K-Nine Security logo painted on the side. A couple of guys in service uniforms stood behind them, squirting each other with a hose.

"I've got to get back to the front desk," Kaye said. "Come back and see me when you're done. I think a story on this place is just what we need. You two behave yourselves," she called out good naturedly. "This girl wants to do a story on us."

One of the men turned off the water as I approached. The other drew a cigarette from behind his ear and stuck it in his mouth. The tip was wet and it took a couple of tries to light it.

The guy with the hose held onto it like it was a giant dick and puckered his lips in my direction. It made me wish I'd taken Janine up on her offer to come with me. She'd have smacked him upside the head, no problem. I didn't have a problem with it either, except I didn't think that would go over too well, and I needed information.

"Hi," I said and ignored the show. "Sorry to bother you guys, but Kaye suggested I talk to you. You got a minute?"

Smokey drew in a long tobacco breath and threw the

rest of the cigarette onto the gravel.

"Trying to quit, huh? My dad used the same technique for years."

"Yeah? Did it work?"

"Not so much."

Smokey laughed. "So, how can we help you?"

"Long story," I said. "But I'm looking for a guy named Cal. I have reason to believe he had a friend or acquaintance who works here."

"He owe you money?" asked Hose Boy.

"No, nothing like that. I met him the other night and we started talking. I thought it would be nice to see him again."

"Don't know him. Sorry." He turned the water back on and returned to washing the vans.

I tried again. "That's okay. It's probably for the best. Anyway, like Kaye said, I'm going to be writing a story on your company, so I hope you don't mind me asking a few questions."

"Ask away," said Smokey, whose name turned out to be Ernesto.

"So, do you train dogs too, or are you strictly drivers?"

"We're professional trainers. In fact, Wade turned most of the security and protection training over to Phil and me, so that he could work exclusively with the drug detection dogs. There's a real demand for this kind of work, but he wants to keep the business small, for now."

Oh, great. A complete change of subject. Now, how am I going to work the conversation back around to the vans? I know! I'll do it super awkwardly! "So do you each drive your own vans or do you have to share them? I shared a car with a roommate once. Major drag. She was a real slob. Kept leaving empty soda cans everywhere." *Unh! Way to go, Alexander. Who gives a shit about my imaginary roommate's clutter disorder?*

Ernesto did not seem to notice. He considered my question as if it were Pulitzer Prize winning material. "Phil and I drive the white vans. Phil's a lot shorter and I hate readjusting the seat and mirrors, so we try to stick to the same van each time we go out. The black van is Wade's."

Suddenly, I couldn't wait to leave. "Well, thanks for all the info. I'll let you know when my story hits the air."

"That's it?"

"For now. Listen, please tell Kaye thanks and I'll be in touch."

I felt two pair of eyes bore into my back as I ran back to my car.

Janine was asleep in the passenger's seat. All the windows had been rolled down and she was swimming in sweat. She woke up as I opened the door.

"Finally," she grumbled. "Can we go now?"

"One more minute. I swear." I took out my phone and punched in Edie Wyncotte's number. "Edie, it's Brandy Alexander. Quick question. What color was the van that Calvin Doyle got picked up in?" Her answer came as no surprise.

CHAPTER FOURTEEN

"Vince, I'm telling you. Wade Stoller is hiding something. Why else would he lie about not knowing Calvin Doyle?"

Vince scowled. "Christ, Brandy. That's all you've talked about since the minute you got here. Will you quit obsessing?"

We were browsing the accessories counter at Meow Ming's, a trendy boutique on South Street, in search of a birthday present for his mother. Somehow, I didn't think her idea of the perfect gift would be a set of $280.00 hand-made prayer beads from a remote Tibetan village—or anything else in the store, for that matter. Mrs. Giancola was more of a crock pot kind of gal.

"I am not obsessing."

"Yeah? Then, what would you call it?"

"Determined curiosity."

Vince cracked a smile. The thing is, though, he had a point.

I was obsessing. Maybe it was because I didn't have a job to occupy my time, so I was looking for connections where they simply didn't exist. But I didn't think so. I'd made Stoller nervous. I could see it in the way he began to tap his foot and couldn't quite meet my eye when I asked him if he knew Calvin Doyle. And he lied about there being a rule against picking up passengers. Edie Wyncote identified his company van, and he's the only one who drives the black one. Sure, Phil or Ernesto, or even his aunt could have taken it when he wasn't around, but that wouldn't make sense, since they each had one of their own to drive. The more I thought about it, the more sure I was.

Vince picked a multi-colored scarf out of a woven basket and rolled the material between his thumb and forefinger. I wrinkled my nose and he put it back down.

"Come on. Let's get out of here. There's an antique shop across the street that sells Depression Era glassware. I saw some really cool stuff in the window. Your mother will love it."

Half an hour later, Vince walked out of Grandma's Attic the proud owner of a Mayfair Open Rose Pitcher. "You were right," he told me. "This is perfect. Y'know," he laughed, "my mother says all she ever wants for her birthday is for my sisters and me to get along. So, one year, we took her at her word. She stopped talking to us for a month."

I grinned. "You know what else I'm right about?" I stopped to grab a couple of soft pretzels off a street vendor. This was an exercise in self control, as I did not order a cherry water ice to go with it.

"Let me guess," he said, and punctuated it with a massive grunt. "Wade Stoller."

"Vince—"

He held up a hand to stop me. "Look, even if the guy did lie to you, it's not exactly grounds for arrest. You're not an officer of the law."

"Yeah, but that doesn't mean he's not hiding something."

"Okay, look. I've got to be honest with you, Brandy. You could have been in serious trouble after that stunt you pulled when you broke into Mario Lewis' house. They could still cite you for interfering with an investigation."

"Are you friggin' kidding me?" I huffed and quickened my step to put distance between us. I knew I was being a brat, but I don't do frustration well.

"What are you so pissed off about?" he bristled, jogging to catch up with me.

I stopped short. "First of all, I didn't break in. And second, there wouldn't have even been an investigation if I hadn't discovered Doyle's dead body. For all we know, he could still be down there, stinking up the entire neighborhood." And then a thought occurred to me. "Did Bobby ask you to keep me out of the loop?" It wouldn't be the first time…or the fourth or fifth.

Vince frowned. "DiCarlo had nothing to do with this."

"Really? Well, good." In actuality, I felt a little hurt. Didn't he care about me anymore?

I waited while Vince caught his breath and then handed him one of the pretzels. He smothered it in mustard and took a giant-sized bite.

"Look, Vincent, I'm not mad at you. And I'm not trying to tell people how to do their jobs. It's just that—" I paused, remembering Sherese's anguished face. "It's just that my interest in this case is—personal."

"It always is with you. That's why you'd make a lousy cop." He took another bite of pretzel, chewed and swallowed. "But you make a hell of a friend. Okay, fine," he relented. "I'll give the investigating officer Stoller's name and suggest he check him out. I'm sure it'll go over real well. They love it when the D.A. tells them how to do their job. Happy now?"

"Thank you. And tell them to check out the guys that work for him, too."

"Anything else?"

I took my napkin and dabbed a glob of mustard off the corner of his mouth. "Nope. That's it."

*****

On the way back to Nick's place I stopped by Carla's

198

hair salon to get my bangs trimmed. I walked through the door and immediately panicked as I spied a young woman sitting behind the counter, filing her nails. Her name was Bonita, and she was definitely not a fan. At the sound of the door buzzer, she looked up. She glared at me and arranged her pouty lips into a fairly impressive sneer.

"Well, that's a little unfair," I thought. "What have I ever done to her?" Okay, so Bonita and Bobby's ex-wife, Marie, were best friends. And maybe I did, indirectly, have a hand in getting Marie deported, after she'd offered to kill me. But that was ages ago. Sheesh. The woman really knew how to hold onto a grudge.

In an effort to diffuse the situation, I extended my arm in greeting. "Hi, Bonita. Not sure if you remember me…I'm Carla's friend, Brandy."

Bonita continued to glare. I stood there for an embarrassing moment before returning my arm to my side. "Is Carla here?" I asked.

Thankfully I didn't need to wait for a response, because at that moment, Carla emerged from the back room.

"Hi, hon. This is a nice surprise."

"Hey, Carla," I babbled, stealing glances at Bonita. "Just thought I'd come by and get the ol' bang-a-langs trim-a-roo'd." I don't know why, exactly, but whenever I'm faced with a socially uncomfortable moment, I start talking like Ned Flanders.

This time even Carla looked at me funny. She took my arm and led me over to a recliner chair at the hair-washing station.

"Honey, why don't we give your hair a wash? Maybe trim some of those split ends along with your bangs. Freshen you up a little bit."

I melted a little at her words. Guess I needed the mothering more than I'd realized.

"Thanks, Carla."

"Just sit down and get comfortable," she told me. "Bonita, come on over. You've got a customer."

"Bonita?" I bolted upright. "Um, do you really think that's a good idea?"

"Oh? Didn't I tell you? Bonita graduated last week from her prison work-release program. And since she's done such a great job cleaning up around here, we promoted her to hair washer." Carla beamed, proud of her protégé.

"That's great!" I replied, a little too enthusiastically to be convincing to anyone but Carla. That's the trouble with genuinely sweet people. They always think the best of others.

Bonita approached, her trademark scowl having suddenly transformed into a grin.

She grabbed a smock and tossed it to me. I pushed a reluctant hand through the armhole.

Carla patted me on my injured shoulder. I bit back a wince. "I'll be through with Mrs. Parnelli in a minute," she said. "Just come to station three when you're done."

"Lean back," Bonita instructed, and shoved my head into the basin. My neck felt like it was resting on rocks, but I did as I was told.

"Um, the other shampoo lady usually puts a towel down to cushion my neck…but this is good, too." Was is my imagination, or was steam rising from the faucet? "Ow!"

"Too hot?"

"Maybe just a tad."

She cranked the heat up some more and began scrubbing my head with her stiletto-like nails.

"Um, Bonita, I just washed my hair, yesterday. Honestly, it's not that dirty. In fact, a little oil is good for the scalp…"

In response, she grabbed a hunk of my hair and twisted it in her fist, pulling the skin around my eyes so tight my cheeks felt like the product of a botched face lift. I elbowed her in the gut and she let go.

"Puta," she muttered under her breath.

Now, I may have flunked first year Spanish, but I knew what that word meant. "Yo, Bonita," I said, jumping out of the chair. "Puta this."

I was all set to shove her into tomorrow, when Carla came up behind me. "Well, I see you're all done here. Great!" She grabbed my hand and steered me down to station three. Conditioner dripped off my head onto the floor.

"She called me puta."

Carla sighed. "Maybe she meant it as a compliment." She began toweling the extra conditioner out of my hair. "So," she said, after a beat, "why are you really here, sweetie?"

"I told you. I wanted to get my bangs trimmed."

"Your bangs are fine."

Damn. The woman was good. "Carla, when you and Uncle Frankie first got together, did you ever worry that maybe you wouldn't fit in with each other's worlds? Or that your friends wouldn't accept him? Or that you might want more than he could give? Or that he played everything so close to the vest, you were afraid you'd never really know him? Or—"

"Sweetie, is everything all right between you and Nick?"

"Absolutely. Why do you ask?"

"No reason." I caught the reflection of her smile in the mirror as she picked up a pair of scissors and snipped away at my split ends. "I'm thinking about having a dinner party next weekend," she said. "Nothing big. Just you and Nick, if you're free."

"Are you sure? I mean, that would be great. But, y'know, Uncle Frankie..."

"Your uncle will be fine. He loves you and he wants you to be happy. If he has a problem with Nick, I'll remind him that he wasn't exactly a dream catch, either. At least not according to my family. And look how well that turned out."

"Uh, Carla, didn't your Uncle Vito try to run him over with his Cadillac?"

"His foot slipped. So, seven o'clock okay?"

*****

"Yo, Sis, Could I, like, uh, borrow Daisy?"

I shifted my phone to my other ear and downed the espresso Nick handed me. I was sitting by the bay window in his living room, watching early morning joggers do laps around Rittenhouse Square. "Who's Daisy?"

My brother coughed. "Oh. I meant the puppy."

"But you called her Daisy. And I thought you were allergic."

"Yeah, well, I have to call her something."

"You're getting attached, aren't you?" I grinned into the phone.

"Th-this is strictly for the purpose of m-meeting women," Paul stuttered. "And you were right, by the way. This puppy is a chick magnet. I have a date tonight," he announced. "So, if anybody asks, Daisy is mine."

"That could be arranged."

"L-let's see how tonight goes, first."

"I'll drop her off this afternoon," I told him, hanging up.

The dogs sat by my side, patiently awaiting the inevitable crumbs from my breakfast cannoli to fall onto the hardwood floor.

"Daisy, you are so in!" I raised her arm and gave her a little paw to hand high five.

Nick stood in the vestibule, strapping an ankle holster onto his leg. He looked up and noticed me watching him. I tried to remain impervious to the growing anxiety that welled up in me, but it was an uphill battle.

He adjusted the cuff of his pants and walked over to me. "What's on your agenda today, Angel?"

"I was about to ask you the same thing," I said, eying his leg.

"Business as usual." He leaned over my shoulder and

read from the notes I held in my lap. "Nothing turned up on Wade Stoller?"

I shook my head. Vince had been good to his word and had checked him out. "Not so much as a parking ticket. Nick, I know he was lying about Calvin Doyle. And it was clear that he was uncomfortable with me hanging around K-Nine Security. I'm thinking of making a return visit."

If Nick wanted to object, he didn't show it. Instead, he picked up his keys and bent down to kiss me. "I'm going on a short road trip, Angel, and I'm afraid you won't be able to get in touch with me. If you can wait on this little excursion, I'd be happy to go with you. If not—" his mouth formed a wry smile— "take the gun. Leave the cannoli."

*****

I'd planned on borrowing Nick's truck to take the newly christened Daisy to my brother's house. As I walked out of the security gate, I found the LeSabre sitting in the loading zone in front of the building. Crap. Nick's mechanic must've dropped off the maroon whale early that morning.

It's not that I'm a car snob. I'm not. At sixteen, my first set of wheels was an ancient Volkswagen Beetle with a broken clutch and no back window. I loved that car. It was totally cool. But with temperatures climbing into the high eighties, I didn't relish the idea of driving around town without a working air conditioner.

There was a note on the dashboard. "Took the liberty of getting the air conditioning fixed. Hope you don't mind.—Nick."

My heart fluttered at his thoughtfulness, and I pulled out my phone to thank him. And then I remembered he couldn't be reached. So, instead, I ruminated (read: obsessed) about what kind of business Nick had that would render him incommunicado. I had to process this with someone, and, as luck would have it, Daisy was as good a listener as Adrian was. She sat in the back happily chewing on the seat belt, while I poured my worried heart out to her.

"Nick and I are…complicated, Daisy. Look, I know it's hard for you to understand, being what—four months old…and a dog. But, trust me, relationships are not easy."

Daisy stopped chewing and sat up. The strap, in tatters, dangled jauntily from her mouth. She dropped it onto the floor of the car and licked the back of my neck.

"What are you trying to tell me, girl? That love conquers all? And that in order for our relationship to work, I'll have to learn to accept Nick unconditionally, the way he accepts me?"

Wisely, Daisy didn't respond. She knew there were some things I'd just have to figure out on my own.

*****

My mom called just as I was leaving the firing range. "Your father's worried about you. He says Jewish girls don't own guns."

I hung a left out of the parking lot and ran smack into traffic. "You raised me Catholic," I countered.

"That's very nice," my mother replied, in a tone that said she didn't think it was very nice at all. "My daughter is making jokes about carrying a lethal weapon in her purse."

Uh-oh. Here it comes. Wait for it, wait for it…

"Didn't we raise you better than that?"

Ah, the age old question. "I guess not, Mom."

I knew my glib remark would cost me. It was met with stony silence. I would apologize, but first, I had to go back to Paul's and kill him for running off at the mouth to my parents. Earlier, I'd made the mistake of asking him if he wanted to join me for target practice. I (apparently, mistakenly) thought that if I showed him how I'm learning to take care of myself, he'd stop worrying about me.

" I'm sorry, Mom. Since I'm in-between jobs, I thought I'd learn a new skill. Beef up the old resume."

"So, what's wrong with accounting?"

My dad chose that moment to jump into the conversation, thus saving me from a life of pocket protectors and nerd jokes. "Nah, accounting's not for our girl. She's a people person, like her old man. Aren't ya, doll? Here, Lorraine, lemme have the phone."

My mother must have passed him the receiver, because, suddenly, my dad's voice came in loud and clear. "How're ya doin, hon? Everything all right?"

"I'm fine, Dad." A car stalled in the right hand lane. I swung around it and barely made the light.

My father lowered his voice, a sign that he was about to say something sensitive. "You need a little cash to tide you over?"

God, yes! "No, I'm good. But I appreciate you asking, Daddy."

"Okay, honey. Let me know if you change your mind. Listen, your mother's chomping at the bit to get back on. I'll talk to you soon."

I love my mom very much. And I know she loves me, too. But, there are times when I'm not sure that she really approves of me. This was one of those times.

"Brandy," she admonished, as she reclaimed control of the phone, "I've been hearing some very disturbing things about you, lately."

"Disturbing things? What things? From who?"

"I can't recall," she sniffed. Once my mother proclaimed something, it became fact. End of discussion.

"Mom, I don't know who you've been talking to, but everything is fine. Really."

"It's that new man in your life, isn't it?" she decided, ignoring my protestations. "The handsome one. I've heard he's dangerous. Maybe you should talk to Father Vincenzo. I'm sure he'll be able to advise you. He's always been very fond of you."

In actuality, the man thinks I'm the devil incarnate, but I didn't have time to argue, because, suddenly, there was a more pressing matter. A dark colored sedan with tinted windows had appeared, seemingly out of nowhere, in my rear view mirror. It was two cars back in the next lane over and gaining on me. A chill scuttled up my spine. It was Donte Lewis' car. I was sure of it. "Mom, I've gotta go." She was in the middle of her signature sign-off, *Call your brother,* when I hung up on her.

I felt something wet on my face and realized I had broken out in a massive sweat. My mouth got all watery, my breathing ragged, and I was pretty sure I was going to throw up. Fuck. A panic attack. Could it come at a less convenient time?

I took a couple of deep cleansing breaths, like I learned at Franny's LaMaze class, and cranked up the air conditioner full tilt. That helped a little, but the added strain on the engine almost sent it into cardiac arrest. I flipped off the air conditioning and sat there battling dizziness and nausea.

Traffic stalled at a red light. I grabbed the phone and punched in 911.

The voice on the line was firm and reassuring. "This is 911. What is your emergency?"

"I'm in my car and I'm being followed."

"Do you feel that you're in immediate danger?"

"Yes. I'm pretty sure they're out to kill me. Could you send a squad car right away?"

"Hold on, Ma'am. What makes you think they're trying to kill you?"

The light changed and we started moving again. I glanced in the side mirror. The sedan was now one car length behind. Traffic in the left lane was moving faster than the right, which meant at any moment they'd come sidling up next to me. I'd be ripe for the picking. Every nerve cell stood on end. I opened the glove compartment, reached in and took out my gun, and laid it on the seat beside me.

"It's a long story, but you've got to trust me on this. The police are looking for the car that's chasing me. Look,

I don't mean to rush you, but do you think you could speed it up a little?"

"What's your name, Ma'am?"

"Brandy Alexander."

"What's your location, Brandy? Be as specific as possible."

"I'm at 36th and Market, heading east. I'm driving a maroon LeSabre. The other car is charcoal grey with blacked out windows. I'm not sure, but I think it's an Accura."

"If you can find a public place to pull over, do it. Lock your car and stay put. There's a cruiser in the vicinity. It's on the way."

Crown Fried Chicken was up ahead. I was going to park in their lot—safety in numbers and all that. But I knew from experience that whoever was driving that car would have no problem gunning me down in broad daylight and maybe take out a few innocent by-standers in the process. I couldn't risk anyone else getting hurt.

"It's too dangerous. I'm going to keep driving. Please, hurry."

I eased the car into the left lane and watched in horror as the dark grey car veered into the right. It was one car back, almost parallel with mine. Steering one-handed, I reached for the gun with the other, wrapped my fingers around the handle and cocked the hammer. I did not want to shoot anyone. But better them than me.

The car in front of the sedan hung a quick left. The sedan zoomed ahead, filling the gap next to my car. Without hesitation, I raised the gun and began to lower the passenger side window.

Suddenly, there was a break in traffic in the right hand lane. I slowed down and edged over, tucking in behind a truck. The grey car tried to switch lanes again but got sandwiched between a bus and a Ford Expedition.

Nearby, a police siren went off. I glanced in the side view mirror and spied a cruiser about half a block away threading its way through the congested street. Up ahead, two more squad cars darted out of a side street, their sirens screaming. Traffic snarled up as drivers scrambled to get out of the way. The cruisers converged on the grey car, forcing it to the curb. *They've got you, you bastard.*

I pulled in several yards behind them and cut the engine. As my heartbeat slowed to a sprint, I realized I was still holding a loaded weapon. Carefully, I reset the hammer and stuffed it back in the glove compartment. Then, I leaned forward and waited for the scene in front of me to unfold. Nothing happened.

Fear turned to curiosity, so I rolled down the window to get a better view. The cops were just sitting in their car. I guessed they were running a check on the license plate.

After a few minutes, an officer emerged from the cruiser and approached the grey vehicle. He didn't look particularly concerned for his safety. He didn't even have his gun drawn. He motioned for the driver to roll down the window.

A driver's license exchanged hands. The cop looked at it and nodded his head a couple of times and then handed it back to the person inside the car. Suddenly, two small heads emerged from the rear window. The heads sported baseball caps. Adorable faces peeked out from under the caps.

The driver's side door opened and a woman in her late thirties climbed out of the car. She had on a white tee shirt with big red letters that said, "Proud Soccer Mom." She looked seriously pissed off.

I rolled up the window and turned on the air, letting the cool breeze dry my clammy skin. I shut my eyes and leaned back against the headrest.

There was a tap on the window. My eyes flew open. A cop stood next to the car, his cheeks flushed from the staggering heat. I turned off the air conditioning and rolled down the window.

His badge said Officer Smiley, a misnomer if ever there

was one.   Officer Smiley's face brimmed with surly attitude. He jerked his head sideways toward the woman in the tee shirt, his voice dripping with unbridled sarcasm. "Why don't you step out of the car, Ma'am? Councilwoman Claire Dobbs would like to meet you."

Turns out, I'd made a tiny error in identifying a city council member as my personal hitman. It was the tinted windows that threw me.

It took over an hour (and a lot of fancy explaining) before the police and Soccer Mom agreed not to haul me down town for psychological testing.

"Um, if you'd just give Vincent Giancola a call, at the D.A.'s office, I'm sure this would all be cleared up in a matter of minutes."

Vincent, albeit reluctantly, corroborated my story.

See? I'm not really crazy or some kind of sick prankster. Rather, my emergency 911 call was a stress-induced aberration from an otherwise perfectly upstanding citizen. I was just lucky they hadn't seen me waving that gun around like a flag on the Fourth of July, or it would have been a very different outcome.

After Councilwoman Dobbs informed me that I'd be hearing from her lawyer, I was allowed to leave. I ran back to my car and called Vince. "Thanks for bailing me out, Vince. I really owe you one."

"I've lost count on what you owe me." He hesitated, his voice going uncharacteristically soft. "I've gotta tell you, kiddo, I'm worried about you."

"I know. I'm worried about me, too."

Under the watchful eye of Officer Smiley, I eased my way out of the parking spot and took off. I was completely unnerved. My life had gotten so out of control, I'd come this close to shooting an innocent woman. In front of her kids! This was not good.

My hands began to shake so hard I could barely steer the car. Great. Not only did I look mentally unstable but drunk as well. I gripped the wheel tighter and got off the main road.

I wanted to talk to Nick. He wouldn't freak out, and he wouldn't judge me. But Nick had already left for parts unknown. "Would it always be this way?" I wondered. *Note to self: Check Santiago's availability before scheduling next emotional breakdown.*

My pity party had just gotten underway when I spotted DiCarlo's Mustang parked in DiVinci's lot. Hello Kitty was perched on top of his antennae, a gift from his three-year old daughter, Sophia.

I found a spot on the street and hopped out of the car. Bobby would definitely freak out and judge me plenty when I told him what happened. But, for some weird reason, I needed to hear him say it.

My eyes took a few minutes to dial up from intense sunlight mode to the dimness of the restaurant. Sanford, the owner, calls it mood lighting. The locals suspect it's to hide the fact that he hasn't redecorated since 1982.

For once, I wasn't even remotely tempted by the smell of pepperoni pizza and fried calzones wafting through the air. I just wanted to find Bobby and unburden my conscience. The restaurant was jammed with diners taking advantage of the lunchtime special. I scanned the room but couldn't locate him, so I headed for the bar and ordered a coke.

Someone in a corner booth called my name. I looked up and immediately regretted it. The voice belonged to my longtime frienemy, Mindy Rebowitz. *Unhh.*

It was too late to pretend I didn't hear her. I gave her a half-hearted wave and got very busy inspecting the snack bowl. Well, someone had to make sure there was just the right balance of Chex Mix and Spanish Peanuts.

I felt a nudge at my side as Mindy's elbow found its way into my personal space.

"Brandy," she crooned, in that annoying sing-song way of hers. "How are you?"

Before I could rustle up a decent lie, she continued, "I

was sooooo sorry to hear you got fired." She tilted her head; a gesture meant to convey sympathy. "You must feel so humiliated."

I stopped sorting rye chips and looked up. "Actually, Mindy, I'm good. In fact, it's opened up a world of opportunities for me. I'm thinking of starting a blog…or trying out for *The Next Food Network Star*. So many options, so little time." I finished off the Coke and threw some cash on the counter. "Speaking of time, I've got to run. "It was great seeing you. Really great!"

I slid off the stool and exited the side door. By this time, I was desperate to talk to Bobby, so I pulled out my phone to call him. That's when I spotted him at the far end of the parking lot. He was slouched against a green Ford Focus, talking to Lauren. I started to wave to catch his attention. Only, just then, he grabbed her around the waist and pulled her close, and gave her what had to be the longest lip-lock in the history of the universe.

I slipped back through the side door and left by the front entrance.

CHAPTER FIFTEEN

The next morning, John met me for coffee at Gleaner's Cafe on Ninth Street.

Gleaner's is a favorite of mine for many reasons, not the least of which is the complimentary Hershey's Kisses that come with the meal. Since I'd brought Adrian along with me, I grabbed a table outside. Without Daisy to keep him company, he'd just been moping around the apartment. I thought an outing might lift his spirits.

John was wearing a Phillies' cap, which surprised the heck out of me. He says that baseball caps are the lazy man's attempt at fashion, and he takes pride in his appearance.

"What's with the hat?" I asked.

With a show of reluctance, he removed it and waited while I gave him the once-over. "Johnny, I can't believe you shaved your head. I swear to God, it looks great."

John ran his hand over the peach fuzz and smiled. "You really think so? Carla talked me into it. I was nervous at first, but I figured it had to be better than masquerading as a French Poodle until the damn perm grew out. It took a little getting used to…you really think I look okay?"

"I really do."

He leaned back and relaxed into his seat.

"So, what did Garrett say about the new you?"

"He hasn't seen it yet. To tell you the truth, I think he'll hate it. Mainly because it wasn't his idea."

"You want to talk about it?" I asked and tossed a bit of my bagel to Adrian. He caught it neatly and swallowed it whole.

John shook his head. I was relieved. Anything I could contribute to a conversation about Garrett would either be insincere or unsupportive. John deserved better than that.

"Let's talk about you, he said. "I heard you called 911 because someone on the city council tailgated you."

"Jeez, John. Where'd you hear that? You know, that's how rumors get started." I ended up spilling the entire story, including the epilogue starring Bobby and his make-out partner, Officer Cutie Pie.

John did a sympathy grimace. "Ooh, Sunshine. That couldn't have been easy to watch."

"Yeah, well, I didn't stick around long enough to find out. And before you go leaping to the conclusion that I was jealous…okay, I'm willing to admit there might have been a small degree of territorial feelings involved."

"How small are we talking here?"

"Okay, technically, I'm talking huge. And I can't understand it myself, so don't go all analytical on me, okay? Look the point is he really likes this girl, y'know? And if I'd come charging up there, all emotionally needy— I just didn't want to wreck things for him." I shrugged. "I want him to be happy."

"You know what you did, don't you?"

"What?" I asked so that I could add it to the list of countless ways in which I'd screwed up, lately.

"You put DiCarlo's needs before your own." He grinned and passed me his Hershey's Kisses. "Our little girl is growing up."

*****

Surveillance work can be excruciatingly dull, which is

why, when I went back to K-Nine Security to do some additional recon, I brought along some company. The other reason is (contrary to popular belief) I do learn from my mistakes, and I understand the value of reliable back up.

Alphonso and I were parked down the block from the building, playing the waiting game until Wade Stoller walked out the door. We could have come by after the place closed to have our little look around the facility. But, breaking into a building full of guard dogs seemed like a really dumb idea. Plus, it's always nicer to be invited.

Still, there wasn't a prayer of doing any snooping with Stoller on the premises. Consequently, we'd arranged for him to meet up with a potential client, a rap singer in need of protection from his legions of fans. Unfortunately for Wade, the phantom rapper lived about an hour's drive away.

"The guy should've left by now. This is no way to run a business," Alphonso complained.

"May I remind you, he's not really meeting anyone? We'll be lucky if he hasn't already figured out that Big Dreddy Locks is a rapper in your mind only. How'd you come up with that ridiculous name, anyway?"

Alphonso grinned. "It's a gift."

I whipped out my phone to check the time. Alphonso eyed it and laughed.

"My five-year old niece has a fancier phone than that. Why don't you replace that relic with something from this century?"

"I did, but they kept getting lost or broken…or falling in the toilet. What? It could happen to anyone… repeatedly." I stuffed it back in my pocket and searched for a new topic of conversation. "So," I settled on, "how's the big romance going with Nicole?"

"Who?"

"Nicole, the woman you were so hot for a few weeks back?"

Alphonso thought for a minute. "Oh yeah, Nicole. I forgot about her. I should give her a call sometime."

I bit my tongue to keep from giving him a good smack and pulled out my phone again. Janine was calling.

"Bran, I need your opinion," she said, skipping the usual conversational amenities. "Do you think it's too soon to sleep with Mike? I mean I know he likes me, but this would really seal the deal."

"Neenie, you have to stop using sex to get the guy."

"Shut up. You do it, too."

"No, I don't."

Janine considered this. "Oh, you're right. I was thinking of Fran."

"Fran doesn't do it either. Just you. Listen, can I call you back? I'm in the middle of something."

I hung up with Janine and caught Alphonso staring at me. "Yes?"

"I'd like to meet Janine. She sounds nice." He flashed me his thousand watt smile and pointed out the window. "There he goes."

I grabbed my binoculars from under the seat and took a look. The black van pulled out of the driveway with Stoller at the wheel. We waited five more minutes to make sure he wasn't coming back. Then we unloaded our equipment (a fourteen-year old video camera my dad had left in the basement when my parents moved to Florida) and headed up the street.

Kaye answered the buzz and let us in. Her eyes roamed over Alphonso, taking in his considerable attributes. Alphonso ramped up the wattage on his smile. "Nice ink," he said, giving a nod to the skull and crossbones on her forearm.

Kaye blushed. "Thanks. I designed it myself." She glanced at the dinosaur of a video camera perched atop Alphonso's shoulder. "Was Wade expecting you? He just left for an appointment."

"Oh, that's too bad," I sighed. "We were in the

neighborhood and I thought we'd come by to get some footage of the place for the piece on local businesses. Unfortunately, we're on deadline and need this right away." I paused, as if the disappointment was too much to bear.

Alphonso glanced over at me and played along. "Tell you what? How about we go ahead and film and then do the interview with Wade later, if this pretty lady would consent to taking me on a tour."

"Oh, hon, I don't know. Wade wasn't real keen on the idea. Said something about protecting his clients' privacy."

"Well, I can see his concern, but let me reassure you, we have no intention of compromising his relationship with his clients. We wouldn't film anything that might in any way jeopardize his business. If anything, this piece will enhance it."

"Well, we sure could use the publicity. Business has been a little slow here, lately. And, between you and me, I think my nephew is a bit on the stubborn side, sometimes. He insists on doing everything his way. Of course, it is his company, but sometimes I wonder. Oh, heck, why don't we go ahead and get started," she decided. "I'm sure he'll come around once he sees how good it will be for the business."

"Great. Alphonso, why don't you start with some outdoor shots, maybe get some footage of Kaye standing under the sign. And then we can move on to the kennels. In the mean time," I scooted next to Kaye and put my mouth to her ear, "something I ate must not have agreed with me, so if you could direct me to the powder room, I'd be very grateful."

"Sure thing, hon. You can use the one in Wade's office. More privacy and a little cleaner." She winked, woman to woman. "It's straight down that hall. First door on the right."

"Oh, thank you." I shot her a grateful smile and watched as Alphonso followed her outside. She had no idea what a gift she'd just handed me.

Wade's office was sparse. A large computer monitor sat on top of a weathered oak desk. There was a matching file cabinet situated behind it and some padded chairs for guests. A plastic palm tree, no doubt a gift from Kaye, capped off the floor décor.

A calendar was tacked to the wall, displaying the month of August. Some dates and times were circled in red. One was starred. I took a picture of it. Next to the calendar were framed pictures of Wade, flanked by several highly imposing-looking attack dogs, sitting obediently by his side. The eyes on one of the dogs followed me around the room as I poked into things I wasn't supposed to. It looked about to jump off the wall and rip my throat out.

Stoller had left the computer on, which I found oddly disappointing. If he'd had something to hide, wouldn't it be locked up tight, instead of so completely accessible to random passers-by? Maybe I was wrong about him…unless he didn't see the need to go to the trouble of turning everything off. After all, who'd be crazy enough to break into building full of professional attack dogs?

A quick scan of his document folders yielded me his client contact information. I checked the one for the security service. No red flags there, but I took some pictures with my phone, so that I could examine it more closely, later. There was a separate folder marked drug detection. The list was small, only three clients in that one. One stood out among the others, only I wasn't sure why. I copied that list, too.

The web browser was open to a page that advertised wholesale dog food. I clicked to another open tab, this one for synthetic grass. Gaah, was this guy boring. There were no more open tabs, so I clicked on his web history and scrolled down. More dog food comparison shopping, the weather report, an article on hair restoration, and, a youtube video. It must've been a good one because he'd watched it over a dozen times.

I clicked on it and almost vomited. The picture was grainy, but there was no mistaking the content. A hand held camera zeroed in on the back of someone's head. The person was female, short in stature, with long, dark hair, a tangled mess. The camera pulled back to reveal the woman's back. She was standing outside in her bra.

Suddenly, the view shifted, and the inside of a car trunk appeared. Once again the camera zoomed in, this time on the telltale, heart shaped spot on Popeye's left leg. Bile rose in my throat. I swallowed hard, cringing at the bitter aftertaste.

As I relived the drama on the screen, the horror of that day came flooding back to me. My chest tightened and my head swam. But even as I fought to stay upright, I knew I'd struck gold.

I ducked into Stoller's private bathroom and closed the door. Turning on the light, I steadied myself against the sink and sprinkled water on my face. The coolness helped to calm me. As the nausea began to subside, my brain struggled to process this new information. Well, I'd figure out what it all meant, later. For now, I had to grab Alphonso and get the hell out.

Quickly, I dried my hands, pushed open the bathroom door and ran headlong into Wade Stoller. He grunted and reeled back as my forehead smacked against his chest.

Fuck all. "Oh. I'm sorry," I stammered, looking up. He was a lot taller than I'd remembered and considerably more formidable.

A momentary flash of anger surfaced in his eyes. "Well, this is a surprise," he said, regaining his composure.

I bit back my first response, *"No shit!"* and chuckled. "A pleasant surprise, I hope."

"What are you doing in my office?"

Okay, guess not. "I needed to go to the little girl's room, and your aunt told me to use the one in here, because it's nicer. I must say the toilet paper is very good quality. Extra soft."

Stoller tapped his foot and the spur on his boot jingled merrily. "I can see that you used the bathroom. What I meant was why are you here in the building?"

"Oh, sorry." My eyes cut automatically to the desk. *Oh, for Crap's sake. When I was on the computer, I moved the mouse and forgot to put it back where it was...okay, Brandy, stay calm. Maybe he won't notice that it's on a completely different side of the monitor now...or that I left the youtube video up on the screen...although that's kinda hard to miss. Shit, shit, shit. What do I do now? I know! I'll talk about his high quality toilet paper some more.*

I began bouncing on the balls of my feet, as if the very idea of what I was about to say was so enthralling, I couldn't contain my excitement. As I bounced I worked my way incrementally back to the desk, effectively blocking Wade's view of the computer screen.

"My assistant and I were in the neighborhood and we'd hoped to grab a few moments of your time to discuss that piece I'm doing on local businesses. Kaye thinks it's a great idea, by the way. She's giving my assistant a tour of the facility as we speak."

Stoller's voice hardened. "Like I already told you, I'm not interested."

"Oh, but that's because you haven't seen how much it can help your business. Here, let me show you." In a flash, I'd grabbed the mouse and clicked out of the video and began randomly clicking on whatever popped up on the screen. "Gee, I know it's here somewhere."

Stoller lunged for me, and slapped his hand over mine. I froze.

"I don't know what you think you're doing, but where I come from it's called trespassing. Now, we're going to walk out of here and find your friend. And you're not coming back. Is that clear?"

I nodded all wide-eyed innocence. "Crystal clear."

Stoller escorted me by the elbow to the front office. Alphonso was just coming in from his tour with Kaye. He raised an eyebrow and I gave a slight shake of my head. Alphonso shrugged and reached an arm around his back. It was a casual gesture unless you were privy to what he had stored in his waistband.

"Um, Kaye," I said, keeping up pretenses for the only person in the room who still bought into our charade. "Wade isn't interested in participating in our news segment, so we'll be going now. Sorry to take up your time."

Kaye flashed her nephew a scowl. "I'm sorry, hon. Like I said, Wade can be stubborn."

I headed for the door and Alphonso fell in behind me. I breathed a sigh of relief knowing he was watching my back.

As we swung open the door and stepped through the threshold, Kaye addressed her nephew. "What are you doing back so soon? I thought your appointment was all the way across town." We didn't stick around for his answer.

I kept quiet until we reached the car. Alphonso threw the camera into the back seat and started the engine. Breaking the silence he asked, "What happened in there?"

"Plenty. He's on to me."

"You sure?"

I leaned my head against the coolness of the window. "Oh, yeah. I'm sure. But wait til you hear what I discovered."

*****

When I got back to Nick's, I found Adrian curled up next to Rocky on the couch. Neither of them seemed particularly psyched to see me, so I tossed them each a treat to get them to like me again. As my morbidly obese Aunt Doris used to say, food is love.

I took Adrian across the street for a walk in the square to compensate for the overfeeding. I thought maybe I'd run across Paul and Daisy there. As much as my brother denied it, he was falling in love with that little girl. I smiled to myself, thinking about it.

As I slipped back into the apartment again, my phone rang. I checked the readout. It was DiCarlo. I let it go to voicemail and slipped the phone back in my pocket.

I was a little hungry, so I made a peanut butter and honey sandwich, and then I started my daily round of phone calls. First, I called the police station to see if anyone had confessed to the murder of Mrs. Gentile's planter. (I tend to go into denial mode when people try to kill me. It's more palatable to think that I was merely an innocent bystander caught in the crossfire of a succulent-hating miscreant) Next, I checked out the jobs on Craig's List. No luck in that department, but I got a great deal on a used kayak.

After that, I called Vince to tell him about my visit to K-Nine Security. He didn't pick up his cell phone so I tried the office. His assistant took my name and put me on hold. While I waited for Vince to get on the line, I thought about how I'd spin the story so that I wouldn't look like a total criminal. Because, technically, (at least as far as I was concerned) I'd done nothing wrong. I had been, after all, invited in.

A minute later, Vince's assistant got back on the line and informed me that he wasn't available. I got the feeling he just wasn't available to me, so I called Janine.

"Yo, Neenie. Do me a favor and call Vincent."

"Sure. But why don't you call him yourself?"

"I just want to see if he'll pick up for you. I think he's avoiding me."

"Why would he avoid you?"

"Because he thinks I'm being a pain in the butt."

"Well, are you?"

"No more than usual."

We hung up and she called me back a minute later. "He's really not there."

"Thanks. Talk to you later."

My brain was on overload, so I went into Nick's

bedroom and crawled into bed. I lay on my back and did some controlled breathing exercises, which might have worked, except that Nick's scent lingered on the pillow case. With every deep breath I took, I was reminded of just what I was missing.

After a minute or so of tossing and turning, I gave up and grabbed a pen and pad of paper out of the drawer. If I wasn't going to relax, I might as well make good use of my time. Bobby always told me that the most important thing in an investigation is to look for connections among seemingly random facts. So, what were the facts? I began to write.

Donte and Mario Lewis, both card carrying members of The Junk Town Gang, dabbled in dog fighting. Mario, Donte, and Calvin Doyle, along with a flame- throwing guy named, appropriately enough, Torch, were in some undisclosed business together. Cal and Donte were afraid their boss would find out about Mario screwing up, so they killed Mario. Now, Calvin is dead and Donte Lewis is missing. No word on the pyromaniac, Torch.

I made a side note. Did Lewis and Torch kill Calvin? If so, why? Deal gone wrong? And where the hell were they now?

Moving along. Wade Stoller tried to hide his association with Calvin Doyle. Plus, he must have had a vested interest in the Mario Lewis incident. Why else would he watch that video over and over? Could Stoller be the boss Lewis and Doyle were so afraid of? And if so, what was his game?

All I had was a gut feeling and a thirty second youtube clip, so I didn't rush to talk it over with the police. My intuition would be a hard sell to those assigned to the case. Especially after the Claire Dobbs debacle.

Somewhere in the middle of perusing Stoller's client list I fell asleep. When I awoke two hours later the sun had already gone down. But even in the darkness, I knew I wasn't alone.

My brain was set to auto-panic, but as I breathed in, all

I felt was a sense of joy and well being. My heart did a happy dance and I rolled over into Nick's arms.

"When did you get back?"

"About an hour ago. You were dead to the world, and I didn't want to wake you."

"I wasn't asleep. Just resting my eyes."

"You were sleeping." Nick brushed my bangs away from my face. "You hate feeling vulnerable, don't you?" he said, softly. It wasn't an accusation, just an observation, and I was grateful that he knew me so well.

I snuggled in closer. "I missed you."

"I missed you, too." He got up and stripped off his clothes and climbed back into bed. I laid my head on his bare chest and listened as his breathing began to quicken.

"So, how'd things go in...uh, where'd you say you went again?"

In response he slid his hand under my shirt and slipped his tongue in my mouth.

"That's not an answer," I said, although it was a spectacular diversionary tactic.

"Will it do for now?"

"For now," I agreed, because even as I pressed for details, those age-old words of wisdom rattled around in my mind. *Be careful what you wish for. You just might get it.*

I untangled myself from his arms and walked over to the curtains and let the moonlight stream in. Nick's clothes lay in a pile on the floor in the corner of the room. They smelled of dirt, and secret, exotic locations, and I was gripped by a pang of fear that was washed away the moment he reached for me again.

Later, we sat at the bar in his kitchen, and I watched while he whipped up dinner; linguine with mussels and a radicchio salad.

"Open," he commanded, and pressed a spoonful of buttery, garlic flavored broth to my lips.

"Oh, my God. This is fantastic." I took the spoon from him and helped myself to more. "Seriously, is there anything you can't do?"

"Actually, there are quite a few things, Angel."

"Name one."

Nick's smile flickered. "I noticed there wasn't a lot of food in the apartment," he said, deftly changing the subject. "Just what were you eating while I was away?"

"Stuff." Mostly dessert, but if Nick could keep secrets, I could, too.

"Touche." He smiled again and handed me a long handled wooden fork. "Dinner's almost ready. Would you mind testing the linguine for me?"

I plunged the fork in the pot and stirred it around a bit and then scooped up some pasta. Years ago, my mother, a notoriously bad cook, (a fact that flies in the face of her Italian heritage) told me that if I threw the noodles against the wall and they stuck it was ready to eat. After years of overcooked pasta that tasted like Elmer's Glue, I came up with my own method to test for doneness. Pop a strand into my mouth and chew. If it doesn't break a tooth, it's good to go.

Over dinner, I filled Nick in on my trip to K-Nine Security. "Aside from the fact that I got caught red-handed, I think it went pretty well."

"You got out alive. That's always a plus."

"True. Anyway, for the sake of argument, let's assume that Stoller is running some kind of illegal operation. He meets Calvin Doyle, they get to talking, and Stoller ends up hiring Doyle to help him with whatever it is he's doing."

"Doyle knows Donte Lewis from the hospital. He brings Donte on board, and through him, Mario and Torch."

"Right. Now, whether Stoller knew about the other guys is a moot point. The main thing is Mario fucks up, so they kill him before Stoller finds out. Except, they didn't bargain on that video going viral. Stoller sees it and realizes that Cal got him involved with a bunch of incompetents." I stabbed a clam off my plate and popped it into my mouth.

"Sounds plausible," Nick mused. "But it doesn't explain how Doyle's charred body ended up in Donte Lewis' basement."

"I'm working on it," I said and made a mental note to hound Mike again.

"By the way," Nick said, "I got some information on the illusive Mr. Torch." He paused. "Maybe we should have this discussion after dinner."

You would think all that talk of charred bodies would dampen my appetite. Sadly, it did not. I took another helping, because, honestly, I didn't know when I'd eat so well again. "Nah, I'm good. So, what did you find out?"

Nick reached into his back pocket and took out his wallet and handed me a piece of paper. I unfolded it and shuddered. It was a copy of Torch's mug shot. One of many, I surmised. I stared hard at the smug smile and eerily vacant eyes. *So this is what it looks like to be born without a soul.*

"His real name is Reginald Harwinton," Nick told me. "By all accounts, he's seriously disturbed. He spent a couple of years upstate in the psych ward of a maximum security prison for, among other things, setting fire to a dog. Even his Junk Town brethren are afraid of him. He operates on his own quite a bit. Doesn't show particular loyalty to the gang, but he's always there when something fun goes down. If anything needs to be tortured, Reggie's your man—which, by the way, is where his nickname originally came from. The blowtorch was a later addition. The word is he'd do anything on a bet or for a buck."

Putting a face to the name was more than I could stand. I folded the picture up and tossed it on the counter.

"What's wrong, Angel?"

"I feel so out of control."

Nick slid off the bar stool and wrapped his arms around me. "I know you do, Darlin.' You want your life back. And since that's not possible right now, you're putting all your energy into solving other people's problems. What do you say we put all this aside, just for tonight? I have something that might make you feel better."

He reached into the cabinet and took out a box of TASTYKAKES.

"Hey," I said, lighting up. "They weren't there this afternoon."

"I picked them up for you on the way home, today."

"I guess it would be pointless to ask on your way home from where." The words came out with an unintended edge. I averted my eyes from his gaze and opened the box. "Thank you for getting them for me." I unwrapped two and ate them and washed them down with some wine.

"Okay," I decided, after a healthy slug of Pinot Grigio. (I don't even like wine, but I'm trying to class up my palette a bit.) "We're going to play a modified version of Twenty Questions. I'm going to ask you some questions and you can only answer with a yes or no. But it has to be the truth. It'll be fun. You'll see."

Nick drained his wine glass and set it on the coffee table. "I think we may have different ideas of what constitutes fun. I'll answer three. So choose carefully."

"First question. Whatever you were doing when you went away, were you in danger?"

He looked at me steadily. "Yes."

"Was it legal?"

"Maybe."

"Yes or no only."

"Then, no."

"Do you love me?"

"Yes."

"Enough to trust me with your secrets?"

"That was four questions, Angel. Game over."

CHAPTER SIXTEEN

"Are you avoiding Bobby?"

"Don't be ridiculous. Did he say I was avoiding him? Because I'm not."

Fran snickered softly into the phone. "So, how come you're avoiding him?"

It was mid morning, and traffic was backed up all the way to City Hall. I was on my way to Sherese's house. I would have called first, but I didn't know her phone number. Plus, I wasn't entirely sure she would speak to me. The last time I'd seen her, we'd parted on a semi-friendly note, but that could change in a heartbeat.

"Look," I said and swung wide to avoid a bicyclist, "I am a very busy person, Fran. What with butting into other people's business, feeding my neurotic impulses, dwelling on all the mistakes I've made, both personal and professional—not to mention a week's worth of *King of Queens* reruns to catch up on, I don't have time to think about Bobby."

"Yeah, okay. So, what did he do to piss you off?"

"I saw him kissing his new girlfriend in DiVinci's parking lot."

"I can't believe it. The man should be horse whipped."

"Sarcasm noted and appreciated. Believe me, I know how dumb this is, and I'm working on it."

"Good, because Eddie's birthday's coming up, and I was thinking of having a party for him. But I'll limit the guest list to just the gang and no extras if it's too awkward for you." Extras, meaning Lauren, who I couldn't help but like, (damn it) and Garret, the poster boy for *hipster dufus*.

And then there was Nick, which brought up a whole other set of worries. After my not so subtle attempt to get him to open up, things felt a bit strained between us.

"I don't mean to shut you out, Angel," he'd explained, afterwards. "But trust doesn't come naturally to me. I don't know that it ever will."

"I get it," I'd told him. *I hate it, but I get it.*

"Invite whoever you want, hon. I'll deal. Unh. I just missed my turn." I hung a quick u-ie and headed back the other way. Someone honked. Obviously, he was driving too fast. Otherwise, it wouldn't have appeared like I'd cut him off. I rolled down my window. "Yo, chooch. Learn to drive."

"Go pay attention to the road," Fran said. "I'll talk to you later."

"Good idea. Love you, Franny."

"Love you, too."

The scenery began to change at around Randolph and Erie. I rolled up my window and turned on the air, mostly to rid the car of the oppressive stench of broken dreams. Crack House Alley was to my right. I turned left at Junk Town and drove a couple more blocks to Garland.

I parked in front of the Rogers' house and walked across the street. Sherese's door was shut and the curtains drawn. I didn't relish re-entering the garbage heap she called home, but I had more questions and I was counting on her for the answers.

Avoiding the broken step on the porch, I went up to the door and gave a tentative knock. Inside, the TV blared. I knocked louder. Presently, the curtain moved and

Sherese's little girl appeared at the window.

"Mama, there's a lady at the door."

"Get away from the window, Ayana."

"Sherese," I called out. "It's Brandy Alexander. I'd like to talk to you."

The curtain opened a bit wider, and I stepped back so that she could get a look at me. It swung closed again, and a few seconds later the front door opened.

Sherese stood in the entryway, her toddler son peering out from between her legs.

"What you want?" There was no hostility in her voice, only curiosity. Something else was different about her, this time, too. She was sober.

"Look, can I come in?"

While she didn't exactly welcome me with open arms, she stepped aside to let me enter. My eyes automatically darted around the living room. Something was different. Where did all the dirty dishes go? And the place smelled…good. Like Pine Sol Disinfectant…or, the equally effective but economically cheaper generic brand. In the corner sat the hobby horse and one of the books I'd picked out for the kids.

Ayana stared at me with wide, unblinking eyes.

"Ayana," Sherese instructed, "take your brother into the bedroom and try to get him down for a nap, okay, baby girl?"

"No nap." The little boy screamed.

Ayana took him by the hand and coaxed him out of the room with promises of candy.

"You wanna sit down?" Sherese shoved a blanket off the sofa and cleared a space for me.

"Thanks." I sat on the edge of the sofa and began. "The reason I'm here is—and I don't mean to stir up painful memories for you, but I'd like to ask you some questions about Calvin Doyle."

"Why? It's not gonna bring him back."

"Okay, this is the thing. The cops believe Calvin was

killed over a drug deal gone wrong. I'm not privy to what all they're basing this on. I do know that Donte's back door had been broken into. Maybe Cal surprised him and they got into a fight, and…well, you know the rest. The point is Donte is their number one suspect. Well, him and some psycho named Reginald Harwinton."

Sherese nodded. "The one they call Torch. He been to the house a few times. Every time he showed up I'd take the kids and leave. That man is evil, and I don't mean it as no compliment. Anyway," she added, "like I told you before, what Mario and Cal was doing was their business. I don't know nothin' about it."

"Maybe you know more than you think. See, I might be wrong, but I don't believe it happened the way the police have it figured."

"Yeah? Well, the cops haven't done nothin' for me so far. If you have any idea what really happened to Cal, I'm willing to listen."

I recounted for her the events that led me to Wade Stoller. "Does the name ring a bell?"

Sherese pursed her lips in concentration. "No," she said, finally. She picked up a pack of cigarettes from the coffee table, took one out and put it to her lips. "Mind if I smoke?"

"Honestly?" I said.

She shrugged and tossed it back on the table. "So, you think that Cal and them others was working for that guy, Stoller. But you don't know what they was doing for him."

"Right," I admitted. "But I'm pretty sure it had to do with his drug detection business."

Sherese looked wistful. "All I know is Cal said he was working on something that could make him some money and he'd take me on a vacation."

Something that had been rattling around in the back of my mind pushed its way to the forefront. "You'd told me that Cal had wanted to take you on a cruise. Why a cruise? I mean it's sort've random, isn't it?"

"Yeah, I thought so, too. But he come over one day and tells me he knows somebody who can get him a free cruise and did I want to go. I said *hell, yeah*. I never been on a cruise before. Shit, I ain't never been out of the neighborhood."

She stood and walked toward the bedroom, talking to me over her shoulder. "I got a what'cha call, a brochure in here. I'll be right back."

Sherese emerged a few minutes later looking annoyed.

"What's wrong?"

"I can't find it. It was sitting out in plain sight on my night stand. Ayana!" she bellowed. She had impressive lung power for a smoker.

Ayana appeared at the doorway.

"Did you take that picture of the ship off my night stand? And don't lie to me."

Ayana took a precautionary side step. "No, Mama. I didn't."

"You sure?"

The little girl nodded and retreated into her bedroom.

"It was right there," Sherese murmured.

"I notice the house was…" *hmm…how to put this delicately…*"spruced up. Maybe you put it somewhere for safe keeping."

"No." She shook her head, her eyes filling up. "I liked looking at it. Y'know?" She was quiet for a beat. Then, "Now I think about it, I haven't seen that brochure since the break in."

"What break in?" *Wow. Did this woman have crappy luck or what?*

Sherese picked up the cigarette and, once again, put it to her lips. This time, she lit it and drew a deep breath, waving the smoke away from my general direction.

"Couple of weeks ago, me and the kids went out on errands. When we came home the house was a mess. Shit everywhere. Every drawer was opened. Clothes and shit was dumped on the floor. Even the couch cushions were overturned. My baby's piggy bank was broke in pieces. I checked around, and the back door window had been kicked in. I had to go and put boards up to keep the rats from climbing in."

"What was taken?"

"Nothin', far as I can tell. I ain't got nothin' worth taking. But it was nasty knowing somebody was pawing through our personal property. Candice, from across the street helped me to clean up," she added, lowering her eyes. "I guess I let things get away from me since Mario passed."

I knew the answer to the next question, but I asked it anyway. "Did you call the police?"

Sherese dragged on her cigarette and turned her head to let out a breath. "What was the use? Besides, I didn't want them snooping around here. I couldn't take a chance they'd find something wrong and bring social services down on me."

I nodded sympathetically, but my mind was elsewhere. "Sherese, the person or persons that broke in probably took the brochure, which is in line with everything I've just shared with you. Do you happen to remember the name of the cruise line?"

"Uh huh. Island Dream Vacations."

I was not in the least surprised.

"We was gonna go to some island I ain't never heard of."

"Don't worry about that for now. The important thing is they were after more than just the brochure. After all, you said it had been left out in plain sight. So, why would they continue their search after they'd found it?" I thought for a minute. "Did Cal ever ask you to keep anything safe for him?"

"Like what?"

"I don't know. Letters, documents, anything that might incriminate Wade Stoller if they turned up? Maybe Cal hid something here as insurance against something happening to him."

"If he did, he didn't tell me."

I handed her my phone number. "If anything comes to you, give me a call."

*****

After leaving Sherese's I needed to regroup, and what better place to do just that than the Barnes and Noble café. "I'll take a redeye, please."

The kid behind the counter punched in my order. He looked bored. "Will there be anything else?"

I scrounged around in my pocket book for more loose change and came up empty. Boy, being unemployed put a real crimp in my junk food consumption. I shook my head. "Thanks. That'll do it."

The window seat was occupied, so I had to content myself with a long table in the rear of the café. I took out my laptop and got to work. Or, I would have, except that someone had left a copy of *Fifty Shades of Grey* on the table, and it seemed only right to see what all the fuss was about.

At around chapter three I reluctantly put it down and started my research. It didn't take long to find what I was looking for. As a reward, I picked up the book again.

"I hear that's fascinating reading."

Startled, I looked up. DiCarlo stood in front of me, grinning. He was in his gym sweats and looked especially sexy…or maybe it was just the lingering thought of one of those fifty shades.

I slammed the book shut and slid it down the length of the table. "I thought it was a book on monochromatic interior design."

"Is that what they're calling porn now?"

"It's not porn. It's erotica…and shut up."

His grin got wider. He pulled a chair out and sat down across from me.

"How'd you know I was here?" I asked.

"Frankie told me this is your new hangout. I stopped in to pick up a book for Sophia, so I figured I'd come by and say hello. Actually," he added, "I thought I saw you the other day at DiVinci's."

"Nope, wasn't me."

"I'm pretty sure that it was."

"You're wrong. It happens. Listen, as long as you're here, I want to run something by you."

Suppressing a smile he said, "I'm all ears, Sweetheart."

"Okay. But first, promise me you won't get mad."

DiCarlo's eyes narrowed. "Do I have a reason to get mad?"

I pinched my thumb and index together to indicate incremental measurement. "I may have stepped ever so slightly over the legal line."

DiCarlo leaned forward on his elbows until his forehead was right up against mine. "How slightly are we talking here?"

"Hardly worth mentioning. And, the good news," I hurried to explain, "is that I didn't interfere with police business." Mainly because Wade Stoller wasn't on anyone's radar but mine.

Bobby blew out a big breath. "Just tell me."

When I got to the part where I checked out Stoller's computer, Bobby gritted his teeth but he didn't say anything. I finished up with my visit to Sherese's and the break-in.

"I'm afraid for her and her kids, Bobby. I didn't want to alarm her, but this was no ordinary burglary. Whoever did this felt threatened enough by what they think is in that house that they came looking for it. And if they didn't find it, they might come looking for it again."

"Calm down, Sweetheart. You said Sherese didn't know if Cal was hiding anything in the house. But if he were, how could she know it was missing if she wasn't aware that it existed? Maybe they already found what they were looking for."

"I hope you're right."

"So what makes you so sure Stoller was involved in the

break-in?"

"Because of the brochure. The first time I went to see Sherese she mentioned that Doyle had promised to take her on a cruise. I thought it was odd at the time. I mean he didn't strike me as a Sperry Topsider deck shoes kind of guy. But, if he was working for Stoller on the sly, it makes perfect sense."

"I'm not following you. Why would the mention of them going on a cruise be significant?"

"Stoller's records show he has three clients for his drug detection business. There's a private rehab center, a high school out in Langhorne, and a cruise line called Island Dream Vacations. They're a small, private company that takes off from Penn's Landing to the BES islands."

I gulped a bit more of my redeye and continued. "I've been doing a little research. Cocaine traffic coming out of those islands is on the rise. Drug enforcement agencies have cracked down hard on cargo vessels, yachts, and the like. So, drug gangs have turned to cruise ships as a way to get their stash into the country. According to what I've read, cruise ship security isn't particularly effective at winning the war against the smugglers."

"Not enough man power, for one thing," Bobby said. "And imagine being the unlucky passenger to run across a multi-million dollar transaction. People *accidentally* fall over the side of the boats all the time. Not a big incentive to turn someone in."

"Exactly. So the cruise ships hire outside agencies to at least give the appearance that they're doing something about the problem."

"Enter K-Nine Security."

"Which looks perfectly legit until you examine the company Stoller was keeping."

Bobby mulled this over in his usual way, fingers drumming rhythmically on the table. A minute went by and then the drumming stopped. "Okay," he said. "Say someone on the ship is smuggling drugs. Stoller is hired to ferret out this person or persons. But—what if he found a way to make it more profitable?" He arched his eyebrows and looked up at me expectantly.

Slowly, the light dawned. "Oh my God, Bobby. How could I not have seen this? Stoller must be on the take to *not* find the drugs. But how would that work? I mean assuming the dogs are properly trained, wouldn't they react to anything that smells like the drug?"

"There are ways to get around it. The dogs are not infallible, especially if they're getting help not to succeed. Anyway, how he manipulated the results isn't important right now. The real challenge is proving he did it."

"There's also the question of Doyle and the Lewis boys. They had to be able to offer Stoller something he couldn't achieve on his own."

"Yeah. But, what?"

"Distribution? They would know how to deal on the streets better than Stoller would."

"That's assuming he got paid in drugs." Bobby frowned. "Bran, everything you're saying makes sense, but it's still just conjecture. Have you talked to the officer in charge of the Doyle investigation about any of this?"

I sighed and drained the dregs from the bottom of my cup. "No. But it's not for lack of trying. And after the Claire Dobbs incident, I'm probably not high on their list of credible sources."

"Claire Dobbs, the council woman?"

"You mean you didn't hear about that?" *Me and my big mouth.*

"This should be good," he said and settled comfortably into his seat again.

"Well, I wish I had time to regale you with embarrassing tales of my ineptitude, but I've got to get going." I stood and picked up my laptop and empty coffee cup.

DiCarlo stood, too. "Hey, you want to hang out tonight? I've got the Peter Manfredo fight on Pay Per

View."

"Can't. Carla invited me over for dinner." (which sounded like a great idea at the time, but, in the light of day, and the re-appearance of sanity, now fell under the category of "What was I thinking?") I had actually thought of cancelling, but Alexanders aren't quitters. We muddle through no matter how ill conceived an idea may be.

"Could I get a rain-check?"

"Absolutely. Listen, Sweetheart, I've got some buddies that patrol the docks. I'll see what I can do to look into this. In the mean time—be careful."

"I will, Bobby. And thanks. I really appreciate this."

DiCarlo reached over and grabbed the book off the table and held it out to me. He teased me with a grin. "Aren't you forgetting something?"

I smiled back, innocent as hell. "I'm pretty much all caught up. Keep it. You might learn something."

*****

My mom called as I was getting ready to go to Frankie and Carla's. We were due there in an hour. I thought about not answering, but she'd only keep redialing until I picked up.

"Hi, Mom. I'd love to talk, but I'm kind of in a rush."

"Your brother met a girl," she interrupted, turning selectively deaf. "What do you know about her?"

I balanced my cell phone on my ear, grabbed my tooth brush off the bathroom counter and loaded it with toothpaste. "Paul met someone?"

"Yes. She has an unusual name. Daisy."

I brushed, rinsed and spit. A big glob of toothpaste landed on my shirt. Crap. I wriggled out of the shirt and walked into the bedroom. Nick was there. He eyed me and smiled.

"Mom, did Paul specifically say he was seeing someone?"

"Not exactly. I called him, and he said he'd call me back, because he was taking a walk with Daisy."

"Are you sure he didn't say he was taking Daisy for a walk?"

"Why would he say that? She's not a dog."

"Uh, Mom, she is."

"Brandy Renee, what an insensitive thing to say. We can't all be great beauties. I'm just happy your brother found someone."

"Okay, Mom. Well, I've got to go. Nick's taking me for a ride in the car." I hung up with promises to call her if I heard anything.

Nick was clean-shaven and dressed in a gray, long sleeved jersey and black fitted trousers. It was the perfect choice; understated, yet classy.

I rooted through my suitcase for a clean shirt. The only thing I could come up with was a lacy pink camisole. It looked like underwear, which it was. I yanked it over my head, tucked in the bra straps and was good to go.

"Nick, do you mind if we take the Jaguar?" I asked when we got outside. "My uncle loves classic cars, and it would give you guys something to talk about. Hey, maybe you could let him drive it. Not far—just around the block—"

He stared at me thoughtfully.

"What?"

"You seem pretty anxious about this get together, Darlin'."

"Anxious? I'm not anxious. Oh, and if Carla suggests we play Charades, just go along with it, okay? She's really into party games."

The Jag was parked in the loading zone. Odd that it never got towed. Nick opened the door for me and I slid in. I leaned over and returned the favor by pushing open the driver's side door.

On the way over to Carla and Frankie's we stopped off at Bon Vivant to pick up some candy. As soon as we got inside, I headed straight for the truffle case eying it as if it were a long lost friend. The woman behind the counter walked over to the other end and pointed to some hand dipped strawberries.

"We have a lovely selection of chocolate covered fruit, if you would prefer something lighter."

Why would anyone prefer that? The fruit takes up space where the chocolate ought to be. "Thanks, anyway, but I think we'll stick to the truffles."

I reached into my bag to get out some money, but Nick beat me to it. He bought two one-pound boxes and handed one to me.

"I didn't think you'd last the ride over, and it didn't seem like good form to bring them a half-eaten box of candy."

"Eh, it wouldn't be the first time." I tore open the box and ate a truffle. After the third one I started feeling guilty about not sharing. "Would you like a truffle?"

He leaned over and flicked the chocolate off the corners of my mouth with his tongue. "I'm good."

*****

Uncle Frankie stood at the screen door as we pulled up curbside. His face was set in a grin of forced enthusiasm. It was the same one he used whenever my mom offered to cook for him.

Carla stood beside him, her ginormous beehive towering over his five-foot ten-inch frame. She opened the door, simultaneously giving Frankie a quick nudge to his ribs. "Be nice," she mouthed.

I figured we weren't meant to see that, so we pretended we didn't.

"Come on in, you two. Dinner's going to be a little while. I forgot to turn on the oven." She laughed. "Hope you're not starving."

I was so hungry I could eat my own arm. "No, that's great. It'll give us all a chance to catch up. Uncle Frankie, you remember Nick, don't you?"

Frankie nodded. "How's it goin'?" His tone, while not exactly hostile, wasn't all warm and fuzzy, either.

We followed him into the house. Nick and I took up residence on the couch, while Carla and Frankie shared the love seat. There really wasn't room enough for two sofas, but Carla likes things "cozy."

"Carla," Nick said, getting the conversational ball rolling, "I ran into your cousin, Benny, today. He said to tell you hello."

Frankie bolted upright. "Benny, the gun runner?"

"Oh, for Lord's sake," Carla fumed. "He's an insurance salesman. I don't know how that silly rumor ever got started."

Frankie cut his eyes toward Nick. "How do you know Benny?"

"He sold me some insurance."

An awkward silence ensued, which I, of course, felt compelled to fill. "Mmm, mmm. What is that terrific smell coming from the kitchen?"

"Garbage. The disposal's backed up. So." Uncle Frankie thrust his chin toward Nick. "How'd you know Benny was Carla's cousin? And while we're on the subject, I never did hear how you and Brandy met." He still had that ridiculous smile plastered on his face, but he was talking through clenched teeth. Definitely not a good sign.

"Funny story." Carla let out a nervous giggle. "I, ah, had actually arranged the introduction—through Benny."

"Did you, now?"

"Yeah. Uh, remember last year when Johnny went missing? Listen, why go over old ground. It all turned out just fine. Would anyone like some iced tea?"

Uncle Frankie stood. "Carla, can I see you in the kitchen for a minute? I need some help with the antipasto."

"But it's already made."

"In the kitchen."

Apparently, Frankie and Carla were under the impression that their kitchen was soundproof. Once the door swung shut, Carla exploded.

"What the hell is wrong with you? You're acting like a total jerk to Nick and you're embarrassing Brandy."

"What's wrong with me? What's wrong with you? You were the one who brought that guy into my niece's life, and I'm just now hearing about it? I can't believe you kept this from me."

"Yeah. I mean why would I keep it from you? You're taking it so well!"

"Look, if Brandy wants to be with him, that's her business. But we sure as hell shouldn't be encouraging it. He's dangerous, Carla. Everybody knows that."

"Who's everybody?"

I slipped my hand into Nick's. "I'm sorry," I whispered.

"Maybe we should let them work this out in private."

"I have a feeling they think they are."

"Frankie, you're not making any sense." Carla continued. "You're friends with Alphonso and he works for Nick. But you don't have a problem with him."

"That's different," he sputtered. "Alphonso's not sleeping with my niece. She's gonna get hurt. He'll break her heart and I'll have to kill him."

"Is that what this is all about? You're afraid of a repeat of DiCarlo?"

Oh, God, don't be bringing that up. I cut a sideways glance at Nick, but his face was unreadable.

Carla's voice softened. "Look, will you give the kid some credit, here? She loves him. And when you think about it, if it weren't for Nick, Brandy might not even be here. She finds trouble all on her own, and he bails her out. If anything, we should be thanking the guy."

Carla had a point. I guess Frankie thought so too, because suddenly all the yelling stopped. "You're right. I'm sorry," he said. "It's just that—that kid means the world to me, y'know?"

"I know."

"All right," Frankie relented. "I'll butt out…as long as

he makes her happy."

"That's the spirit, hon."

A minute later the kitchen door swung open and Frankie emerged with an enormous pot of spaghetti. "So, who's hungry?"

*****

"Three words…first word…sleep…Sleepless in Seattle!"

"Yes!" Carla shouted. "We win again!" She leaped to her feet, no easy task in four-inch stiletto sandals, and took a victory lap around the cramped living room. Uncle Frankie high-fived her as she jogged by.

"Congratulations." Nick offered. "You guys are an unstoppable team."

"Congratulations," I grudgingly conceded, having never fully mastered the art of gracious losing. Personally, I thought the teams were a little unfair. Carla and Frankie knew all each other's references.

We'd gotten through dinner in about ten minutes. It's amazing how much can be accomplished when there's no pesky conversation to get in the way. Now, we were in party game purgatory. On the up side, beating Nick seemed to put Frankie in a much better mood.

Uncle Frankie squeezed my leg. "Don't worry, Midget Brat. You'll make up for it next round."

"You bet I will. We're mixing up the teams. Frankie, it's you and me against Nick and Carla." I turned to Nick. "Sorry, Santiago, but I need a fighting chance of winning and you're just slowing me down."

"Competitive little thing, isn't she?" Frankie laughed.

We played another round and Nick and Carla won. Crap.

*****

Nick was subdued on the way home. He was too polite to be moody, but I sensed something wasn't right. This was confirmed for me once we got back to his place. He pulled into the loading zone and turned to me, the engine still running. "I've got some paperwork to catch up on, Darlin. I'm going to head over to the studio."

My heart began to pound. I knew the evening had been hard on him, but still, it felt like a big, fat rejection. "Talk to me, Nick."

"What do you mean?"

"Listen, Frankie didn't mean all those things he said. He's just looking out for me. And now that he's gotten a chance to know you, it'll go much smoother next time…if you want there to be a next time…were you bored? I'm sorry. I know it's not the kind of evening you're used to."

"I wasn't bored, Angel. It was fine. They're good people."

"So, then, what's wrong?"

Nick didn't answer. Instead, he unhooked my seatbelt, pausing to brush his lips against my cheek. "I'll see you later."

Fighting my instincts, I got out of the car and unlocked the security gate. I wanted to give him space, but it took all of my will power not to turn around, jump back into the car and choke an answer out of him. It was a lonely walk back to the apartment.

My cell phone rang just as I reached the elevator.

"Brandy, it's Mike."

I was in no mood to talk, but curiosity got the better of me. "Hey, Mike. What's up?"

"The cops have located Donte Lewis."

"Are you serious? That's great! How did it happen? Did he confess? What did he say?"

"Not a whole lot. He's dead."

CHAPTER SEVENTEEN

"What?"

Mike filled me in as I climbed into the elevator and made my way to the fourth floor.

"A couple of hikers stumbled across Lewis' body in a shallow grave in Tookany Creek Parkway.

"Where, exactly?"

"I don't know. Somewhere near the golf course. Looks like whoever killed him was in a hurry…either that or they didn't give a shit about Lewis being discovered. He was just sort've dumped there."

Near the golf course… which, I happened to know from my obsessive internet searches, was about half a mile from Wade Stoller's house. I said as much to Mike.

"If you're suggesting that Stoller killed him, why would he dump the body so close to his house?"

"Good question…unless someone else did the dumping."

"Who'd you have in mind?"

"Oh, I don't know. Someone on his payroll who didn't have the work ethic to do the job right." And, seeing as three out of four of the major players were already dead, that only left Barbeque Master Chef, Reginald "The

Torch" Harwinton."

I let myself in to Nick's apartment and collapsed onto the couch. Adrian sauntered out of the bedroom and began whining at the front door.

"Sorry, baby," I whispered softly. "Nick's not here."

He seemed disappointed. Or maybe I was projecting.

I turned my attention back to Mike. "Do you know how Lewis was killed?"

"From the preliminary report, it looks like he was shot in the chest at close range. I don't have any of the details, and it'll be a while before they're available." Mike coughed and cleared his throat. "Look, Brandy, I shouldn't have shared that much, only, I feel like I owe you for setting me up with Janine. But—if DiCarlo asks, you didn't hear it from me."

"Got it."

*****

The readout on the clock in Nick's bedroom said three a.m. Instinctively, I knew I was alone in the king-sized bed, but I reached an arm out, anyway, hoping to be wrong. I wasn't.

I sat up and turned on the light and grabbed my phone. Halfway through his number I disconnected and placed the phone back on the nightstand. I spent the next ten minutes playing the *What If* game. *What if he got into an accident…what if he's lying in a ditch…what if he's lying in someone else's bed…in someone else's arms…No. He told me there's no one else, and Nick would never lie to me…But, what if…*

The front door opened without warning. Quickly, I lay back down and squeezed my eyes shut and waited for Nick to enter his bedroom and slip into bed beside me. My breathing slowed. *I overreacted. Everything's fine.* I waited some more.

A half hour passed before I finally admitted to myself that he wasn't coming in.

*****

"He didn't even hear me leave, Janine. Or if he did,

he didn't try to stop me. For all he knows I could be dead."

Being the knee-jerk reaction kind of gal that I am, it took me less than five minutes to gather up Rocky and Adrian and go. I tiptoed past Nick, who was sprawled on his back, asleep on the couch. He hadn't even bothered to undress.

"Is that why you left?" Janine asked. "So you could milk some grandiose reaction out of him to prove his love for you?"

"Of course not!" *You're Goddamn right it is. I'll show him. I'll leave and get killed and then he'll be sorry, and…oh my God. What am I? Five?"*

At least I'd left a note.

Dear Nick,

I appreciate everything you've done for me, but you need your space, even if you're too kind to tell me. It's safe to come home now. I've found new temporary housing.

Brandy

It was passive-aggressive to say the least. To say the most, I felt hurt and was being a manipulative brat. Nick had done nothing wrong. I was punishing him for…for what? I didn't know.

"I screwed up, Janine. What am I going to do?"

Janine yawned. She was an awfully good sport for having been woken up in the middle of the night. "You're asking me for relationship advice?" she laughed. "Well, whatever I'd do, do the opposite."

I called him at eight a.m.

Nick picked up after five rings. His voice was low and filled with sleep, and a hint of his southern roots clung to his words. "Hey, Darlin.' Why are you calling? I'm just in the living room."

Unh! He didn't even know I'd left. "Um, Nick, we need to talk."

There was a soft beep on the other end of the phone. "I'm getting another call, Darlin'. Can I put you on hold for a minute?"

"No, that's okay," I said in a rush. "I just wanted you to know I'm at Janine's. I'll be staying with her for a while."

"Any particular reason?" he asked, evenly.

"I, uh, left you a note."

There was a split second of dead air as Nick's *call waiting* clicked again. Ignoring it, he said, "Is this about last night?"

The question caught me off-guard. "Yes… No…I don't know. Everything feels all messed up, and I don't know why."

"You're right, Angel. We do need to talk."

Uh oh. He's agreeing with me. That can't be good. "Look, take the call," I told him. "We'll talk later."

"Te amo," he said, softly.

"Te amo."

*****

I spent the afternoon fending off a full-blown anxiety attack. *"Why do you always have to analyze the crap out of everything?"* asked Tough Girl Brandy. *"Just shut up and enjoy the sex."*

"No. You shut up," snapped Sensitive Brandy. *"You know what Nick and I have goes way beyond sex. But there's something inherently wrong here, and ignoring the fact won't make it go away."*

"Why don't I just pop you one and put you out of your misery?" asked Tough Girl Brandy, which was a rhetorical question and didn't require a response. It did, however, cause some concern over the voices in my head. *Note to self: Call mom to see if schizophrenia runs in the family.*

I had to find something useful to do. I settled looking up the docking information for Island Dream Vacations. The cruise ship coming in from the BES Islands was scheduled for arrival the next day at six a.m.

I took out my phone and scrolled through my photos, zipping past the shots of Rocky and Adrian decked out as elves for this year's Christmas cards. (FYI, friends and family love receiving pictures of your pets in funny costumes. They rank right up there with annual holiday newsletters and fruit cakes.)

Finally, I found what I was looking for—the photo of Wade Stoller's August calendar page. He'd marked off the 16th with a notation underneath. *6:00 a.m. I. D. V.* Perfect. I emailed the photo to Bobby and gave him a call. It went straight to voicemail. "Call me, ASAP," I told him. "It's important."

Next, I called Vince. His receptionist said he was in a meeting. I then tried Mike Mahoe, but he was out on patrol. As a last ditch effort I called Richie Burns, the traffic cop I used to hang with in my Godfrey days. He had a "situation" at Ninth and Wharton. In the never-ending cheese steak wars, a couple of customers from Pat's and Geno's gridlocked the intersection as they duked it out over a lone parking spot. He said he'd get back to me.

Having exhausted my list of everyone I knew that carried a badge, all there was left to do was to go down to the docks myself and…and what? Make a citizen's arrest? *Wade Stoller, stop in the name of the law and my possibly unfounded allegations!* The idea was ludicrous even to me.

I thought about calling the DEA with an anonymous tip, but I couldn't afford to blow this. Instead, I went stir crazy waiting for someone (anyone) with authority to return my call.

When I couldn't take the waiting any longer, I jumped into the car and swung by Johnny's to see if he wanted to work out again. After all, it was so much fun the last time.

I didn't have any clean shorts, so I put on a pair of sweat pants that I'd commandeered from Nick. They were big in the waist, so I rolled them down until they rested on my hips.

Arriving at John's I got an idea. It would be funny, I thought, to play my Rocky ringtone and dance around with my arms raised like Sylvestor Stallone did in the movie. The boxing gloves were in the trunk of my car. I retrieved them and shoved my hands into them to complete the ensemble.

As soon as I rang the bell, I turned my back to the door and hit the ring tone simultaneously raising my gloved hands high in the air. The sweat pants eased their way south, but all he'd see was the top of my underwear. No big deal.

John's door opened. Immediately, I began belting out the words to *Gonna Fly Now,* as I sprung into an improvised Rocky victory dance.

"Can I help you?"

Hmm. That so doesn't sound like Johnny.

My gloved fist-pumping slowed, and I dropped my arms just as the sweat pants slipped again, dipping well into Refrigerator Repair Man range. At that precise moment I remembered which pair of undies I'd grabbed out of my suitcase that morning…the emergency ones with no elastic on the waist band. *Uh oh.* Frantically, I tried to pull them up, but I was literally all thumbs.

"Is John home?" I asked. With my back still turned, I sat down on the step and tried to wriggle my ass back into Nick's sweat pants.

"John's indisposed," replied the voice that, unmistakably, belonged to Garret. Who else could spit out a phrase with such pomposity?

Sweat pouring down my face, I worked my underwear back over my hips and stood up. I turned around, my cheeks burning with embarrassment.

"It's uh, nice to see you again, Garret."

"Is someone at the door?" John walked into the living room and peered over Garrett's shoulder. I waved a gloved hand in his direction.

"Hey, Sunshine. This is a nice surprise. Isn't it a nice surprise, Garrett?"

"Well, it was a surprise, anyway. She mooned me."

"Jesus, Garrett. Not on purpose. Look, John, Garrett says you're busy, so I won't keep you. I'll talk to you later."

"Bran, wait." I noted with satisfaction that John nudged Garrett out of the way. He grabbed my wrist and pulled me inside.

'We're not busy. I'm glad you came by."

Garrett shot him an annoyed look. "But we were going to watch that PBS Special on Monarch Butterfly migration from Mexico to Pacific Grove. I'm sure it would just bore her."

"She has a name, Garrett. It's Brandy. And if Brandy's bored, we can turn it off." There was an edge to John's voice that I hadn't heard since the time he called the Banana Republic to protest their return policy on holiday novelty items.

"Suit yourself," Garrett shrugged. "I'm going to go watch it in the bedroom."

"He's mad," I whispered when Mr. Personality left the room, "I should go."

"You're staying."

"But he saw my ass. I'm not comfortable."

"Look, Sunshine." John shoved me onto the couch. "It's a matter of principle. If you leave now, he'll think he's won."

"John, what part of *he saw my ass* did you not understand?"

"Stop whining. You're missing the big picture here." John ran his hand lightly over the top of his head. The hair had started to grow back and he was looking more like his old self again. "Listen, kiddo, I never should have let this go on for as long as I did. You've knocked yourself out trying to be nice to Garrett and he's thrown it back in your face. It's about time I grew a pair and told him to knock it off or get out."

"But—but I don't want you to die alone—or worse yet, end up with that guy who smelled like bug spray."

"I won't," John grinned. "I'll move in with you. Besides, the truth is this whole thing isn't even about you. Yeah, I know you think everything is about you. But this is between Garrett me, and how I feel about myself when I'm with him. And I gotta tell ya, I don't feel too great."

I stood and gave John a hug. "You guys have some talking to do. I'm gonna go."

John nodded and walked me to the door. "I would've given anything to see the look on his face when you mooned him."

"It never happened." I pointed a warning finger at him. "End of conversation."

*****

I was alone at Janine's and feeling fairly rudderless. On my way back from John's, Nick had called. We made plans to get together for a late night dinner. He sounded weary and distant, but the latter could have been my imagination. Despite Tough Girl Brandy's best efforts, I was projecting all over the map.

Then, there was the whole no job thing. At the rate I was running through my savings I was going to lose my home. Plus, it felt unsafe going back there anyway, because the Junk Town Gang kept trying to blow it up. Or were they?

With the exception of the first hit on the house—and the guy had confessed he'd gone rogue—there was no real proof that the JTG was trying to kill me. But if someone wanted me dead, they'd be the logical choice to pin it on. I didn't have to stretch my imagination to figure out who that someone was. God, I wanted to nail the bastard and get on with my life.

DiCarlo called me at eight o'clock.

"Did you get my message?" I asked.

"I did, and I'm way ahead of you, Sweetheart. I went and talked to somebody who talked to somebody and they're going to be there to greet your pal Stoller and the ship, tomorrow. And don't bother asking me any of the details. These people could lose their jobs if it became known they were working off a hunch and a favor to me."

"Fine."

"That's it? No argument?"

The truth is I was happy to turn it over to someone else. I didn't need to know the details. And anyway, I figured I'd find out soon enough. Because when the ship came in, I was planning to be there.

"You're not thinking about going down there, tomorrow, are you?"

"Pfft. Don't be ridiculous."

DiCarlo groaned. "Alexander, I swear, if you were still my girlfriend—"

"You'd be the luckiest man on Earth," I finished for him, although I was pretty sure that's not where he was headed. "Listen, Bobby, I promise to stay out of everyone's way. There's nobody who wants to get this guy more than I do."

*****

Nick and I were supposed to meet up at his apartment. I was almost there when my phone rang. I pulled over to the curb anticipating he was calling to tell me that he was running late or that he wouldn't be able to meet me after all. "Hey," I said into the phone.

"Brandy?" *Hmm. female. Definitely not Nick.*

"Yes?"

"It's Sherese." There was a hitch in her voice like she'd been crying.

"Sherese, what's wrong?"

"I—I found something. I think it's what you was lookin' for."

"What'd you find?" I asked my pulse quickening. If all went right the next morning, Stoller would be arrested for drug smuggling or at the very least for purposely turning a blind eye to someone else doing it. But that wouldn't necessarily tie him to all the murders. I needed proof that he was involved, and, just maybe, Sherese had found it.

"I don't want to talk on the phone," she told me. "You said to call if I found somethin' and I found somethin'. I need you to come over right now and get it. I don't want this shit in my house no more." She stopped and caught her breath and added, "And don't bring nobody with you. I don't want people knowing where it come from."

I did a quick mental calculation. It would take me at least an hour to schlep across town, pick up whatever it was Sherese had and get back to Nick's. *Unh!* I started the engine and pulled out into traffic. I'm on my way."

I called Nick to tell him of my change of plans.

"No problem," he said. "There's a Cuban restaurant not too far from there. It's on the corner of Listern and Girard, and it's open until two. I'll meet you there in an hour."

Cross town traffic was surprisingly sluggish for the lateness of the hour. There was construction on Broad Street, so I had to take a detour to get to Sherese's. I'd have to hurry to meet up with Nick.

After what felt like an eternity, I turned onto Sherese's block and parked directly in front of the house. In the stillness of the night the neighborhood creeped me out, so I reached into my glove compartment and took out the Clear Knuckles I'd bought last year. In case of emergency, they were much more my speed than a loaded pistol. Not that I'd given up completely on the idea of carrying concealed. In fact, my aim was improving on a daily basis. Unfortunately, my judgment was still in its formative stages.

I exited the car and jogged up the sidewalk. The sofa was still out on the street looking forlorn and a little bit embarrassed. I felt sorry for it.

Sherese's porch was shrouded almost completely in darkness, with just the barest of light peeking through the living room curtain. I knocked briskly and waited for her to answer.

After a minute she called out from behind the door. "Who is it?"

"It's Brandy."

I listened as the deadbolt turned. Sherese opened the

door and stepped out of the way to let me in. Her face was turned and cast in shadow, and I sensed that something was wrong a split second before the door slammed shut behind me.

CHAPTER EIGHTEEN

I spun around and found myself staring into the eyes of a lunatic. A lunatic wearing a carpenter's tool belt with a blowtorch hanging from it. A scream rose in my throat but nothing came out.

Reginald Harwinton chuckled and pointed the business end of a Sig Sauer pistol at me. His other hand was fisted in Sherese's hair—or the patchy remains of it, anyway. Most of it had been singed off, leaving her scalp burned and blistered.

"We been waitin' for you. Ain't that right, Sherese?"

Sherese stood stock still. Beads of perspiration had formed on her upper lip, and I watched as they travelled slowly down her jaw line.

"I said, 'ain't we been waitin' for the bitch?'" He yanked hard on her hair so that her head flopped back and forth in assent like a drunken rag doll. "That's better. I don't like to be ignored."

Sherese stole a glance at me, and I could feel the pain in her dark, pleading eyes. It pushed the fear out of my own. My heart beat slowed, and an unnatural calm washed over me as my brain clicked into survival mode. No. Warrior mode.

I took quick note of the enemy. He was shorter than I'd envisioned, about five foot nine, with hair that hung in thick dreads and draped over one eye like a curtain. The hand that held the gun was large and sported long, dirty fingernails. He opened his mouth and smiled wide showing a missing front tooth. All in all, he was quite the catch for some lucky girl.

My eyes swept the room in search of something I could use as a weapon. The coffee table that once held a week's worth of dishes and cutlery was maddeningly empty. Sherese couldn't have picked a worse time to become a model housekeeper.

I tucked my left hand into my right to hide the Clear Knuckles and forced myself to return his smile. "Mr. Harwinton? Or may I call you Torch. Actually, I was hoping to run into you."

His smile faltered. "Is that so?"

My voice held steady betraying no emotion. It seemed to throw him off-balance. "Well, we're running in the same circles lately. Mario Lewis, Calvin Doyle. And I'm pretty sure you're the one who's been taking pot shots at me. I thought it would be nice to have some face time. Get to know each other better. We have a lot to talk about."

"Yeah?" he asked, amused. "Like what?"

"Wade Stoller for starters. You've been working for him, right? He hired you to kill me and make it look like the gang did it, didn't he? The only thing I don't get is why."

"Cause you a nosy bitch is why. You need to learn to mind your own business."

Funny, he wasn't the first to point that out to me.

"So," I said, ignoring his excellent advice, "Let's see if I got this straight. Stoller was using his dog sniffing business to help smuggle drugs into the country. He hired you and your friends to distribute the drugs. But Mario fucked up. So, he asked you to get rid of the mess. Only, Cal told him he'd left evidence behind, so he sent you to look for it. But you haven't been able to find anything."

"Not yet I haven't. I need for Sherese to cooperate."

He puckered his lips and leaned into her, and laid a slobbering kiss on her mouth. Sherese recoiled, as the tears she had kept in check now streamed down her face.

"That's right, Baby," Harwinton crooned. "You give me what I want, and I'll give you what you want."

Wow, this guy had a tough time reading social cues. Sherese was clearly not enjoying his overtures, romantic or otherwise.

My bravado was beginning to wane and my legs were on the verge of collapse. We needed to buy some time, so I decided to take a gamble.

"Okay," I bluffed and prayed Sherese would go along with it. "Maybe Cal did leave something at the house. Something that could put Stoller away for life. But, if we gave it to you, how do we know you wouldn't kill us anyway?"

Harwinton's face contorted into a cruel smile. "You don't get it, do you, bitch? It ain't a question of if I'm gonna kill you. It's a question of how you gonna die. Now," he pointed the pistol directly at my chest, "I could do it quick and merciful—" he paused and stuffed the gun into his belt and, with a showman's flair, pulled out the blow torch— "or slow and painful." Lovingly, he fired it up and grinned as a jet of blue and orange flame burst from the nozzle.

Sherese's knees buckled and she pitched forward. Harwinton caught her and yanked her back up by her remaining strands of hair, and she whimpered like a wounded pup.

Stoller's insane lackey shook his head, as if marveling at the peculiar nature of man. "You know, whenever I set fire to a guy, it's always the same. They turn into little girls. They be wailing their heads off as the pain gets worse and worse. And pretty soon they smell their own flesh burning, and they start making noises that ain't even human. It's a beautiful thing. Like nothin' you could ever imagine." He pressed his face against Sherese's. "Cal was funny. He cried like a baby before I even got started."

I felt my bowel spasm. Ever since I was a kid I've had an unholy fear of being burned alive. And if I've learned anything over the course of the past year, it's that nightmares do come true.

Harwinton cranked up the flame. "Now," he demanded. "Why don't you show me what y'all got?" He took some tentative steps in the direction of the bedroom.

"No!" Sherese screamed. "There ain't nothin' in there."

"Really? Cause you acting like you hiding something." He beckoned me forth with the flame of the torch and propelled Sherese forward.

And that's when we saw her. Sherese's young daughter, Ayana, stood motionless in the hallway, her eyes wide with fear.

Oh, holy mother of God. How could I have forgotten about the kids?

Harwinton shot her a chilling smile. 'Well, what we got here?"

The little girl stood mutely rooted to the spot.

"Sherese, why don't she speak when she's spoken to? Seems I need to teach your girl some manners." We watched, horrified, as he turned the flame toward the little girl.

"Don't you touch my baby!" With the strength only a mother protecting her child could summon, Sherese wrenched out of Torch's grasp and knocked the lit canister from his hand. It sailed across the living room and landed in the corner.

"What 'chu doin' you crazy bitch?" Rearing back, he made a massive fist and punched her in the stomach. Sherese flew backwards from the force of the blow and slammed her head against the wall. Her body went limp as she slid to the floor.

I dove for Harwinton knocking him off-balance. He toppled over onto his stomach, and I followed suit, landing squarely on his back.

"Mama!" Ayana ran to her mother and knelt down beside her, crying.

"Ayana," I shouted. "I'll take care of your mom. You go get your brother. Now! Take him out the back door to Candice's and tell her to call the police."

I watched her run off in the direction of the bedroom and then turned my attention to the monster I'd landed on. With little effort, he flipped onto his back and grabbed me by the arm. I brought my leg up and kneed him in the nuts. Harwinton let loose with a torrent of curse words and tried to work the gun out of his belt, but in his rush, he only managed to push it farther down into his pants.

With my free arm, I landed a Clear- Knuckled blow to his chin, momentarily stunning him. Before he could react, I slugged him again. His head bounced against the floor and he lay there not moving.

Suddenly, I became aware of a weird, orange glow emanating from the corner of the room. *Fuckin' A. The drapes are on fire.*

I scrambled to my knees and tried to rouse Sherese, but she was out cold. Quickly, I grabbed her by the ankles and maneuvered her toward the front door.

As the fire steadily grew, the air became thick with smoke, infusing my lungs with a heavy, burning sensation. I watched, terrified, as the flames spread to the couch.

Oh my God, oh my God, oh my God. What do I do?

There was a sudden tugging around my waist. I dropped Sherese's legs as Harwinton dragged me to the floor and straddled me. His face was shiny with sweat, his breathing labored, his pupils so enlarged they looked like Oreos.

His hands reached for my throat and clamped down. "You god damn cocksucking bitch," he rasped, tightening his hold.

I thrust my arms up between his and broke his grip on my neck. Harwinton tried to reposition when something else caught his attention. I followed his gaze with my eyes.

The blow torch lay about a foot from my head.

"Slow and painful," he hissed.

Simultaneously, we reached for the canister. As the fleshy part of his arm hovered over my face, my South Philly grammar school training automatically kicked in. I bit him. Hard. Harwinton flinched and pulled back leaving himself wide open. I reached up and shoved my thumb directly into his eye.

Enraged, he flung out his other hand and smacked me in the mouth. It hurt like hell, but it was just the diversion I needed. I twisted away from him and snatched the canister off the rug and brought it up to one side of his face. I couldn't think about the moral aspect of what I was about to do. It was either do it or die. So I did.

His screams were everything he'd described; long, piercing, animal-like wails as his dreads burst into flame and slapped at the blistered flesh on his face.

With frantic desperation he leaped to his feet and made a jagged run for the front door.

Sherese began to stir. She sat up and coughed; her voice barely audible over the din of the fire. I rushed over and stuck my arms underneath her and dragged her to her feet.

"We have to get out of here, Sherese. Don't talk. Here, cover your mouth with your shirt and let me lead you." She was too confused to argue and docilely allowed me to lead her through the kitchen and out the side door.

Out on the street a crowd had gathered. Judging by the muted sounds of the sirens, it would be a few minutes before the emergency vehicles arrived. I wondered, briefly, where Torch was, but I didn't let myself dwell on it. Wherever he was, he was a hurtin' buckaroo.

I spied Roger and Candice King in the crowd. Candice held onto Ayana's hand and tried to comfort the traumatized child. An immediate and all consuming fear came over me. Battling our way through the crowd, we reached the Kings.

I crouched eye level to the little girl. "Ayana, honey. Where's your brother?"

Ayana began to shake all over. "I couldn't find him. I looked and looked."

Sherese howled and flung herself toward her rapidly disintegrating home. Roger scooped her up holding her in his protective arms.

The fire engines were still a ways away and time was running out. If there was any other choice, I would have taken it in a heartbeat. But there wasn't. I raised my eyes to heaven and thanked God for chocolate, my friends and my family and made a dash for the side of the house.

Half way there, I heard my name. I turned and saw Nick running to catch up with me. "Are you okay?" His face was pale; his jaw set as he silently checked me for injuries.

I nodded, barely able to speak. "The baby. He's still in the house. I have to go."

Before I could finish the sentence he pulled me by the arm and handed me off to one of Sherese's massively large neighbors. "Don't let her near the house and there's a thousand bucks in it for you." To me he stated quietly, "I'll find him, Angel."

"No. I can't let you do this," I sobbed and struggled to free my arm from the neighbor's grasp.

Nick gestured to the guy, who grabbed both my arms and twisted them behind my back.

"Go easy," Nick admonished. "I expect her back in one piece."

In less than a year's time I had witnessed the Zen side of Nicholas Santiago, the gritty, and the sophisticated. But as he entered the burning building I made a mental note to add one more. Super hero.

Mere seconds had passed, but it felt like an eternity. I watched in helpless wonder as the fire grew to seismic proportions, spewing thick black smoke from the chimney. There was an enormous popping sound as the front window exploded spraying chunks of glass onto the lawn. Burning embers floated from the sky and landed on my arms. Ash got in my eyes and filled my lungs, but I barely noticed. All I could think of was Nick.

And then, the unthinkable happened.

As I strained my eyes against the dark, smoky night, suddenly, the roof collapsed. Candice picked up a shrieking Ayana and held her close, shielding her from the debris. Sherese moaned into Roger's shoulder.

"We need to get them over to our house," Candice instructed her husband. She turned to me, her voice gentle. "You should come, too, honey."

"I'm fine where I am, Candice. I need to be here for when Nick comes back."

Roger patted my shoulder. "Of course you do. We're right across the street if you need us."

Rescue workers now filled the narrow street. Fire fighters leaped from their trucks, and, in a flurry of orchestrated activity, unleashed torrents of water on the burning building.

The captain stood on the sidewalk barking orders to his crew. He was a big man in his late forties. I thought I recognized him from the gym. I pushed my way through the crowd to reach him. "Captain Greco," I read off his name plate.

"Ma'am, please step back onto the pavement. We need to keep this area clear." He cut me a quizzical look. "Hey, aren't you related to Frankie Brentano?"

"He's my uncle. Listen, there are people trapped in the house. A man and a little boy. Please. You have to help them."

Captain Greco gazed at the inferno and then back at me. "We'll do everything we can, but I've got to be honest with you. It doesn't look good. I figured if you're Frankie's niece you're tough enough to handle the truth."

Oh, for the love of God, man. Why would you think that? Lie to me!

I was on the edge of full-blown hysteria, when a deafening cheer rose up from the crowd. A man had emerged from the side of the building. He walked slowly, as if he bore the weight of the world, which, in a way, he did. In his arms he carried a squirmy thirty pound package. The man was drenched in sweat and covered in soot, and he never looked more beautiful in his life.

Ambulance workers rushed to Nick's aid. One of the EMT's took Sherese's son from his arms while the other tried to place an oxygen mask over Santiago's's face. He waved them away and sank wearily to the pavement.

My heart filled to overflowing, I knelt down beside him and threw my arms around his neck and kissed every inch of his magnificent, grimy face. "What took you so long?" I joked to keep from bawling.

"He wouldn't leave without this." Nick held up the hobby horse, now blackened from the fire.

And then I lost it completely.

"C'mon, Angel. Let's go home."

*****

At noon the following day, Fran, Janine, Carla, John and I sat in the comfort of a cushy, red leather booth at my brother's club, tossing back Rolling Rocks while I recounted the evening's events. Okay, technically, I wasn't "tossing" so much as sipping my beer through a straw. My mouth was still pretty sore from where Torch had hammered on me. I guess I didn't have much to complain about, considering what I'd done to him, but still…

I'd gotten about three hours of sleep and was running on empty. First, I'd had to give my statement to the cops, and then there was the overnight stop at the hospital after Nick almost hacked up a lung on the way back to his car.

"I'm okay, Darlin'," he'd insisted.

"Humor me." I was consumed with guilt over the fact that if Nick hadn't come looking for me when he did, he never would've been put in such danger. "Please."

In the end he let me drive him to Jefferson where he

was greeted with a hero's welcome and a private room. As if his looks alone wouldn't have warranted such treatment, the on-duty nurses had seen the news footage of his dramatic rescue of Sherese's son and flocked to his bedside to offer aid and comfort.

Unfortunately for them, I was occupying the other half of the single bed.

"You need to go," instructed Nurse Terri DuCote.

"Make me."

Nick squeezed my hand. It could have been a sign of affection or a sign for me to shut up. I preferred to think it was the former. He turned to the nurse with a disarming smile. "There's really no arguing with her. She'll just sneak back in, in the middle of the night, so do you think you could make an exception, just this once?"

Nurse DuCote blushed and returned the smile. She looked back at me and nodded. "Personally, I wouldn't leave him, either, honey."

Nick fell asleep quickly, but it was fitful. Just as I began to doze off he jerked awake, calling my name. When I asked him about it in the morning, he said he didn't remember. And, for the first time since I'd known him, I got the feeling he wasn't telling me the entire truth.

While I waited for Nick to sign his release papers, I checked my voicemail. There were 34 messages, including one from WINN. Something about an exclusive in exchange for giving me my old job back. For the next fifteen minutes I tried to come up with creative ways to tell them to go screw themselves. I settled for *I'll get back to you.* It might not have been the most personally satisfying response, but as my dad always says, it doesn't pay to burn bridges.

Nick's car was still at Sherese's, so I offered to drop him off there.

"You broke out in a sweat just saying the words, Darlin.' I don't think you're up for a return visit just yet. I'll ask Alphonso to pick it up for me."

Instead, I took him back to his apartment. I pulled into the loading zone and cut the engine.

"Are you sure you're okay?" I asked. "Do you want me to go upstairs with you?"

"I'm absolutely fine. I've got a meeting scheduled for this afternoon, but I should be finished by six. If you're not busy, why don't you come over?"

"Okay." I was quiet for a minute, my thoughts going to the exact place I had forbidden them to go. *Stupid thoughts*.

"What's wrong, Angel?"

"I was so scared, Nick. I really believed I was going to die. Not just die, but that it would…you know…really, really hurt."

Nick unbuckled my seat belt and brought me onto his lap. I leaned my head against his chest and listened to the beating of his heart. It calmed me.

"But here's the thing," I added, because I desperately needed him to understand. "As scared as I was for myself, it was nothing compared to how scared I was for you."

"You don't have to be afraid anymore, Angel." He looked on the verge of saying more but changed his mind. With great tenderness, he swept the bangs from my eyes and kissed me on the forehead. "I'll see you at six."

Paul walked over to the table with a tray full of sliders and French fries. Daisy trotted alongside him and hopped up onto the booth and squeezed her furry little self in between Carla and me. She sat happily awaiting a slider.

John cast an eye at the puppy and then to Paul. "Hey, isn't this a health code violation?"

"No," he said, and set a slider down in front of Daisy. Maybe my mother was right. This looked like love to me.

Carla put the mini burger on a plate and cut it up into bits for the puppy's consumption. Daisy waited politely until she was through and then ate it all in one giant slurp.

John made a face. "Am I the only one grossed out by this?"

The rest of us looked at each other. "By what?"

He shrugged and picked up a burger.

"We'd almost finished our meal when DiCarlo showed up. Judging by the dark circles under his eyes he'd logged about as little sleep as I had. We all slid over to make room for him in the booth.

"You look like hell," he told me.

"Thanks. That's the look I was going for. And just for the record, you don't look so hot, yourself."

"Not funny, Alexander. You could've been killed."

Carla reached behind me and cuffed Bobby on the back of the head.

"Ow. What was that for?"

"We're celebrating here. So, unless you have something positive to contribute, go find Frankie. He's in the back room playing pool."

Bobby reached over and snagged a burger. "Then, I guess you don't want to hear my news."

We turned a collective eye on him. "Did the police find Torch?" I asked.

"Yeah. He hadn't gotten very far. He was about five miles west of Sherese's house when they picked him up. He'd hit a telephone pole and was passed out in the front seat of his car. He's in pretty rough shape. Third degree burns over most of his face and hands, but he'll live."

I did what I had to do, I reminded myself.

Carla gave me a sympathetic pat on the knee.

"The good news," Bobby continued, "is that Harwinton sang like a bird. He confirmed your theory about Stoller, by the way. They picked him up at the docks early this morning. Surprise, surprise, traces of cocaine were found on his dogs' noses."

"His dogs snort cocaine?" Janine blurted out.

"It's how he kept them from finding drugs on the ship. By numbing their noses." DiCarlo turned to me, his expression half admiring, half incredulous. "You had it figured right all along. I don't know if you're the smartest person I know or the luckiest."

I suspected it was a little of one and a whole damn lot of the other, but I wasn't going to think too hard on it. I was just happy that the nightmare was over, and things would finally go back to normal.

*****

Apparently, I spoke too soon.

My hands were full of take-out; Mexican, Indian, Italian, and your classic American fare, so I leaned against Nick's security gate and rang the bell with my shoulder. Earlier, I'd tried to get a hold of him to see what he wanted for dinner, but he didn't pick up the phone. So, I got a bit of everything.

I wanted the evening to be perfect. Janine said she'd keep Rocky and Adrian for me one more night. She did my hair and make-up—well, as much as I'd let her, and gave me full run of her wardrobe. I chose a pale pink tee shirt dress that came down to my ankles.

Janine wrinkled her nose. "You look like a giant penis. Here, let me do this." She whipped through her closet and pulled out a shimmering, black, micro-mini dress with strategically placed cut outs on the front.

With great reluctance I put it on. "Great. Now I look like a street walker."

Janine stood back with a satisfied smile. "My work here is done."

Nick answered on the third ring. "Come on up, Angel. I was just about to hop in the shower. I'll leave the door unlocked. Just let yourself in."

Nick was still in the bathroom when I got to the apartment. I set the bags down on the counter and took out the containers. Then, I started thinking about Nick, naked, and I decided to wait for him in his bedroom, in case he was hungry for something besides dinner.

A large, black duffle bag sat half open on his bed. *Hmm*...I peeked inside and found a pile of neatly folded clothes; jeans, sweats, fatigues and dress shirts. Next to the

267

bag lay two beautifully tailored suits, a sports jacket and a couple of expensive ties.

Suits…fatigues…WTF?

"Hi there."

I jumped a mile. "I wasn't looking in your bag."

Shit. Why'd I say that? My hand was still stuck inside the damn thing.

Nick walked over to the bed and grabbed some jeans from the top of the pile. He was naked, alright, but even that temptation didn't do it for me. Staring at his duffle bag, I was out of the mood.

"Going somewhere?" I asked.

"I'm afraid I am, Darlin.' I'm leaving, tomorrow."

"How long will you be gone?" My mouth felt like cotton and the words sounded dull in my ears.

"Hard to say. Maybe a month."

"Can I ask where you're going, or what you'll be doing? Or is that strictly need to know?" The sharpness of my tone surprised even me.

"What's wrong, Angel?"

"Nothing."

Nick settled in next to me on the bed. "You're upset because I have to leave."

"I'm upset because you're choosing to leave. Why now, Nick? After all we just went through, why do you have to leave now?"

I wanted to shut up. Told myself to, in fact. Quite sternly. But the words just kept coming. "We almost died last night. That's a major event in my world. I thought maybe we'd take a half a minute to appreciate being together. But, instead, you're off and running to God only knows where for God only knows what. At least I hope God knows because you're sure as hell not confiding in me."

His voice was infuriatingly calm. "It's the work, Angel. You're making it personal."

"Because it is personal. And you do it every time. It's a

pattern with us. I get myself into a mess, you bail me out and then you disappear. I don't blame you for leaving. Taking care of me is exhausting."

"That's not it."

"Then, what is?"

Santiago leaned forward and extracted a hand rolled cigarette out of a wooden box on his night stand. He put it to his lips, thought better of it and stowed it back in the box again. Staring at me with unwavering eyes, he spoke slowly and deliberately.

"Look around, Angel. You and I are the only two living things in my apartment. I live this way by design. I can't commit to a person, a dog, or a cat, or even a houseplant. I'm sorry, but I can't be who you want me to be."

Suddenly, I felt sick to my stomach. I tried to interrupt to tell him to forget it. We could go on pretending that we could make it work, because I loved him that much, but he wouldn't let me.

"I care about you, Brandy Alexander. More than I ever thought I could and definitely more than I should. But it doesn't change who I am, and, somewhere down the line, I was bound to disappoint you."

It would have been a great kiss-off speech, except that I wasn't really listening, because, at that moment, something caught my eye. It was the tiny silver cross that dangled from his right ear. *The cross that once belonged to his mother. Oh, my God. How clueless can I be?*

I slid off the bed and stood eye level to him. He started to rise, but I placed my hands on his chest and shoved him back down. "It's my turn."

That got his attention.

"Y'know what, Nick? I'm sure you believe every word of what you just said, but none of it's relevant, because I've finally figured out what the real problem is."

"Okay, I'll bite. What do you think the real problem is?"

"It's not your job that keeps you from being able to

269

commit. It's fear."

"Interesting theory, Darlin'. Fear of what?"

"Me."

He actually cracked a small smile at that. "Brandy, I'm sorry, but you're not that scary."

"Yeah? Well, here's the thing. You know I'm not the most introspective person in the world. I feel what I feel, and then I stuff it down with a Hershey bar so that it doesn't interfere with my life. I'm not saying it's the best way to manage my emotions, but it makes it a hell of a lot easier to recognize when someone else is doing it."

"Angel, is it possible that you're attributing emotions to me that I just don't have?"

"No. It's not. Those feelings are there. They may be covered up by twenty years worth of scar tissue, but they're there."

I paused, letting my words sink in. "Nick, you loved your mother more than anyone else in the world, but you couldn't keep her safe. So now, your entire life is about keeping people at a distance so that you don't get hurt again."

"Brandy—"

"I'm not finished. Look, you've given me so much. You accept me, you clean up after me, you love me. But you won't commit to me. Not fully, anyway. Because you're afraid one day you won't be there to keep me safe, and you're going to lose me. So you blame it on your job, or act like you're just not that guy. You don't *do* commitment."

"Look, Angel—"

"Still not finished. The funny thing is you once said that I wanted a guarantee that we'd have a future together, and you couldn't give me one. Turns out you're the one who wants a guarantee. And I wish I could give it to you. Only, I don't have that kind of power."

I waited a beat, but he didn't say anything. "Okay, now, I'm finished."

Nick cut his eyes to the wooden box, and I could tell he was dying to grab a smoke. Instead, he grabbed me around the waist and pulled me close, and pressed his cheek against the exposed skin on my belly. I wrapped my arms around him and blocked out everything but the rise and fall of his breath.

After a few minutes, Nick broke the silence. "So, where do we go from here?"

And with sudden clarity, I knew.

I unwrapped my arms from around his neck and straightened my spine, closed my eyes and said a silent prayer. *God, give me the strength to get through this without chocolate.* And then I began. "I love you, Nick, and that will never change. But I'm an all or nothing kind of girl, and I won't settle for anything less than all of you. So, until you're willing to take that leap of faith, and commit to someone, something, *anything*, we don't have a prayer of making it." My voice began to crack, betraying the resolve I'd so carefully constructed. "I'm going to miss you, Nick. Be safe, and have a good trip."

His expression was stoic, but there was no mistaking the pain reflected in his eyes. "Eres el amor de mi vida, Angel. I want to give you what you want. What you deserve. I just don't think I'm capable of it. I'm sorry. I don't want to leave you like this."

"You're not. I'm leaving you."

EPILOGUE

"Yo, Sunshine. Look alive!"

"I can't move. I think I twisted my ankle."

"You can't move because you've been buried under a blanket of TASTYKAKE wrappers for the past three days, and your nonstop crying has sapped you of all your strength. Believe me, Bran, no guy is worth that amount of crying."

"I wasn't crying over Nick. I was crying because all the cupcakes are gone."

"Uh huh." John squinted and pulled his baseball cap down over his eyes. The afternoon sun cast stubby shadows on the Art Museum steps as we stretched our out-of- shape bodies in preparation for the long trek up. "You ready?"

"As I'll ever be." I knew John was only trying to help, but I longed to climb back into bed and watch Reality TV until my brain turned to apple sauce.

I'd left Nick's apartment without a backwards glance and managed to make it all the way to the elevator before dissolving into a soggy little heap.

I knew he felt awful. But he would never promise something he couldn't make good on, and I never would have wanted him to. I just wished he could.

"Race you there." John took a tentative step up. "Whoo hoo! Only seventy-one more to go."

My pocket began to vibrate. "Hang on," I said. "My phone's ringing. Hello?"

"Brandy? "

"Yes?"

"This is Judy Harrison, from Jacob's Place. How are you?"

Super depressed, actually. Nick has commitment issues and I'm going to die alone. "Great, thanks. Are you calling about Popeye?"

"I am. When Mr. Santiago came to pick him up, we forgot to give him a copy of the adoption papers. He said he was going out of town and wouldn't be reachable. I was hoping to drop off the papers with you."

"Nick adopted Popeye? When did this happen?"

"Day before yesterday. I'm sorry. I thought you knew. This has been a real blessing. He's the only person Popeye has responded to. I warned Mr. Santiago that it was a big commitment, but he said he wanted to do it…and he mentioned something about a leap of faith. Not sure what he meant by that."

My heart filled with inexpressible joy. "I do, Mrs. Harrison. I do."

Lifting my eyes to the mountainous stairway, I took off running, taking the steps two at a time, never stopping until I reached the top.

ABOUT THE AUTHOR

Shelly Fredman is a native Philadelphian who long dreamed to be Mrs. Illya Kuryakin from The Man From U.N.C.L.E. Having failed to reach that lofty goal, she switched her affections to fictional characters and situations that she could control with the stroke of her keyboard. This quest for power resulted in The No Such Thing As...Brandy Alexander Mysteries.

Shelly and Brandy share feeling of pride in their hometown, and even though Shelly has moved to the west coast, she has always been, and forever will be, a Philly girl at heart.

Made in the USA
Charleston, SC
03 June 2013